# Speculations
# about Jakob

Uwe Johnson

# Speculations about Jakob

*Translated by*
*Ursule Molinaro*

A Harvest/HBJ Book
A Helen and Kurt Wolff Book
Harcourt Brace Jovanovich, Publishers
San Diego  New York  London

# Speculations
# about Jakob

**ACKNOWLEDGMENT**

Many thanks to Venable Herndon and the
Pennsylvania Railroad for help with
this translation.—UM

# I

But Jakob always cut across the tracks.

— But he always cut straight across the sidings and the main line, why, because, on the other side, outside, all the way around the station to the street, it would have taken him half an hour longer to catch his streetcar. Seven years he was with the railroad.

— Look at this weather. What a November. You can't see ten steps ahead of you for the fog, especially in the morning, and that's when it happened, in the morning, and everything so slippery. Doesn't take much to slip. Those crummy yard engines, you hardly hear them coming in weather like that, much less see them.

— Seven years Jakob was with the railroad, let me tell you, and anything that rolled on rails, if it rolled anywhere, he heard it, believe me

below the high signal tower with its large glass eyes a figure came walking straight across the dim foggy freight yard, stepped surefooted and casual over the tracks, one rail after the other, stood still under a green-glowing signal arm, was blotted out by the thunder wall of an outgoing express, moved forward again. Perhaps Jakob could be recognized by the slow steady straightness of the walk, hands in his pockets, chin out, he seemed aware of all the comings and goings on the tracks. As he came closer to his tower, his outline evaporated more and more among massive dark monsters of boxcars and

asthmatic locomotives which, obedient to the thin piercing
whistles of the brakemen, crept phlegmatically, in jolts, along
the wet smeary rails in the early morning fog

— he if anybody. Explained it to me himself, what with
physics and formulas, amazing how much a man picks up in
seven years, and he said to me: Just stand still if you see something coming, never mind how far away. "A train that's on
its way is right on top of you," he said to me. He'd have
known that fog or no fog.
— Yeah, but an hour before they squashed a brakeman, up on
the hump. Don't you think that guy knew it too?
— That's why all the excitement. Even if they dished up all
that stuff about tragic accident and great contribution to the
socialist cause, and honor to his memory and so forth: the
man who dreamed that one up is sure to know better. Go ask
anybody in this whole lousy station if you can still get a travel
permit to West Germany these days, and Jakob had just come
back that same morning, on an interzone train. Guess who
he'd gone to see?
— Cresspahl, ever heard of him. He's got a daughter.


**GESINE**
*My father was sixty-eight last fall and lived alone in the ocean
wind that fell stark and dark on the land, on him, on his house*


Heinrich Cresspahl was a powerful wide man, heavy, slow-
moving, with a head like a weather-beaten turret, under short-
cropped gray hair. His wife had been dead these eighteen
years, he missed his daughter. Only a few pieces stood along
the walls of his workshop, he had taken down the signboard
of his craft a long time ago. Occasionally he'd repair a precious antique for the County Museum, or for people who
passed his name on to their friends. He went about the coun-
tryside a lot in a corduroy suit and high boots, looking for

old chests and peasant cupboards. Sometimes horse carts would stop in front of his house, pieces of furniture would be lugged inside; later, cars came from the big cities and carried rich brown artfully crafted pieces with dull-gleaming ornaments off to distant places. That's how he kept alive. Tax forms correctly filled in, a bank account modestly in keeping with the cost of living in a small out-of-the-way town, no suspicion of illegal revenue.

### HERR ROHLFS

*Sixty-eight years old, cabinetmaker, domicile: Jerichow, Ziegeleistrasse. I could and could not figure out what the Secret Service wanted from him. Those memos from Jerichow Local, nagging, private denunciations mostly: said thus and so, insinuated such and such. Sang publicly at the Jerichow Inn (don't think the Inn is a "public" place in a town that size; they all know each other, well okay: publicly at the Inn) the song about the dog that walked into the kitchen where he shat upon an egg, the cook he raised his ladle up and beat the dog to dregs, and all the dogs assembled and praised the cook's great skill, and scribbled on the tombstone: and still he shat, and still and then the dog came back into the kitchen and I forget what happened after that, and all right all right I get it. And that's the kind of information those people put on paper. Submitted for your serious consideration. They seem to think agents have their own club songs, going to wear spy buttons soon maybe. Dogcatchers. That's the kind of stuff that makes them angry back there, makes other people angry too, other people who wouldn't mind letting Cresspahl enjoy a quiet old age. Until I noticed the man had a daughter, born in 1933, Jerichow High School, English Lit. in Leipzig, Interpreters School in Frankfurt am Main, am Main, and since the beginning of the year (something those Jerichow clods hadn't noticed; Cresspahl probably hadn't told them:) with NATO Headquarters. I leafed through the other reports without warming up to any of them, everything such run-of-the-mill*

*X-ray work, just plain stupid, and around noon I drove back
to headquarters, asked to see Lagin and showed him the file,
if it's got to be done I might as well be in on it. "Ah—
galoobooshka," he said. Knew it all by heart, fantastic memory,
wanted my report. I reported to him. He reported to me. Coordination. Eto ooyazno. Coordination. Summary. On my way
out I said: "Yezly ana ostayetsa galoobka na kryshe . . ." He
didn't understand at first, they have a different way of putting
it, then he laughed. "Lootsche varabeya," he said. He was
very nice, not at all formal, at any rate this was a one-
man job. The birdie in the bush. I still had an evening at
home, but felt rather distracted, uneasy at times. After all, my
previous assignment had been a nice job, that's what they
promoted me for, and being earmarked for special mission is
in itself a promotion, but did it have to be this business and
right now, how could Cresspahl still run around singing such
songs, I can also be demoted, it isn't over yet. And the trouble
about the baby. I realize my daughter's got to be asleep at 8
P.M., she's two years old, I realize that, but all I did was lift
her up a little to say goodbye, well all right. About midnight
I went downstairs into the street. Hänschen was reading in
that eternal technical home study manual of his and yawned
for me to see, he started the motor and said: "Vacation might
have lasted a bit longer," and I said "Jerichow has a beach,"
but it was around the seventh of October and I felt better
again; we'll just have to wait and see. It was the beginning of
October and fall weather and we drove all night away from
Berlin and the sky kept growing bigger and whiter and there
stood the Jerichow churchtower rather modestly behind a hill.
The dogcatchers of Jerichow have two one-family houses on
Bahnhofstrasse, lightless-sinister, rather run down, the garage
right next door,  the only thing missing is a sign out front. I
identified myself as Herr Rohlfs, had a room cleared out for
myself and Hänschen, they asked about Cresspahl's file the
first half-hour. They're very miffed, don't appreciate music and
songs, but I'd never heard the name before, and did they think
the file had gone to Headquarters in the meantime? Not bad.*

'It isn't easy working in this town," they said, and I asked, "How are the bathing facilities around here?" They thought the weather was too cold. That boy, he sometimes thinks on two tracks, he's going to go places.

They may have taken me for a State Secretary on vacation. The town isn't as backward as it looks, a stranger doesn't attract attention, they really didn't stick their noses and tongues too far into my business; most of them supposedly took me for the accountant from the State Purchasing Office: because they get to see him so seldom, says Hänschen. Well, we took a little stroll, I did find out how to get to the beach, Hänschen stood shivering beside my clothes and absolutely refused to come into the water, he thought my little dip quite out of line. And in the evening we sat around knocking the mud off our shoes. By and by I went to visit a few people in Jerichow, a pretty a pleasant town, I said, too bad one can't stay here; they all thought so too. Especially the Postmaster, stiff-necked, right-thinking, a civil servant, stamps sold regardless of who is who, letters stamped and sent off without delay, as if I hadn't seen the mail carrier read the postcards, and the privacy of the mails is one of the basic human rights. But how does a Secretary of State sign? and there you are. Must be loyal to the authorities, was also loyal to the fascists, why of course, Herr Mesewinkel. Better be careful not to get my names mixed up one of these days. That same day, I was just about to call home, hope my daughter is all right, when I saw him for the first time, Cresspahl, high and large, standing in line at the stamp window, corduroy crumpling about his legs, jacket worn sloppy and spotted, glasses. The glasses had got caught in their case, stubborn, head to one side, he fingered at them, said: "and then gimme also twenty twenties." She seemed new here, not familiar with the dialect, he tried to explain to her, "for a letter," he said, twenty stamps at twenty pfennigs each. I was able to study him in detail, I was next in line. He stalked powerfully to the door with his large back, stopped and bedded the glasses—with reverence I must say—in their dented metal case, "Morning," he said and thumped around *the church to the Ziegelei, stood with someone at the corner, talked. Let him, I say. I don't bear a grudge against anyone, I'm not old enough. But the cause of socialism will triumph and last for ever and ever, and casually exit from the Republic just like that and hop down to the Mediterranean, can't have that. She's too young for that, at least you can probably talk to her, you have to talk to everybody.*

But if someone should happen to ask you:

HERR ROHLFS
*But if someone should ask me: the details of the subject's personal description could stand improving. Gesine (first name underlined) Lisbeth Cresspahl. Well now. The name is common in these parts, can happen, Lisbeth was the mother's name. Lisbeth Cresspahl, died in 1938. The grave thickly overgrown with ivy, not fenced in, and there are quite a few fancy fences right beside it. On the stone only the name (not Elisabeth), not the maiden name, no quotation from the Bible, no cross, only the dates. Well then, Gesine Lisbeth. And what am I supposed to do with—height: medium. Way back then. Five years ago. Eyes: gray. Could just as well be green, it's so gloomy in the passport office, everybody has dark gray eyes; and what did they put down for hair color? dark. Date of birth, citizenship, special characteristics: none. I wouldn't know how to do it better, but this way it's of no use to anybody. The passport picture from that solemn musty photo studio next to the two-story Consumers Store, The Modern Photo Shoppe, Good morning Miss Cresspahl, please be seated. Turtleneck sweater all the way up to the chin, the head a little more to the side please, the left ear is too low*
— *Never mind my ear.*
— *And how about a little smile?*
— *No. This is for a passport.*
*Or: "S' only a passport picture." The face very eighteen-year-old hair dark perhaps not real black straight back the skin tight and suntanned over strong cheek bones nonchalant earn-*

*est stubborn eyes, color of eyes: gray. Win this woman dlya*
*dyela sotsyalizma. Eto ooyazno. The birdie in the bush*


For eight years Heinrich Cresspahl had seen his daughter to
the front door. He leaned against the frame, had a last few
words with her so to speak, she standing before him, hands
behind her back, not looking at him, looking up with a laugh
on her face, jumping around him, making a fist at him, scolding him, walking beside him to the curb, another quick
look at him and a nod before she walked along the wall of
the local Soviet Headquarters to school, and later to the station; and Cresspahl standing huge in front of his house, protruding into the landscape with his pipe, experiencing whatever weather it was that day. Besides, he'd say more or less
the same thing every morning. And when his daughter was
just beginning to acknowledge his words with a polite rebellious curtsy—during several spring weekends in the fourth
year of the German Democratic Republic—Cresspahl did not,
one morning as expected, walk diagonally across the street into
Ilse Papenbrock's store for his daughter's rolls, because that
night she had not stayed until breakfast. Anyhow, during the
years that followed, Cresspahl bought nothing but rye bread,
Ilse Papenbrock was told his daughter had gone away on a
trip. For three and a half years she had to be satisfied with
that information; imagine a young girl traveling about the
world all that time without a father's protection! and the
world was so big.
Jerichow used to be a rural town, most of it owned by a
single noble family: a thousand and one houses along the
Mecklenburg stretch of the Baltic coast, with the wind blowing stark and dark all year round . . . ; an hour's walk to the
beach, past the quarry and then through fields. They had re-
built the tile works after the fascist war and set up a furniture
factory, which brought more life into the streets, so that Herr
Rohlfs looked like a late summer vacationer. A man lived
there, Cresspahl by name, in a long one-story house at the

quarry behind the old, burned-out tile kilns across from a
fenced-in park around the villa of the Soviet Headquarters.
Toward the end of the war, the owner of the tile factory had
abandoned his villa, furniture and all, without a second
thought, but the two covered wagons—strays from a Pomeranian convoy—turned without stopping at the open gates of
the mansion and came to a halt in the street in front of
Cresspahl's house, and since Cresspahl happened to be standing at the door, he took the refugees in and divided the larger
half of his house among them. He himself withdrew with his
daughter into the two rooms adjoining the workshop; Lisbeth
Cresspahl had died in 1938, her daughter was twelve years
old that April. She was called Gesine. One of the two Pomeranian families moved on after the announcement of the Pots-
dam Treaty; but Frau Abs who had come alone with her son
in the other wagon had wanted to wait here because of her
husband, and for permission to return to her Pomeranian town,
that had burned down: as the children in Jerichow would
sing each May, that May it had a meaning for them and gave
them an inkling of the size of the world. Next year Frau Abs
sold wagon and horses for a supply of wheat and potatoes and
went to work as cook in the hospital; in Pomerania she had
also been a cook, but on an estate. The first summer and fall
Jakob worked with the horses in the villages around Jerichow;
in town during winter there was little else for him to do but
to bootleg for the victorious Soviet Armed Forces. He also
watched Cresspahl work at his craft, it was Jakob who cut
the letters in the door of the workshop, CRESSPAHL HARD-
WOOD INLAYS: but at eighteen he started as brakeman at
the Jerichow station. At that time Gesine Cresspahl was ad-
mitted to Senior High School, Jakob had no such notions for
himself, besides his mother considered it pointless; Gesine
was fifteen then, she still accompanied him on errands, they
still felt like brother and sister. Then Jakob's job took him
south as far as the Elbe, where Cresspahl's daughter would
meet him between two express trains, when she came home
from school on weekends back to Jerichow to her father and

to Jakob's mother. And then one night she arrived in Jerichow during the middle of the week and talked in the kitchen for two hours to Jakob and his mother and Heinrich Cresspahl, and the bony, bitter-faced woman stood at the table, arms crossed and head bowed, motionless, and said nothing to anything Cresspahl said, and kept silent during Gesine's vehement replies, and yet she was the only one to face up to the farewell at daybreak in front of the house: Child — Child: she said, and Cresspahl avoided this form of address in the copious letters he sent his daughter across the border. Because that's where she remained, across the border, in the other Germany, interpreting in a headquarters of the American Armed Forces.

And once and for all Gesine Cresspahl had accepted Jakob's mother as her own, the way she had accepted Jakob as an older brother who had been given her as a present; what can a father do for a daughter who's lived in Jerichow for twelve years as though it were the world, now the war had come to Jerichow? he can talk to her, but he can no longer make up her mind, moreover Cresspahl had always let her have her little secrets. Rigid and inaccessible she had cowered on the back stoop in the sharp April sun and gravely watched the unknown woman who stood in the half-uncovered wagon handing her sewn-up baskets sacks milkcans down to Cresspahl and who wanted to stay. Pomeranian sounded very different from what they speak in Mecklenburg and it has words of its own, she didn't understand them all. And in the evening when she returned with Jakob from the lake behind the quarry where they had ridden the exhausted dusty horses, she stepped only haltingly up to the bench under the birch and studied the unknown woman's hardened grief-skeptical face before she said: "Well, good night then." With equally patient, labored cordiality Frau Abs accepted Gesine's politeness and answered, in a just-as-cautious High German: "Yes. Sleep well"; but she had once again become aware of a life in which children are supposed to go to bed early and to sleep well.

GESINE

*She cooked my meals and showed me how to fix my hair, she helped me, even away from home. I know the evening I kept my hands behind my back, Gesine: she said, touching me gently, politely on the shoulder with her horny hand; I know her half-voiced rattling words. I know her face: it is long and bony, the narrow dry eyes already well along toward old age, I've had a mother all this time.*

After Gesine and Jakob left Cresspahl's house for the world, Frau Abs lived by herself. Cresspahl was waiting out his life, nobody could live it for him. "Ah but that one's so far away," she would say when Cresspahl came into the kitchen at night with a letter from across the border, often with a lengthy special page slipped in for her; she had no answer, there was nothing now she could do for Gesine. She sat quietly at the table, her hands folded in her lap, and told Cresspahl to tell his daughter this and that, but soon she'd get up and start her brooding solitary evening on the other side of the hall. Jakob didn't write very often, his visits were far apart in the year; with Jakob there, she'd sit longer in Cresspahl's part of the house and hide her warmth less stubbornly: on such evenings one could sometimes guess at her girlhood face, see its traces. Actually she had accepted this household unreservedly since the very first evening on the back stoop: after the flight from the war, her life had anchored itself in human habits again as though she had found a new home with a young girl to look after; that's what she realized one evening, during Jakob's October, when she found a gentleman named Rohlfs waiting for her outside the hospital kitchen who drew her into an intimate concerned conversation about socialism and the Western capitalists' passion for war and the advantages and disadvantages of one or the other, the influence they have on each and every life, for instance on the life of the Cresspahl family, which unfortunately was hardly a family any more

since the only daughter seemed to be absent, and Frau Abs
had been a mother to her so to speak? and she said

HERR ROHLFS

*"No," she said, denied it right into my face, and everybody in
this town will tell me how she used to go to the beach with
her and that she'd wait at the station and that they walked
through the streets together like mother and daughter; once
a year she takes a trip, and where does she go, to the woman
who sent those letters of which I read one which starts without
any form of address but with "I was thinking about you this
morning when I" and now nothing at all. She only lived in
that house and has nothing to do with the Cresspahl family:
she says, and says it to me with such calm that I said I must
have made a mistake and please excuse me. She didn't understand a thing except that I was asking about the girl; and I
won't ask her again if I can help it. Fine: I say. I can't take
that kind of calm, with fluttering eyes and secretly trembling
hands, I'm not that old, I don't like to see anyone scared into
lying. It wouldn't have worked out. And I say to Hänschen,
"Well, how about a dip today you and I?"; he finds the water
too cold, I say "Then let's get out of here. Let's drive down to
the Elbe."*

THAT FALL JAKOB was twenty-eight years old; in no previous
October had he been so aware of time. On his job the minutes
had to be employed thriftily, carefully weighed; he knew each
one individually. Vertical and horizontal lines divided the
sheets on the slanting chart-board before him into time and
space sequences of scheduled and unscheduled events; with
his various pencils he'd mark the train movements in his sector
from block to block and from minute to minute, but of the
famous changes of season he actually noticed only the difference in light. After he was through, the minutes did not make

up a day but a timetable. This fall now: as I was saying: he
did not become aware of time only when he locked the door
on the train sheets the microphone the loudspeakers the telephones and walked down the long gleaming corridor under
the cold white neon rods to the staircase that opened to the
outside and that made him see the difference in light. In the
other light lay the drabness of the bald industrial street,
cranes screeched in the yard, rumbled above kinky mounds of
scrap, in the nimble electric dumpcarts the load shuddered at
every violent jolt of the brakes, shop windows shone white and
green, at the streetcar stop people stood uncomfortable in the
windy wetness along the desolate sooty walls in the half light:
it stayed with him all through work. From the wide windows
of his high pale red tower above the yards he could see the
rails curving away as far as the Elbe bridge, fast and small the
trains rolled heavily under him, from all over the vast network
the switch-engine crews pushed and pulled cars and strings of
cars into long trains with much running and whistling back
and forth alongside the stocky locomotive, from the sheds
hammer blows leaped thin and sharp into the thick hissing of
steam. On the other side of the Elbe, however, his sector
stretched between poles and telephone wires far beyond the
fog-padded horizon steadily parallel to the Western border.
A scale diagram of the tracks between block signals and stations hung in front of him above the loudspeaker, and when
voices from somewhere in the vast plain announced or asked
about a train in the official jargon, Jakob would picture the
unseen station in his mind and the signals ahead of the train
which to him were a code symbol made up of letters and a
number, and from the time and the mileage he'd know what
the train's position should have been according to schedule
and where it actually stood, in its own and everybody's way,
when you're late you're automatically in the wrong. Then he'd
plug himself in, flip the switch and tell the microphone how
he'd like things to be, flip back to listen, at last the voice of
the Chief Dispatcher, the C-D (sitting far away overlooking
his station) spoke up and explained what Jakob had pictured

for himself in the remoteness of his tower: a one-hundred-twenty-car freight with gravel lumber peat coal radio sets marine turbines tanks (a TF, perhaps 1204) was pulling into track two under the talking C-D, the yard signals changed position, the express—which Jakob had watched pulling out below him half an hour ago (clock time: 2:07 P.M.) and which the information over the loudspeaker reassembled on his sheet into a thick black downslanting line, away from block signals and time points already passed—thumped by on the main line.

That fall the coal shortage and the rundown condition of much of the rolling stock made it almost impossible to keep on schedule. High up in the mighty tower the dispatchers sat morose and disgruntled at their microphones, because finally all the lines were tied up in knots by blocked overdue trains, no part of the timetable ever matched the other and each shift ended as confused as it had started. Moreover, each decision was a matter of state morality, no answer solved the problem, placing the guilt on him whose job it was to give it. Jakob though held his temper pretty well. Conscientious and with a kind of equanimity he leaned back in his chair, his long dark head pensive, conciliatory, bent to one side, picturing with narrowed unfocused eyes all the movements in the plain below which his deep hesitant voice discussed with the microphone. "No, not me. You maybe?" he said. "That's what you get from smoking. Our domestic cigarette industry. Talk to him, he can't blow up your tracks. Nonsense. Tell him to keep his shirt on"; sometimes he'd nod as though the person at the other end were standing right in front of him. Each incident dragged a bristly tail of mutually-conditioned consequences behind it, probability became uncertainty in one's own sector, and if a train happened to run on schedule for once, it might all be spoiled by the delays which a neighboring dispatcher telephoned through to the tower with sighs and regrets. When the tangle looked hopeless and covered all over with burrs, Jakob would nod and wordlessly hike the corners of his mouth—with curiosity rather than anything else—to see if one more train might not be squeezed into the minute-side of his train sheet as an interrupted thin blue line. Green meant clear, the competition went by its official name "green tracks," on-times and delays were counted afterwards as so many merits and demerits, enough on-times earned you a bonus. But the endless administrative memos and the party pep talks hardly knew or referred to anything but the time-table which Jakob hardly managed to remember, what with the complications of his job. If one of the train sheets had been transparent and placed over the other, timetable and actual running record would not have matched any better than the northern and southern stellar systems: said the dis-patchers that fall; Jakob was not the only one to scribble his reports on the available back of the hectographed sheets.

Seven years ago he had started with the German State Rail-road as a brakeman in an insignificant Mecklenburg town on the Baltic. He had been apprentice, flagman, assistant operator in most of the stations in the North Elbe division: so he knew a lot of people on the line, everybody called him Jakob (al-though he was a dispatcher now); perhaps this was because he was so patient with everybody. On the photos in the dis-play case of the Sports Association "Locomotive" he stood without any particular distinction between the outside left and the center forward of Handball Team I, and the photos of the city rubble clearance also showed him everywhere so tall and with such broad-shouldered calm that the onlooker im-mediately thought or said: "That's Jakob. That one, see, the one that looks so solid."

— That one? You'd think he was a fullback. The way he looks.
— Yeah, you'd think he couldn't run. But he can, just try to get the ball away from him. He hasn't been playing for two years or so. You can get fed up with all that cheering and fanfare, and he's never been one to go for grandstand stuff, you know: there comes the ball, the guy sidesteps, pirouettes, or does a handstand: nothing like that, and in one game he had a guy who tried to cover him every second, you won't get a

single goal! he kept yelling, and didn't give up until Jakob
let go of the ball and simply stood there and laughed. Some
things you can't start all over again. If that's what you mean
by fed up.
— And when do you get a Sunday off with all that overtime.
— Yes. His job had something to do with it of course.

Sat behind his locked tower door not looking around, talking
away into the world, marking the steady stream of distant
events which appeared on his train sheet as a curve, traces of
time that passed without stopping. Tugboats swam down the
wide gray river under flat spreading layers of smoke, wet air
hung thick and dirty over the city, the sky stayed white all
day.

HERR ROHLFS
*Fine: I say. But after two whole days a man ought to know
what he needs, so what's the matter with him? no idea. I know
more or less what a dispatcher does, central authority for the
entire sector, locked door, priority on all telephone lines, quick
precise thinking, efficiency, they all say: take it easy, even on
the street, constant overtime, tension. One of them, Bartsch by
name, acts pretty jumpy. No idea. He can't just be a dispatcher. Here's the shift schedule, here his hours: fits. Home
from work, bed, back to work. If he gets home a little late
once in a while, it's because the stores were packed. Sometimes
it's the bus, the rush hour: well, and what does he do on his
own? of his own free will I mean. There's always something
we like to do. Take a look at his bank account: can't spend
half his money the way he lives. How wrong can you be: a
week ago I saw him in Jerichow sitting with Cresspahl at the
inn, that's quite a distance from here, and when somebody
wanted to sit down at their table, they asked for the check
right away: not that I care much about Cresspahl's opinions.
It's Jakob I was interested in, I drive out there after him, I
look at his daily routine, and there I am left standing almost*

*like one of those intellectual blockheads who doesn't know
what to make of socialism. Or rather, I'm sitting behind
Hänschen in the car, pulled over to one side of the street,
waiting for the streetcar, waiting for Jakob to cross the freight
platform, since he always cuts across the tracks. "Foggy, huh?
Let's make a turn, Hänschen, and then let's get around that
streetcar so I can take a look at him, easy, step on it, now he's
in the street, see him?" Good evening Jakob.*

He turned the transparent pass case over and showed the other
side to the woman conductor who said thank you and took
another look and nodded with rapid practiced glances. Then
she climbed from the platform onto the rear steps and asked
him if she might please pass, and Jakob pushed back half
a step without saying a word and let her through. He looked
at the girl's long blonde hair tied in a pony tail as she stood
against his shoulder in the breathless crush of afternoon traffic; when the car heaved gently, heavily at the curves, he
could see her face: friendly dreamy inaccessibly young and
intelligent beside his wedged-in arm,
and the closeness had no future. And
his life was open to anyone who cared to look. Later, in the
bus, after he had shopped in the overcrowded, now brilliantly
lighted stores on the market square, he sat in the front, next
to the exit, and saw his motionless reflection jolt in the misty
windows at the quick deep lurches into every pothole in the
street; he put two ten-pfennig pieces in the conductor's hand
and said "twenty," the conductor shoved the ticket at him and
repeated "twenty" in a mechanically rising wornout tone. His
mind was a blank. At one point he thought of the girl student
pressed against his shoulder and how she had paid no attention at all to his staring, now the mere closeness was a pleasant
memory. But perhaps his stares weren't the attention-getting
kind any more. He looked at the other passengers with that
hardly noticeable attitude of fatigued intimacy that guarantees
fast painless forgetting. At every stop, the door next to him
hissed open and shut. When his street was called out, Jakob

stood up with his bag in the dim swaying box, the conductor
rang the bell, through the exploding door Jakob stepped into
the cool clear-shadowed darkness of the street between high
evening houses. He cut across the road, across the sidewalk
and into the house, for a while the sound of his feet on the
warped wooden stairs lingered in the street. Below, the wind
was quiet. Then steps approached from the other end of the
street, crossed the sidewalk, passed through the house into the
courtyard. The span of a glance, a figure stood with dusk-
gray upturned face under the light that Jakob had switched
on in the kitchen. Again steps slurring and sighing on the wet
pavement, again the deep cool breath of quiet rain:
patiently the eyes learned Jakob's comings and goings in the
city, and not personal was the attention that began to trail
him in the middle of October—in the evenings or during the
waxen half-awake early-morning rides in the streetcar or on
his walks through the long deaf corridors at work—hoping to
learn about his character and reputation. The eyes had no
scruples and avidly seized upon each detail solely for the sake
of finding out (as a lover might pursue a mistress he has never
met) yet this was an assignment, and the hirelings the wage
slaves wore attitudes that could be changed and checked,
they forgot what they saw, derived neither benefit nor experience from it for their own lives. Thus, reports and speculations
grew out of meetings and neighborliness and telephone conversations and indifferent glances exchanged in city convey-
ances, and took shape on tape recorders and typewriters and
in the intimate atmosphere of whispers and were sorted out
and bundled and stapled together and stored in a windowless
room of an unobtrusive blinded tenement in the northern suburb for a man who gave a different name to everyone he met,
who therefore, even nominally, could not muster anything but
a general and public concern for Jakob's well-being. The great
of the land were casting their eyes upon Jakob.

— And what about Cresspahl's daughter?
— I don't know. I mean: perhaps he made the trip just to go

to the refugee camp. That's what Sabine says. As I was saying.
— Sabine says. But Sabine went alone on vacation last summer. You know they split up don't you. It simply came to an
end. And I've seen them, the way they behaved with each
other afterwards. She'd say something like "Good morning
Jakob," and he'd make a friendly face and say something like
that back. You understand? they were still fond of each other,
only love was over between them for good.

The German Railroad employees didn't get holidays off. All
the never-ending requirements of the service allowed—after
months of alternating work and sleep—was an accumulation
of one's overtime to approximately two full days, referred to
as a "rest period." Once, during a rest period that October,
Jakob went to Jerichow. With his mother he walked from the
hospital to Ziegeleistrasse (his mother was quiet and well
liked, and at that time Herr Rohlfs knew no more than what
he had read in the Hospital Personnel files). He spent the
evening with Cresspahl at the inn listening to him discuss the
world situation; they had a table to themselves and the fact
that they got up and left as soon as a third person came to sit
down might, after all, have been a coincidence. This was the
one exception in October.
Twice he went to bars around the freight yard and near the
port with men from the railroad—of whom Jöche and Peter
Zahn and Wolfgang Bartsch were known, although Bartsch
was with them only once and went home early. Jakob didn't
drink too much, their conversation sounded like shop talk,
more vehement later on when they discussed the difficulties
they had to cope with, Jakob didn't say much, he seemed to
be looking on. Tall, in friendly conversation, he walked with
the others to bus and streetcar stops, excluding no one from his
good night ( " 'Night then." — "See you tomorrow at lunch."
— "Have a good ride home." — "We'll get there. Oh, and
what I wanted to say . . . " — "I'll give you a ring." — "See
you tomorrow." — "Have a good ride home." — "It's already
morning. Good night." — "Good night. Good night"), ap-

peared sober and cheerful at work. And he had hardly more than four free evenings in two weeks. Herr Rohlfs learned about Jakob's regular attendance at meetings, sessions, reconstruction programs, but these he did not classify as exceptions.

On an evening in the middle of the week Jakob was seen in the Rathskeller with a lady. The lady sat beside him, almost as tall as he, only narrower; held her face carefully, daringly brazen against Jakob's nearness; he looked straight ahead, registering her many words with pensive, almost motionless mirth. Many diners found themselves looking toward that table, perhaps because her elegant light suit stood out in the fall weather and next to Jakob's uniform which at least told you Jakob's profession and consequently made the young lady seem more familiar to the onlooker, more accessible to criticism. If you can say: that one, the one with the guy from the railroad, it's as though you knew him, and therefore knew her a little too, "and she sure was good to look at." A blonde, with hair pulled straight back, a few lighter curls around the self-assured teasing face. Her jacket hung over the back of the chair, she was sitting on the edge, the skirt tight and firm around her body. Once she got up, Jakob turned, for a while she stood there with him looking at her. Then dinner came, the rest of their conversation seemed to stay on an even keel. A comparison with the slowly assembled photographs revealed the girl's name as Sabine. The former landlady said she was not in the habit of discussing such matters with her roomers, so far as she knew Herr Abs had stopped coming to see her sometime back in the spring; later Sabine had moved out. And if she might express an opinion: it was unlikely that Herr Abs had gone on seeing her after that. So? No, those were precisely the things she didn't stick her nose into, although apparently some landladies did. Jakob sat next to Sabine, his back against a column under the painted, low-vaulted ceiling and helped her to everything and showed her every attention (felt her eyes on his face and the big dull ache of weariness he would have liked to deny for her sake. The face obeys and smiles,

now just sit it out as you always have), she didn't seem restless. Later, Jakob rode from the Rathskeller to his tower and
Sabine spent half the night in the Melodie, a dance-bar behind the Rathskeller where an expensively dressed gentleman
of about forty who didn't look like a railroad man had been
waiting for her. The manager said the gentleman was con-
nected with Surgery, City Hospital II, well let that be, and
he thought he'd seen the lady before somehow, in different
circumstances, ah yes, with someone from the railroad. Sabine
worked in the Head Office, the one Jakob reported to, from all
over the division young men of Jakob's age would telephone
her on all kinds of official pretexts, a conversation with Jakob
had not been recorded in a long time, I told you. So then
what?
So this:
Jakob's city was large, letters arrived in great quantities from
other cities beyond the border. Awkward and heavy, the mail-
bags tumbled from the interzone expresses onto the electric
wagons that carted them off to the branch station. At the central post office, employees raised the bags over the sorting
tables, shook out the packets, tossed them here and there, the
cord was jerked out of the vise grip of the notched block, one
bulky bunch of letters after another disappeared into the various city zone boxes, other bundles piled up for the rural routes.
The yellow stake trucks came rumbling across the bridge one
after the other, in the morning and at noon every zone box was
crammed to bursting. Regularly, and particularly one night in
October, certain zones—according to instructions from the
Route Supervisor (who had been instructed in turn)—were
sorted once more, four letters were pulled out and shoved into
an officially stamped and stapled manila envelope and they
missed their delivery the next morning. On Gesine's large
yellow envelope the Italian Post Office had stamped a notifica-
tion concerning the defense of the Atlantic by the victorious
American Armed Forces, Jakob's name and street number had
been typed, there was no return address. When things got too
warm for the glue, it buckled unevenly and set the letter free,

the envelope was dried and pressed and fluoroscoped. The contents consisted of forty cigarettes, brand: Phillip Morris on which no duty had been paid, and a written communication. The cigarettes were contained in two equal packages of twenty each and wrapped in a piece of paper torn from an American family magazine, one side of which praised air travel on a certain type of plane and the other a movie star. The paper on which the communication was written bore the imprint of a medium-sized pension in Taormina, Sicily, under which nine lines had been written by hand; of these photocopies were made. Still that same morning, Jakob's and another letter were returned to the carriers' room, at home that afternoon he found a letter from Gesine with 40 Phillip Morris. He used the wrapping paper for the sandwiches he took along on the night shift, and after the third puff Wolfgang Bartsch finally noticed that Jakob's cigarettes usually didn't taste like that. "Do you have Parsch bring them in for you?" he asked, Parsch was a train conductor Jakob knew. "No," said Jakob, "they're a gift from the Administration." And Herr Rohlfs smoothed out the thick springy photostat and read several times what she had written in her large unbroken round hand with sharp bottom loops in the very blue ink of a hotel-pension in Sicily overlooking the Mediterranean: "Dear Jakob, I'm bumming around the world, in the rain this place looks like the Rehberge, nobody has an umbrella like my old dad. Whom I must honor and you must greet for me. And don't forget your loving half-sister Gesine Cresspahl. Thank you for your long letter on bridge-building." Released, the letter snapped into a roll which Herr Rohlfs slipped through the rings of the birdie-in-the-bush binder, while retaining in his memory the somewhat doughy look of the writing on the photostat and Gesine Cresspahl's old, now for ever unalterable passport photo from the archives of the Jerichow police. During the following days Jakob passed many mail boxes without anybody seeing him post a letter, and besides Herr Mesewinkel knew by now from his impersonal interest in Jakob's existence on this earth: that Jakob worked hard on letters to Gesine and actually thought them out in his great indulgent head.


— BUT ABOUT THAT Cresspahl never breathed a word. I don't think even Jakob knew.

— I don't think they even talked about it. Jakob must have guessed as much. After all, when you look at it closely . . . it just sort of closed in on Cresspahl. So then, Wednesday morning Cresspahl came thumping through Jerichow on his way to the station, looking huge in his black coat and hat, lugging two big suitcases, and people wondered of course, but that morning the cat had his tongue. They stared after him and said Look, there he goes. We won't see *him* again, and he's lived here all his life. And all because of that daughter of his. Wouldn't you know? he just took off. And at noon Jakob's mother came to the station and boarded a train for the county seat, the line runs through there anyhow, and from there, who knows, you can go where you please. But it wasn't Frau Abs who came back that evening, it was Cresspahl, empty-handed. The very same evening someone called the hospital, wouldn't give his name, only wanted to let them know. Wanted to let them know that Frau Gertrud Abs, fifty-nine years of age, residing somewhere on Ziegeleistrasse, well, she wouldn't be in to cook the next morning. Must have thought: in a hospital somebody's got to do the cooking, and if he worried that much, he probably had something to do with it.

That evening on his way home from the station through the dim-lit twilight streets Cresspahl was in a vile humor; every now and then he'd let out an angry grunt. He didn't mind carrying two suitcases to do someone a favor (and so he'd calmed her down on her last evening in this stranger's house where the war had washed her and whose comforting familiarity she was about to leave), but he'd have wished her last years might

have been different. At any rate his house stood empty now,
the prospect of new tenants was unpleasant to him, and such
were the times (Cresspahl said "the toims"): that, for the sake
of honesty, one had to settle for falsehood and subterfuge,
dishonest even to oneself, and a joke only later. He more or
less expected certain dangerous consequences (although Frau
Abs had said nothing about the new catastrophe, he couldn't
think of anything), so he about-faced in front of the war
memorial in the market square and stalked with defiance into
his nightly inn. With Peter Wulff he went into the living-
quarters behind the barroom and put in a long-distance call,
instead of letting Peter Wulff—whose voice was smoother and
not so far back in the throat—do it for him. "We'd none of us
thought we'd ever lay eyes on you again," he said when Cresspahl came back and sat down beside the bar with all its
various bottles, and placidly downed the colorless liquor and
set the glass right back on the shiny zinc. Fat and firm-fleshed,
the proprietor bulked over him and mused about Cresspahl's
situation behind his jovial confidential balloon face, while he
drew much beer from the tap and chatted with several customers. "But you went somewheres," he asked casually, leaning
forward to put the second glass on the rim of the bar. In the
noisy room his words were no more than a pantomime, exactly
like Cresspahl's face, to one side, with high raised eyebrows,
and what Cresspahl said was only a sound among many others,
politely he said: "Yes. Went to the Chamber of Commerce,"
and added with an indignant cough, "Never mind, it's all the
same shit": and so started the second rumor, "He just went
to the Chamber of Commerce," which contradicted the first:
"Yeah, now he's gone to the West."
After half an hour Cresspahl thought the call was taking a
long time to come through, in spite of the bad-tempered intense eager discussion he was having from his place at the bar
about last Thursday's fighting on the Israeli-Jordan border (on
a twelve-mile front); but a sudden defect in the tape recorder
was the cause. Until they got the lines plugged together and
Cresspahl stalked around the bar to the back, and one quiet

lazy spinning spool fed the magnetic tape to another and the
long-distance operator said:

"This is Jerichow, go ahead."

"This is your obedient daughter," she said. The connection was
crystal clear, the sounds had an almost bodily presence. From
the very first word her voice had an undertone of the hesitant
Low German drawl, polished by many languages. Now you
could hear Cresspahl get up again from Peter Wulff's armchair and pull the door shut, he cleared his throat.

"Dear daughter" said Cresspahl: "since you're not writin'
. . . " She had not written and so he permitted himself this
call in the middle of the night. And did it have anything to
do with the fall that was dripping out of the sky, damp on his
daughter's head? "Aren't you writin' to nobody?"

"Yes. To Jakob."

"You're not very happy."

"No.

Father, dear, everything is so wet, I'm hung up in the dark in
my room, and if I invite somebody up to cheat the loneliness
for a while, they're all so clever. I do nothing but talk from
morning to night, just think if I had to answer for all those
words. Nothing's wrong though."

"I'm cheering you up."

"Yes."

"Are you still there? Are you still there? Are you still Hello
are you still there"

"Yeah I'm still here and I'm telling my daughter she's keepin'
her window open when other people have had the heat on for
weeks."

"You heard the streetcar pass."

"Everything."

"It isn't so cold you know. The wind hits flat against my
windows, you're right, they're both open, it smells so of city;
remember the neon sign across from me? it keeps jumping up
under the eaves and I'm lying here by the window and it all
seems so strange. Someone sends you his regards. I'll be leaving on a trip around midnight."

She doesn't write to anybody: said Cresspahl: and then off she goes head over heels. Meantime he'd gotten a letter from Berlin from the Academicians. "Gesine."

"Nonsense. I'm alone in the world, my father sits in Jerichow in the wet fog. I'm not going to see anyone special, it's business."

Cresspahl asked how long the business would take.

"Quite some time. Are you standing at the door?"

That's right: said Cresspahl. "Put a scarf around your neck so you don't catch cold on your trip. And you might leave some money and the keys. Someone's coming to see you, an ole woman, comin' for good."

"Holy Cresspahl" she said, terrified, "why!"

Children shouldn't ask their father about things he doesn't know himself: said Cresspahl reproachfully.

"Badly brought up," she said.

"End of conversation" said he.

"No!" she said.

"Yes. End. Dear father. Your loving daughter. End."

but the two men, the two belated pedestrians who took turns walking past Jakob's house, noticed that both his windows were dark that night. And next morning he came out alone and crossed the sidewalk and took the first bus alone; once he'd climbed into his tower he was on ice for the rest of the day. Later, after Jakob's landlady had gone to work, a pretty young girl rang the doorbell. An eight-year-old boy came out on the landing, he was just getting ready for school, there was toothpaste in one corner of his mouth, it had already dried; he said Jakob wasn't there, he let the lady look into Jakob's room, it was empty, and so these two also went about their respective occupations in the early morning, with a yellow band of sunlight still above the high roof tops, it threw a neat shadow across their backs and on the almost dry pavement under the tousled trees. Much earlier, however, still during the windy night, Herr Mesewinkel had set some motion into the world with several telephone calls, for one hour at the

Berlin border all passes in the express trains were carefully
held under the light and read, and at the East Berlin Station
passengers for the first night train, scurrying between suitcases
and with nighttime haste had to make one more halt and wait
before a weary conscientious policeman at every exit: in blue
uniform with a red armband until, at 2 A.M., there were no
more trains arriving from the north and Herr Rohlfs stretched
out to sleep on the couch in the back of the room that had
been cleared out for him, here as elsewhere, and pulled his
coat up to his chin but did not switch off the lamp. Early the
next morning, while the sky sank lower under the whiteness
and the quiet damp devoured the colder shaft of sunshine, his
car shot out of the southern residential suburb, crossed the big
Elbe bridge and jumped a hundred miles to the north, he was
driving himself and did not take his time, the roads weren't
meant for that. His driver lay curled up in the back seat,
gathering strength for the return trip. At noon, under a light
rain, the car stopped in Jerichow in a street near the station,
pulled halfway up to the muddy trampled front garden of a
deserted looking one-family house and waited, still and stiff,
ready to pounce, for a short while, until a worried stoutish man
came wading through the mud and stumbled into the seat
next to the driver; with a peevish officious voice he began in-
viting Herr Rohlfs into the house and was still leaning over
with outstretched hand when the car jolted forward over the
turtle-shell cobblestones, past rainsodden horse carts up to
the station fence, and Herr Rohlfs contemplated dreamy-eyed
the single platform between the dull dirty tracks while cursing
the man ahead of him in a pedantic and inventive fashion.
The man said nothing now: even his silence attested to Herr
Rohlfs' superior knowledge. The heavy, long, high-slung, spat-
tered car turned abruptly, throwing a large pancake of mud
against the station fence and crept hurriedly onto the wider
though rougher pavement of the main street with its one-story
houses; at the two-story Consumers Store it ran around the
church with its spire like a bishop's mitre; from there it got
lost on the way to the cemetery and finally stopped as though

perplexed behind the old tile works next to the high jagged
wall of the ramshackle cooling shed which was still standing.
Herr Rohlfs inspected the long house with its peaked roof
among bare trees in the farthest corner of the wet garden,
while the man who had joined him translated the view with
his hands, pointing from the desolate courtyard of the tile
works to the quarry in a depression on the ocean side; the
driver was still in his seat, indifferent, by himself, his head
backward, blowing the smoke of a cigarette in sudden deep
sighs through the slightly open window. Herr Rohlfs typed
what the stoutish man was saying on a graceful flat portable
across his knees (Herr Rohlfs seldom wrote by hand); the
elder bushes were rustling beside the cooling shed. Soon after,
the car backed up and climbed the grassed-over path between
the tile works courtyard and the wet garden, turned sharply
in front of the Soviet Headquarters and escaped with rapid
bounds from the mud into Ziegeleistrasse, hurried toward the
bishop's mitre, sped around the cemetery and raced into the
bluish distance, away from Jerichow . . . where the wind blew
stark and dark from the ocean and fell on the land, on my
father, on his house: as Gesine once wrote in a letter, she's the
daughter, she's not here any more.

As the first gray cloud blobs of evening rumpled the sky over
the misty pale track field, Wolfgang Bartsch arrived with his
key in Jakob's tower to relieve him. He stood as though undecided and in argument with himself, leaning on the table,
looking, listening while Jakob gave a ruthless report with his
pencil; without paying much attention he lit a cigarette in
his round rosy blond bespectacled face. "We're all doing our
best," he said clearly, with reserve and bad humor, but then
he showed some interest and sat down in the swivel chair and
drew a line to mark the end of Jakob's shift. He hadn't even
expected a look for an answer, and Jakob didn't give him one.
He dumped the ashes and the countless matches out of the
tray and telephoned the main office to check out. He held the
mouthpiece up to Bartsch's face for him to say "hello there,"
the main office voice in the telephone echoed "hello there."

One of the loudspeakers crackled, Bartsch bunched himself into position. He nodded to Jakob's "Take it easy"; in the corridor, his urgent nervous voice could still be heard, a little muffled. Jakob pulled the key out of the lock and walked down the corridor, his coat thrown loosely over his shoulders, his briefcase in one hand, toward the blended twilight of the staircase. On the panel beside the elevator the light slipped jerkily from one number to the next toward the top, halfway up it usually stopped. Jakob pressed the button, the light kept climbing. He stood in the musty stridently illuminated cage without leaning against the walls and rebuttoned the collar of his uniform; but we're all doing our best: Bartsch had said. Jakob smiled and shook his head. Wolfgang had gone on for a degree. That was already four or five years ago, but somehow Jakob remembered it as though it explained Wolfgang's bitterness, a leftover from school or somewhere else. The elevator thumped to a stop on the ground floor, from above the bell was calling. Jakob handed his key through the watchman's tiny window and said, "Take it easy." "Take it easy, Jakob," answered Jenning, half turning his head. He'd known Jakob for five or six years, must have been one of his apprentices about 1951 in a block tower north of the station. But Jakob walked right on. He showed the two police guards at the door the broad diagonal stripe of color across his pass, they looked without looking and went on with their conversation in a muffled southern singsong. He slammed the heavy iron gate shut behind him and walked off, across the tracks in the thin drizzle. (He turned the pass over and showed the other side to the woman conductor); the hours between the blinding hectic shifts seemed so similar, he couldn't tell one from the other. The city was an unvarying landscape, its streets were interchangeable in his memory. The sky was white.

The brightness of the day had almost faded when Jakob jaywalked across the street from the bus stop. That day a car stood parked behind the bus, three steps ahead of the street lamp. Jakob paid no attention and walked right on between the fender and the curb in the daylight that wet fog was

smothering more and more, until the rear door of the car
swung open and stopped him. Out of the car's low void he
heard someone say his name, in a hand stretched toward him
he saw, clipped under the shiny crystal of a flashlight, a narrow leather case, open, containing a thin sheaf of paper—the
kind on which money is usually printed. "Well," said Jakob,
sounding more curious than anything else, and he wasn't
saying it to anyone in particular, not even to himself; he
walked around the back of the car and got in from the street
side. The car bounced forward, its motion pressed him comfortably back into the seat; he set his briefcase down, they
passed the bus, its headlights shone through the rear window
on the driver's neck between his cap and the frayed rim of his
rubberized collar. Jakob pulled a cigarette from the case he
felt pressed into his hand; he lighted it, concentrating on the
flame because of the unknown face beside him. There was
an ashtray hanging from the hand rail on the back of the front
seat. Fatigue weighed on his body and on his thoughts; heavily
slumped back, he saw the headlights sweep along housefronts,
shiver over the pavement, over cars, tree trunks, swerve around
house corners, fences. At one point he was startled to discover
that he wasn't thinking of any one person in particular; it
made him feel uneasy then he forgot about it. In the business
district they slowed down, the great brightness from shop
windows and street lamps and headlights flashed into the car
from time to time. Jakob remained sitting where he was,
smoking, until they stopped at a lonely gate in front of a
lighted staircase and Jakob followed the man from the car
down a brilliant corridor between many doors behind which
he heard radio music, talking, typing. They entered a windowless cube of a room and sat down opposite each other in
noiseless armchairs at a chess table under a wooden lamp with
a silk shade. Jakob was studying Herr Fabian's face. (This was
the name he used, with a slight bow, to introduce himself to
Jakob.) Whose face was one of those Jakob didn't associate
with of his own accord, nor would he have looked at it closely
if he had happened to encounter it with his eyes on the street

or elsewhere, it was one of those he'd never have taken as be-
longing to a special type or profession at first glance, or even
given it a second thought. The face turned toward him with
attentive soft-brown eyes that were appraising other things
beside Jakob, and Jakob thought that the wide hunched forehead and the corners of his mouth in the square fleshy face
would want to give up very little of their assumed rights; Herr
Fabian's dreamy eyes lost their dullness when you looked more
closely. Jakob smiled as his memory went over the evening,
followed him—more and more surprised—to this room, to different cigarettes, and the face smiled again without a reserve
of irony: but he was having his little joke with the rapid
change in his expectations, and that precisely brought them
to terms during their goodwilled inspection.


— So what do you think they said to him. Probably gave him
the thumbnail course in history from the Theory of The Surplus
Value up to the intensification of the class struggle by the
avant-garde . . . they're right, as long as they keep talking.
— Never mind, I wouldn't have wanted to listen to that from
where Jakob was sitting.
— Jakob could thank his lucky stars for being alive in times
like these, because he'd never had to experience the irrationality of life,
— Which came into the world with capitalized private ownership of machines and raw materials and money, so that the
capitalist can hire a man's labor and invest the product of the
labor endlessly to satisfy his needs
— He uses the product of labor for his anti-humane purposes
as well as his vanities
— Yes, and often the product's value is double the wages, and
triple, you live on cheating and—let's call it exploitation. If
one fires you, you've got to go to the next, and if you just
stand there and scream they sic the police on you, who get
paid for that, they've got to live too. So just add it all up.
Jakob's father went to South America for a couple of years.

— They must have known about that. And they must have told him that a man can make a mistake. Say he sets out for the distant promised land. Suddenly the distance becomes annoyingly oppresive, becomes proximity, capitalists happen to live there too, they've just been waiting for a young Pomeranian farmer. So in the end he preferred to go back to the misery at home, because it was home. That's probably the kind Jakob's father was, and Jakob too, maybe.

— No, with Jakob it must have been something else I think. But when Jakob's father got back, the worker still couldn't buy the things he had produced with his life for the money they gave him for it. Apart from that it was just home and anyway the—what did you call it: irrationality you called it, was still mighty prevalent at home: that's what they told him probably. Another beer?

— Yes. And the capitalists bred criminals to enforce exploitation, and the criminals played on individual prestige and had everybody going around saying everything is dandy and may it last forever. And they couldn't get their fill of it at home, so they spread war all over the world, Jakob could have died in it, then they choked in their own stench. And the conquerors had their will with the Land of Evil.

— That's just about what they must have told him, without mincing their words: and why is the advancement of socialism just? because capitalism was unjust. At last, a kind of justice that doesn't explain itself. Yes, two more beers here. Put it on our check.


HERR ROHLFS

*I based my reasoning on the facts. I told him that the Soviet Union abolished private ownership of machines and raw materials and the wage system—not to mention the land reform, he'd be aware of that himself—when they liberated us from the fascists, and after so much filth, incredibly, a new State was born which managed labor fairly and channeled the surplus between wages and labor value toward the common*

*good; in times such as these all sorts of people could be happy
and why not Jakob? Didn't he think it was worth the effort?
I asked him, he nods politely with his large tired face, I wasn't
sure he'd been listening, he just sat there, looking, but thoughtful. And for a while we merely listened to the damn radio next
door, religiously we listened, some stupid girl chorus with an
eternal teasing refrain, it seeped nostalgic endless out of the
wall as though it were the greatest: a kiss from a miss that
brings you bliss, miss kiss bliss: that's what they sing about.
"I do have a certain overall perspective," Jakob began after a
while, slowly, the way he probably always speaks, but he
didn't want to talk against the music from next door, perhaps
he was also missing his sleep or dinner, that's the way he
looked, but where could I get anything to eat in this place?
And it's just because I'm able to have an overall perspective:
he said: that makes my job more difficult. Because he meant:
he said: that men in all walks of life will send each other
things and go on trips, and that the social order (if he might
use the term—; suddenly I sat transfixed, immobilized with
suspense, something in his way of thinking struck a chord in
me; by and by, it dawned on me that it was similar to my own:
as though argument and point of objection were known to me,
not that I had ever used it! but maybe I also just sit like that,
friendly, listening, and let the conversation reach a certain
point determined solely by instinct, then I speak my piece and
twist it in the opposite direction; not the subject but the tech-
nique must have felt familiar, must have struck me, although
I realized it only much later, maybe that was precisely why I
failed to call him to order. Looked at him as though I couldn't
move, if he might use that term—;) the social order changed
the motivations and circumstances of human behavior merely
on the surface. That was based on my facts, wasn't it? The circumstances in Jakob's sector are then, generally speaking, the
same as in all other sectors, namely, the third, and sometimes
the second tracks were torn up by the Red Army and are missing. The French did the same: I thought to myself, but that
wasn't Jakob's point. I sat still, like a bird in a trap. Moreover,*

*the German Democratic Republic, in realizing its first five-year
plan 1950–1955, was forced to build up its own heavy industry
to the detriment of railway transportation, "some of our lines
have had the same rails since 1929, we never get enough new
ones, and now we're in the second five-year plan," the things
one finds out, I've asked a lot of people, nobody cared about
that, and he says it so casually, like a statistic; why, doesn't
he give a damn! "Every summer and every winter we make
up a timetable and have them tell us where the slow spots are,
and we divide the minutes into smaller and smaller segments,
trying to make it accurate to some extent and then, the very
next week, they notify us of three new slow spots," I can still
hear him. As though he were giving someone a brief intro-
ductory lecture on local railway conditions, that someone is
sitting across from him and can't hold still with all that information. All right, and besides we've got to remember that
traffic now is about three times as heavy as it was before the
war, and of course the lines used to play a very different, much
less important role in the railway system of the undivided
Germany. Most transcontinental freights: he explains to me:
run through his sector on their way to the Scandinavian ferries
and to Hamburg, getting them through on time was important for the prestige of the German Democratic Republic,
he always pronounced the whole name unabbreviated just as
I do, and what do I mean by it and what does he mean? And
the only direct north-south connection in the country runs
through his sector, the routine traffic of local and express
freight and commuters is not insignificant in this city, the first
Elbe port this side of the border: what liberties he's taking I
thought, I'd realized that for some time, until I understood
that this, then, was his hampering overall perspective: "the
way things are I won't be able to get the trains from either
direction through my sector on time this fall. Besides, a little
way up there's the intersection where the West German
Hamburg-Berlin expresses cross my tracks, they've got to be
on time, and I have to hold my trains at the bridge," trying to
stay on time is no longer a matter of pride or pleasing the*

*passengers, but the primary condition of such an overcrowded schedule: one's overall perspective sometimes made one marvel that it worked at all: he said. "And not enough coal," he added, hesitating for the first time, without going into an explanation. How can you refuse your friend coal just because he has no dollars? That's how it is with your socialism, my good man. But he didn't stop because he distrusted me, he just didn't want to be irritating. Not for a minute had it occurred to him that I might be concerned with anything but his job, so this would have been beside the point. He still hadn't recovered from the pressure of his day. If he should give in a moment and let his thoughts wander, it would mean the end of thirty people or twenty thousand marks down the drain, he's responsible to himself for that, the job's got to be done and he had to bear all that responsibility on top of it. And his job is really this responsibility and nothing else, I thought; I'd have liked to ask him about his life. What a serious-minded man, I thought.*

— Now let's admit that there's more to it than just a difference in the distribution of the surplus value, it really does represent a plus; when they don't yak so much about their hospitals and paid vacations I'm perfectly willing to admit it.
— Then you might just as well say too, why don't you, that justice is evident at first glance
— So obvious it hits you right in the eye
— And isn't it up to us to show the only viable path into the future to the other two-thirds of the German land still groaning under abuse and irrationality? It's supposed to be a noble task. No fainting at the sight of hardships. And nevertheless.
— Yes. And nevertheless and still. Jakob knew that as well as I do (one wouldn't think so), I can imagine how he always thought ahead, he could picture the whole route and where it ends, no U turn, detour, one way street: and nevertheless
— The victorious capitalists abused the defeated and encouraged exploitation through private ownership and reinforced

retrogression in life's evolution on earth, once again the criminals weren't far away. Because the capitalists don't like the way their neighbors distribute the surplus value, they prepare for war and want to free the worker of the freedom he has finally achieved; with all the means at their disposal, they strive to undermine the strength of rational existence, they do not hesitate to use unscrupulous devices, they appeal to all your outmoded notions and hire you as the handyman of reaction: I say, do you hear, they are despicable and doomed, shouldn't everybody stand up against their criminal doings for the sake of socialism's national evolution? And who told you for sure that Jakob's the way he says he is?

— You get yourself into a rage the way a squirrel jumps, except that a squirrel can jump faster than you; you say just what they want to hear and yet, somehow, you sound as though you knew better, what's your objection, what the hell can be said against it?


HERR ROHLFS

*but of course at this point I couldn't ask him about his life, so I trusted that he had listened in his usual thorough manner, and maybe I did give an answer (although for any third person the conversation must long have seemed senseless meaningless) when I said that by now any means seemed justified against stagnation and regression, against a change back to the old: against all those who resist the change toward the new, the future. While I was saying all this, we kept pushing cigarettes toward each other and offering each other lights, showing each other all kinds of courtesies, I practically felt my wife could have stepped into the room, into the conversation, with a plate of cookies and a fresh pot of tea, and afterwards Jakob would have watched my loving long-haired daughter kiss her father goodnight under the understanding eyes of the guest (as though I'd have wished to have Jakob as my guest); it was all right with me that Jakob knew what I was driving at; although I don't think he's ever afraid, not of any-*

*thing. And it seemed to me at first that he talked beside the point intentionally when he changed the atmosphere of casual conversation to annoyance and spoke angrily, stretching in his armchair as though he were dissatisfied all over, letting me know that the call to order should have come at an entirely different point, not at the one to which we had after all progressed, and that he was aware of that too: "If I'm supposed to know such people, I'm most probably like them," he said. I realized his anger was forthright and not implying anything else: "but I'd like to say I don't feel that way." "The people I know all do their best," said Jakob; and he probably wasn't even trying to lie. How about his work, was his work harmful to the future of socialism? No. Definitely not. Yes, but can one ever do enough for the socialist cause? So it couldn't be helped: I had been overhasty and half in a fog, he caught me unawares, it was I who had ignored the rules, and so he said nothing about what time it was and that at midnight he had to go back and sit in his tower until the naked morning with his responsibility for coal and all those different human lives, he simply stopped talking. But it had been said and repeated, it was there in all its reality: no one can ever do enough for the socialist cause, shouldn't one discuss that with everybody, Jakob?*

— That may be, but Jakob's mother had to leave because of it. And surely he (because I have the impression that it was just one, only one man could tell him that:) had no intention of doing her harm, simply his presence, his very existence, the fact that he moved around and spoke the way he did, drove her away; and if it was just one man he must have been forced to come right out and admit his part in her leaving which might have looked like decency (he considers his profession like any other, these things can regrettably happen on his job, but he, too, has a mother: you've got to believe that he understands without him having to say so), so Jakob probably said he didn't deny it.

— Yes. But that covers a lot of ground, for instance: that kind of work is essential and consequently the sacrifices that go with it are justified. To me it's more a proof of Jakob's patience. Anyhow, if somebody had told *me* on an empty stomach during my sleeping time before the next shift that my mother had left and that I'd never see her again here, and now Jakob's mother. She had counted on staying for good you know, just think how she must have searched among the eleven years of dearly bought possessions, all she could take was two suitcases, and now Jakob. What can you say to a thing like that: far away from home, plunged back into misery, having to flee again. Right? She's over the border, and now: she passed through Jakob's station, right under his tower, the train made its stop from 5:03 to 5:12 platform three, track five, and you know how it is with an old woman. She thinks of everything in advance, plans it exactly, this comes after that, and then the excitement sets in (Jakob was her only child, your mother never believes you might possibly be grown up and able to take care of yourself, she had to see him once more, one last time), and her careful planning gets all tangled and knotted like a rotten net. Anyhow, she must have wanted to telephone Jakob, she tried, but the pay phone in the station connects to the local exchanges, not to the railway exchange; on the second try she dialed the right number, it was Jakob's number, but someone else's on the city exchange, and she didn't want to leave her train now that she'd finally boarded with those two heavy bags

which had even given Cresspahl trouble in the sprawling station at the county seat, but afterwards he sat, innocent and placid, in the express that was going to the former German capital with connections across the border. Cresspahl went back out on the platform with her and exchanged tickets, later from her seat in the train she saw him standing, remaining, long, old-fashioned, cranky, at the very end of the platform, that's when the sun came out once more and fell pale and speckled through the dirty glass roof

— And while she's settling into the seat Cresspahl got for her, thinking this way and that, not knowing what to do in her haste, they start the train up ahead with such a sudden clumsy jolt, and before she has time to look for Jakob's tower (he probably told her), the train's been creeping forward and clickety-clacks faster and faster out of the station and away from Jakob. Can't have taken Jakob long to figure that out and if somebody had told me that. . .

— But why, do you think, didn't she leave word with Cresspahl, why didn't she say anything to Cresspahl, with everything depending on him, what do you make of that?

— That's honesty. Don't forget how old she is, what they taught her in school. A promise is a promise, keep thy tongue from evil and thy lips from speaking guile: she wouldn't even lie for her own advantage, even if it hurt no one. Perhaps they made her sign something, the written word is the written word. And after all it wasn't about Cresspahl, but about her not getting mixed up in the class struggle (since she had no idea what it was all about anyway). No. For her there was only getting out (okay I know: desertion) and telling Jakob one last time: Be sure to eat properly, and don't smoke so much, keep well.


"No," said Jakob as though repeating it for the fourth time, Herr Rohlfs nodded, he leaned forward and said "I beg your pardon," although Herr Kowalke (who wasn't really called Kowalke, though he might be used to assuming still another name at such points in these conversations) although Herr Kowalke had not offered (not to Jakob) extra time off, Western trade magazines, foreign travel, expense money, exit permits to West Germany, but had merely said, "Faith and loyalty don't go unrewarded." Jakob was not nervous. He felt immobilized between lampshade and chair arm and table edge, he left the cigarette lying in its thick quiet smoke and did not budge, still not quite accepting the reality of the news: he really held it away from himself as though it were some abstract product of the conditions of the conversation which, in itself, was understandable only from a distance. "There is nothing I want," he said, and the throbbing undercurrent of his heart made him realize that he had just described his life during that fall, the lazy abstaining anguish moved inside him as though he had always known it, beginningless somewhere in time. He had been trying something with his life which had turned out like this: because the time ("the toims") was and were such that a man had little say in his own life and had to take on the responsibility for things he had not started. So a man floats back and forth between his job and a furnished room according to rules and routine, sometimes it surprises him that this is humanly possible. But it evidently was. And after Herr Rohlfs had finished speaking of faith and loyalty with his air of sincere curiosity, consideration, surprise: the pledge to silence meant nothing bad and wasn't aimed at anyone, everyone concerned would be informed (they hadn't touched upon that yet), because the right thing had to be said at the right moment—, Jakob signed his name slowly and meticulously, pledging absolute silence about this, his temporary absence from everyday life; Herr Rohlfs would meet Jakob again Tuesday evening, as a Herr Rohlfs at the bar of the Hotel Elbe, today was Thursday, he hoped Jakob might still catch up on essential sleep, unfortunately it had not been possible any other way. They leaned back and smiled again and once again, their smiles were not meant for each other but for the evil conditions of present-day existence. Jakob let himself be driven back through the night to his tower. When they reached the center of the city, he tapped the driver on the shoulder and asked him to stop; he got out and stepped into the noisy blue haze of the Melodie Bar where he bought cigarettes and sandwiches. When he came back to the car, the driver opened the front door for him; he was a very jaunty young man who behaved toward Jakob with athletic irony, as though they were old buddies, but Jakob climbed wordlessly into the seat beside him; the driver stopped his smiles and winks. Only at the gate did he look sideways. His foot was already on the brakes when Jakob nodded; with a muffled purr the car glided with large luminous eyes diagonally up to the gate in the quiet rain. Jakob grabbed his coat and briefcase from the back seat and without a word he walked past the murmuring guards to the stairs. He stood beside Wolfgang Bartsch and looked into the widely spread clusters of light signals and lamps in the fog blanket below, and inhaled the delicate smell of cinders and damp air and heavy rubbing of iron on iron, while they discussed the job; Jakob thought: he's one of the best dispatchers, that's all I know about him. But then a voice from a loud-speaker said "mawnin" as Jakob had said "mawnin" when he walked in, and Wolfgang replied: "mawnin" which meant good morning and was the night shift's greeting, this was his return to the world. From the shadows he could see that Wolf-gang's forehead trembled constantly just above the eyebrows and that his eyes blinked in the glare of the lamp; he found himself nodding, remembering. "Mawning, Wolfgang," he said before he walked over to the cot in the rear. As he stretched out under the light coat of his summer uniform, Wolfgang had finished and swiveled around in his chair; his face was half in the dark and blurry, but the slight surprise in his voice was friendly and familiar. "Mawnin, Jakob," he said, "you still have three hours to sleep." "Yes," said Jakob. But he fell asleep expecting to be waked up.

JÖCHE, anyone know Jöche?
In the morning he'd run his train across the bridge into the cool red sun. He'd lean on the accordion gate of the locomotive and spit cigarette smoke into the rushing dirty airstream. The tower slid toward him through shrouds of lumpy light. He blew a call for signals, the tough hollow whistle tone rose from the hurried rumbling of the train and geysered up in front of Jakob's window, stood and fell away. Jöche's turned-up long

bony face shifted sideways as it moved away from the tower,
withdrew into the cab, the train clanked across the switches
and into the station, the signals changed behind it, the tail
lights fused with the early day. Jakob pushed the window
shut. Lack of sleep stretched weightless transparent lucidity
behind his forehead, the prospect of a changed existence came
to meet him as he returned to his neat clearly laid-out job;
anyone know Jakob? As to Martienssen, he came for the relief,
stalked in on his stick, he had worked on the German Railroad
three times as long as Jakob, his hair had been combed back in
single straight wet strands, stiff gray arches stood up at the
temples, all the wrinkles in his face flowed backwards, brisk
and grumpy he said, "Take it easy, Herr Abs," to Jakob, who
replied "easy" with a brevity that pleased Martienssen; no fuss.
Martienssen found his conduct relaxed and to the point.
Afterwards Jakob went into the restaurant on Industriestrasse
with its damp sober smell of the still orderly new day. Jöche
was sitting almost alone at one of the narrow tables, near the
window, his hook-nosed angular face bent over the steaming
broth, he was busy coming back to our undangerous everyday
life. A locomotive consists of numerous tons of artfully assembled steel with inhuman strength, it races ahead wild and
irresistible on its tracks and can't escape them and slams into
the switches with all its weight which grows in proportion to
the square of its speed, the heavy hurry of the power engine
is felt in every one of its parts: Jöche didn't mean to say it
was fear. It was the awareness of swift danger mixed with an
attack of great sobriety. Two years, and he still hadn't got
used to driving a locomotive. He knew each movement by
heart, every precaution came to him by instinct, but after work
he liked to sit quietly for a while in a house that stood still, at
a window that didn't move, and let the quiver of racing steel
ebb from his nerves at underarms and temples. It was the job
he had wanted, apprenticed for during years of machine shops
and schools; aloud he never said how things stood. But Jakob
walked in through the door and saw Jöche sit there in that
kind of tough calm which he knew and recognized.

— That's what they told me at the end of my run: Cresspahl's gone to the West. With two suitcases and his hat, no one could make out what he was saying. So he's gone to the West. (Everybody thought he would, eventually.) Look I'm from Jerichow, so it wasn't just another bit of news; it changed the whole town, I think of myself arriving in Jerichow and Cresspahl no longer there. You understand? If I tell that to Jakob, he'll bang his fist on the table, or ask—not believing a thing: "What are you saying, what did you say?" and after all, it means all kinds of things to him and I didn't want to stick my nose in it. But now I had to change all that, a man can change his mind if he feels like it, and I thought: well, he must already know. Or, since he couldn't know: perhaps he's been expecting it. And anyway: Jakob is as steady as a rock. Because he was just sitting there, as though wondering what was going to happen next, or something like that. But actually he'd already heard the third rumor and he probably hadn't heard it just as a rumor either, then he lets me talk.
— Do you blame him?
— No. I don't blame him.

He lifted Jöche's cap to the window sill and sat down across from him, they said hello. Jakob ordered what Jöche was having. The door to the kitchen stood open, the waitress was scrubbing the floor. From the tables against the back wall words and smoke rose thinly toward the ceiling and fused with the large heavy light that slanted in on Jakob and Jöche. Jöche was saying Cresspahl had left Jerichow and passed away to the West. Jakob immediately took in the harsh high voice and the wary look, absorbed it with that complete all-engulfing sympathy of a long-standing, never-questioned feeling of trust. But he nodded sideways, without looking up, when the hot clear broth and the rolls were placed before him: so Jöche took back his eyes and looked at his own hands noisily working on the crisp roll. Two young men sitting at a wide window, one in the clean, well-pressed elegant uniform with three stars on the braided silver epaulettes, the other in the sweaty sooty oily engineer's coveralls, they were used to each other, had been friends for six or seven or eight years, with time their jobs had taken different tracks, but not until today had their lives been different; Jakob knew, Jöche found out too late. Jakob didn't come to his decision before the brief moment of looking down. Only a while ago he had got up and gone to the window to see Jöche go by in his locomotive and wave to him as he always had and now too, that's when the change struck him, he had stood at the open window, looked down and not waved. He pushed his cup away and said with his prepared face: he wouldn't be surprised if it were true.

All morning he acted that way with Jöche, not surprised; as though it were true. Jöche is a special name. His mother had called him that, and the kids in schools, his girlfriends always started out saying Jochen but ended up saying Jöche, only Muschi Altmann had said Jöche from the start, but she was the one to marry him. During the one last school year in Jerichow that Jakob spent next to the long lanky eager boy, the name Jöche stood for willingness, good-natured conduct, the volunteering for public chores had disappeared in the meantime, the friendliness was still evident. Jakob sat heavy, pensive, well-intentioned in his wide motionless body in front of Jöche, however what Jöche took for a reflection of sadness in Jakob's face was something else. Jakob was surprised that out of the murky shame inside him lights of irony were gradually beginning to flicker, making him say something like: "Jöche. I can hardly believe it, Jöche." How had the news reached Jöche? The news had traveled down from the coast with the locomotive crew: said Jöche, "What people won't say," said Jakob, thinking to himself: they saw Cresspahl get on the train, but not off, now they're weaving the whole story around Cresspahl, as though things were the way a man sees them. For a breath length he also got lost in his mother's panic, walking the long stretch from the hospital through Jerichow to the station, fearful, trying to look casual, running past the raised green signal of the angry stationmaster, scrambling onto the incoming train, she'd never been good at lying, then she faded again. Occasionally it occurred to him to accept Jöche's tale as true, then he'd see Cresspahl, tall and powerful, march to the station carrying suspicious suitcases, wanting to ride away into the world to join his much missed and loved daughter, "because, naturally, she's behind it all Jöche." "That's what I thought too," said Jöche and a brittle laugh spilled from Jakob's chest, he felt it joyless in his eyes, the rest had been more a violent kind of breathing. "Must be hard for such an old man," said Jöche; Cresspahl had, after all, been alive for seven decades, four of which he had spent in Jerichow, in the stark dark winds, and Jakob said, "Yes. That's it. Jöche," he said, looking into Jöche's well-meaning presence, feeling defenseless. Jöche thought about fathers' love for their daughters, shook his head, sliced the air with the side of his hand, twisted his mouth to contempt and looked so totally reliable that Jakob didn't feel like leaving. Meanwhile their conversation switched to the mighty of the land and they agreed on the ineptitude of the solutions they proposed; Jöche did most of the talking, after they had downed a few glasses of the liquid that lifts your spirits and strengthens your patience against the things to come. Behind Jakob stood his fatigue and leaned forward with him and smiled his understated smile and applauded Jöche's presence in everything; so everything seemed to happen all by itself and as though nobody had to decree the inevitability of their unadmitted separation. When they parted in the market square under a hard blue sky that was pulling warmth out of the noon sun, Jöche turned on the streetcar steps and waved his hand, and Jakob raised his arm as he had wanted to that morning. Now his entire behavior returned, unused, from Jöche and detached itself piece by piece from the morning: as though he hadn't uttered a single word or accepted a single glance or communicated in any way.

When you dial a number on the telephone, each figure transmits a coded electric impulse to the corresponding relays of the central office, the relays sift the impulses (the pre-selector raises its arm and automatically finds an open exchange selector) down the line and to the telephone of the desired connection. These automatic installations are admirable. This also applies to the public pay phones at the city's important intersections in their yellow-painted glass-and-metal booths. Jakob pulled the door in until it clicked into the lock track, movement and noise from the market square seeped thickly through the gap. As he dialed the number of the railroad office, his left hand with the receiver hung on to one corner of the phone box, the thin second hand raced around the watch face on his wrist. Besides normal mental and physical fitness, a man must be able to prove possession of a good reputation and an accurate watch to find employment with the railroad. At first he'd still had the old pocket watch passed on to him by Herr von Bonn of Bonnin, that's about all it was worth; this one now was a gift from Cresspahl's daughter two years back, he had a watch, he could watch the time. But how does something like a good reputation fit into the admirable multitude of events within the span of time? because one thing happens after another and means this in opposition to that and is irretrievably lost in time: whether you notice it or not, want it, condone it, or would rather, in the end, take it back. Anyhow, the morning had passed with Jöche and could no longer be salvaged whole and begun anew, one's good reputation can easily be washed away by such an irresistible stubborn flow of time. After the buzzer on the operator's board in the railroad office had sounded for twenty seconds, the speaking line opened, a voice repeated the number. Jakob said good morning. "Abs" he said and "D-1, please." Dispatcher's head office. The dispatcher's head offices are assigned to a Government railroad department, they are under the jurisdiction of the administrative offices (O-d-1), and those in turn are under the Ministry of Transportation (H-d-1, the Chief Dispatcher). "I'll connect you," said the voice after a brief pause, to let Jakob know he had been recognized, but Jakob said nothing and remembered to say thank you only later, after the connection had already pushed deep into the railroad's own lines, after he'd already been switched over to dispatchers. He had no idea who had handled his call, confidentially asking no questions, then the delay slipped his mind again. He wedged the receiver between coat collar and tilted neck, patted his pockets for cigarettes. Outside the booth the streetcar was grinding around a curve, shrieking; it put the brakes on and came into view panel by panel through the gap in the door; car motors were idling at the pedestrian crossing. Tenacious and obstinate his thoughts covered up the sight, the imagined sounds mixed willfully with the movements in his head. A man is responsible for his life but not for relays: he thought: but now the relays weren't doing their part, Herr Rohlfs also abstained, who then was to blame for Jöche's going, who could justify the inevitable? "Yes," he said and repeated his name when the line opened again and the dispatchers' operator said "Dispatchers." "Abs, shift supervisor, please," he said. The shift supervisor was Peter Zahn, yesterday he had sat in the cafeteria with Peter Zahn, they had looked at the girls together and after a while they had again talked about marriage in their usual arrogant ridiculous way, matter-of-fact Peter Zahn had stayed in his chair, matter-of-factly he had said "hello there Jakob" and still, his face had shown a reliable expression of greeting in the slightly murky blue eyes; now we shall see, thought Jakob. "Hello there," said Peter Zahn, leaning forward on his desk, then he said "hello there, Jakob," then nothing more. That was less than yesterday. In the public phone booth on the market square Jakob took the cigarette out of his mouth and nodded his brittle smile, before he said, "Peter, I need two days rest." Now he could feel Peter's hand over the mouthpiece, then someone walked through his office, slamming the door, finally Peter answered jeering: "Rest. Rest!" The next shift on Jakob's section was supposed to start in two hours. But Jakob said nothing of overtime and rattled nerves, because he had allowed Herr Rohlfs plenty of time to let them know, faith and loyalty should be worth that much. "Until Monday morning? Will that be enough? Second shift then?" asked Peter who had not leafed through his lists. "Take it easy," said Jakob in conclusion. "Hey, Jakob," Peter said quickly, but Jakob had not moved. "Give me a call Monday," he said, and Jakob said nothing for a short while. Then he said yes, they said goodbye, all in all it was not less than yesterday but so changed, it couldn't be recognized: and could Jöche help it if Herr Rohlfs hadn't phoned him as well? So a man has little to do with his presumably unique movement through time which is: today and here, and the most important is that which must be done first, which claims the future for itself and the dignity of the past besides.

First of all.

As to the circumstances of the more recent past, an approximate agreement is generally assumed to exist, that's because you remember you were there. The approximate agreement is not very clear-cut in the public speeches of contemporary speakers, Cresspahl would say: most of them were probably there, but each saw a different house burn down. And houses never look alike anyway: he would say and in the same way Jakob's distant view had completely deviated from the general agreement (and in the same way perhaps from Sabine, yes: such things can happen). Because at the age of fourteen he had come upon the end and heritage of the German war, having no part in it, however. To the extent that he didn't understand, didn't know what to make of the soldiers of the defeated army who arrived in Jerichow at the straggle end of the exodus, grimy, tired, without discipline or decency, and begged for bread and water, and stole like vultures and numbly continued along the coast, westward, as though to escape what they had left behind. He found their weapons and uniforms in the quarry, they were none of his business, he picked them up like a beachcomber. Then, quiet or boisterous, in another cloth, the pursuers came driving through the streets in low clattering carriages drawn by small fast horses with queer bridles with pierced rifle butts and were dignified because of their victory. Dignified because of the German Plague that became known with their arrival, dignified because of their orders to bring in the harvest. He was sixteen then and supported his mother working on farms and bootlegging for the victorious Soviet forces. But each half-liter bottle of liquor

or brandy or kirsch netted him approximately a fourth of the
price and with the interim currency of the Allied Powers in
Germany he bought a wardrobe and beds and put them up in
the dim three-windowed room beside Cresspahl's furniture; if
this thing had several angles, he concerned himself only with
this one alone. Surely he also thought about the hazards that
were supposed to have befallen a woman who lived on Bau-
strasse, whose husband worked at the town hall, at the hands
of a victorious Soviet soldier in the woods; but he had no part
in the insults because of which a wild embittered band of
fighters in their conquered zone of Germany roamed about
beating and shooting and getting drunk and paying for everything with their own money; he got along. And in the sharp
peasant smell of their tobacco, and in the surprisingly belted
blouses of their uniforms, and in the foreign language he
guessed the extraordinary size of the world and the multi-
plicity of human life. The scantily recut, redyed uniforms of
the new German police seemed always an afterthought, as did
their missions (the long, sweating man in his unevenly faded
cloth arrived on a rusty bicycle in the farmyard on a hot summer day and explained his uniform to the peasant woman and
showed her his papers, but badge and uniform proved nothing, because the eggs were still being handed over at gun
point to individual marauding Soviet soldiers and therefore
there could be no question of delivery to the city, he incessantly wiped the sweatband of his cap and repeated what he
had said too often, and the mocking suspicious face of the
peasant woman who did not tell her dog to stop growling), but
Jakob did not wish to deny dignity either to Herr Fabian or
to Herr Rohlfs, to the extent that he had become aware of
their reality and to the extent that anything has dignity when
it succeeds another (and when anything is more worth wishing
for than those things of the past). However, he had no part
in this dignity.

Traveled nevertheless on an express north to Jerichow on
tracks that carry and guide the artfully mobile contraption and
found himself subject to the conditions of public passenger

transportation (although with a service pass) and spent the whole afternoon in the realm of physics, steam pistons, and air brakes; the weather looked like evening rain; arrogant, irresponsible, disgusted he sat at the window of the dining car and let the landscape swim past, his eyes following the wires from signal to road gates to switch to main signal to intermediate signal to approach signal, he rode along under the telegraph wires that were humming with train positions and block clearances and he knew that some dispatcher was watching over it all somewhere, over safety and danger and being on schedule, and he went over the procedures, the causes, the conditions and found them necessary, all of them. And may have acknowledged that he was not altogether reconciled, calmly, with visible surprise.

— To think that Cresspahl must have sent him a telegram. What does Cresspahl telegraph in a case like that? Or maybe ask yourself: what can one say in a case like that?
— You can't say what happened, I'd not hint at anything even, but what can you think up, and it has to sound urgent, because he couldn't have asked for two days rest without something tangible to show for it, and gone up there.

Jakob had rented a furnished room in one of the flat-chested gawky houses in the quarter near the port, the floors were warped, the walls spotted with mildew, each of the narrow rooms had the musty smell of constant humidity. He was standing in the middle of his landlady's kitchen on the spotty sheen of the linoleum, feeling his briefcase dangle in his hand as he looked around. On the kitchen table breakfast plates were stacked, the newspaper had fallen beside the coal bin, outside the window in the deep narrow courtyard the light hung like lead. But the dish on the kitchen cupboard was empty. Jakob turned around noiselessly and walked out into the hall. Later, in his room, where he had already laid out a clean shirt and his pyjamas and shaving things beside the briefcase on the bed, the bell rang, in his pants, a towel around his wet neck, Jakob went to the door, this time it was the telegraph boy. He thanked him. He was in a hurry by now, perhaps he was also too deep in thought so that he remembered the telegram only in the dining car when he happened to slip a hand in his trouser pocket as the waiter wrote out his check, he broke the seal and read what Cresspahl said about it. Yes, but Cresspahl hadn't thought up anything. YOUR MOTHER GONE TO THE WEST: CRESSPAHL.

— And he told me early that morning that he wanted to go up there. You must have arrived around the same time, wasn't that on Friday?
— Yes. That was on Friday.

# II

— Not before Friday

**JONAS**

*did I set out from Berlin. I didn't bother to look in at the Institute. I stood at an open window, waiting for the train to start, and when a gentle jolt set the station pavement in motion, a goodbye-face sliding past, a baggage cart, and the floor widened under my feet, I knew that the trip had begun and I crept behind my coat and fell asleep at once; I'd had a little too much the night before. But after they checked the passes I couldn't get back to sleep because the train radio also had its opinions, culture and politics and entertainment, the fat complacent basso voice kept singing in my head: Here I am. And why I came. Sign this paper with my name? Never knew it was my duty, here it suddenly rhymed with beauty. I guess I never had a yearning. For reading, writing, higher learning. But loved to chase a pretty skirt. Never asked if I might flirt. And yet he too once loved a maid. It always hurts to be betrayed. During a pause I got up and fussed noisily with the door on my way out, so that no one heard me switch the loudspeaker off. After a decent interval I came back in, it had been switched on again. I looked at the other passengers, all loyal well-meaning faces, anyhow they had already settled any possible question or argument. I'm usually not that irritable. It might have had to do with my departure; just because I didn't understand the music maybe, I simply couldn't see what it was all about, I heard it merely as noise. So all*

*kinds of impatient thoughts occurred to me: all those seven
people had been complete strangers three hours ago and now,
just because they were sharing the same rolling box, they
already referred to themselves as We, we'll get there at such
and such a time, and since that matched the music for me,
and I couldn't see what the music was about, I felt caged in
among the wet steamy coats and went into the dining car
where I sat a good part of the noontime away. And after lunch
I noticed Jakob.*

*I sat in the narrow row of tables, with my back to the bar, and
watched five young soldiers on the other side talk confusion
and howl at regular intervals, wild with beer. I learned that
"A-K18" had been part of their training; surely not a film
camera, a rifle clip more likely, or a machine gun equipped
with some ingenious spring device that lets it hurl several
cartridges through the air toward a target in rapid succession
and at enormous speed, as is its function (no child can
imagine that sort of thing), they had also been trained for
"M-T"s. And when they started telling each other about
"M-S"s and said: "We were sorting tools, I couldn't get away,"
I looked around to see if anybody else was watching them
besides me. But their sound volume was such that no one
could pass them up. At a large table in front of them, a railroad official was conversing with the waiter, next to me a
one-time lady of society was painfully sipping apple juice, at
the end of the tables on my side sat two Russian officers facing each other in silence, completely wordless content and
present, quietly drinking coffee, occasionally glancing over
at the Germans. I acted the foreigner, forced myself to look
indifferent, stoic-faced, to observe the waiter. Who was standing politely beside the railroad man with three stars on his
shoulders, not in an attitude of serving the customer, rather
as though they were bestowing respect and honor upon each
other with a matter-of-fact conversation whose subject had
no further interest. When the waiter left, I clung to Jakob
(I didn't know him then, once I had heard his name men-*

*tioned, I was seeing him for the first time), at once something took hold of me, lifted me up, set me down again. I found myself completely attentive, as only once before in my life. If I remember correctly, I immediately began searching for words. Which I discarded again, one after the other, they all described a characteristic, this man didn't seem to have any. It was like this: his exterior engraved itself at once, ineffaceably, in me and if I now say, think: "he was tall and broad-shouldered and solid, that day he looked a little gloomy (not sad) to the observer," he could be mistaken for anyone who merely resembled him. "He was sitting at the window; outside, the country was drifting past in the fog," because we ("we") were deep into West Mecklenburg by now, because there was brushwood, brown and rigid it stood out over the shivering green of the meadows, toward groups of trees blueing with evening haze, very remote a forest's blurred detail, and over it all hung the sky, heavy, monotonous, the inhuman silent grayness squeezing a glowing strip of sunset out of itself. He was looking out, his head slightly, casually inclined, to me he seemed to be part of it, no it wasn't that, not yet (for a long time I had been aware solely of the window, of the train's hard singing haste), but there was something peculiar about his movements. He was pondering wondering about something, today I know what it was and that it required a wide-awake, a totally unsentimental approach, that's when he moved his face. He tautened the skin over his cheekbones, or his cheekbones arched out, but he didn't know he was doing it. It was moving unintentionally, outside the context of thought and conscious self-control, perhaps it had another context underneath, here I'm forced to say "self-assured lack of attention" . . . as though he had spent his whole life in the woods. Also the gentle astonished curving of his eyes down to his hands: all the rules and regulations we know by heart and recite when we move were contained in him, absorbed within him on the other side of speech, and since I had been searching for a name, I called him "like a*

*cat so unscrupulous," I knew it was wrong, and "proud, sus-*
*picious, affectionate" apply only to an extremely far-fetched*
*part of his meaning. Rather I should have said: I saw a man*
*who looked lived in. He didn't notice my staring. I must have*
*been staring. He sat thoughtfully above the high slim-stemmed*
*glass the waiter had brought him and every now and then he'd*
*take a sip of the warm-colored yellow-brown liquid; I was*
*sitting diagonally across from him, we had nothing to do with*
*each other. The flaming strip on the horizon was shrinking,*
*breaking up, shattering into small spots, the country was*
*sleeping—for I don't know how long. He got up before I did.*
*Changing into the Jerichow local I lost sight of him; I thought*
*it had all been by accident.*

When the evening train arrived in Jerichow, Herr Rohlfs had

HERR ROHLFS

*long been sitting in the station restaurant, over dinner. The*
*race had been a little unnecessary, also cost plenty of gasoline*
*as is usually the case when the bill doesn't count; but I didn't*
*know what else to do with the evening up there. I like the air*
*here better. Five minutes ahead of time Cresspahl was already*
*standing on the platform outside the window behind which I*
*was sitting. I had a clear view of him under the lantern; he*
*was chewing on his pipe, constantly wrinkling the skin around*
*his eyes. Your mother gone to the West. An ole woman comin*
*to see ya. He's got a hard head, well, we shall see. If he doesn't*
*have a finger in something after all. I had ample time to finish*
*my dinner before the train pulled in, I paid but continued to*
*sit over a glass of beer. A large slow shadow emerged from*
*the half light, walked toward the lantern and turned out to be*
*Jakob. I felt pleased with myself to be able to say, so soon,*
*"now he's doing this, later he'll act like that," but then it*
*occurred to me that this trip of his depended as little on his*
*own decision as the streetcar schedule, it was my fault, so to*

*speak. You can't talk about fault in this case: she could have chosen to stay; I can't help it if she didn't understand. Now let's see how Jakob goes about a thing like this, then we'll be able to talk. He had traveled in his uniform. But they kept standing there, who were they waiting for? Humm, I know you: I thought at once, I didn't know him at all, but I like that kind. Those young college fellows from the big city, even on trips to Jerichow they're still dressed as· for a fashion show, in clothes they've bought in the West, and then they wear these suits under an open coat as though it were nothing —which it isn't at all. We sent them through school on our money, we've thrown it after them, we've taken our trouble over them, time and again we've said to them: there, that's what it's for, don't forget now, and here they are running around with a smooth smart face, gentlemanly, reserved down to the handshake (they were shaking hands), full of conceit about the independence of their opinions. I don't know him at all, I didn't know how he fits into this business, what's his connection with Jakob? Cresspahl knew him, slapped him vehemently on the back, but he stood his ground the young man did. Cresspahl became very animated during the introductions, well, okay. He explains to Jakob who it is. He seems as much a stranger to Jakob as he is to me. But Jakob, he looks at him, then he smiles as though they did know each other after all, still, Cresspahl is pointing to him*
*— This's Jakob.*
*— Good evening.*
*— Maybe you've met?*
*but Jakob shakes his head. Now he's saying something. Could be "No. But. . ." He was standing there, straight-backed, then he bowed with a few (friendly) words. Who'll tell me about Miss Cresspahl's love affairs? Cresspahl. Cresspahl tells a lot, a different story to everybody. The dogcatchers would issue a questionnaire. I can't ask Jakob about that. I can't ask anybody. Unless I go sit in the Jerichow Inn, if I weren't a stranger to most of them. For instance tonight Hänschen is*

*going to have a good time for himself at State expense. Publicly, at the Jerichow Inn.*

To Jonas, Cresspahl's kitchen didn't look as though he lacked a woman around the house. The two large windows

JONAS

*cut bright rectangles into the blackness of the garden (I assumed the garden was out there), the floor was scrubbed, bright with cleanliness, I couldn't detect a single grease spot on the tiled table top, and the lamplight was pouring directly down on it. I stood with my back to them, retracing the carvings on the massive sideboard. Shiny with use. It must have been extremely old; he seems to eat in the kitchen. I waited. They waited for me to turn around. I leaned against the sideboard. Cresspahl and Jakob were sitting on stools facing each other across a corner of the table, Cresspahl said (we had hardly said a word on our way to the house, all I knew was that Jakob's mother had gone to the West): "She left Wednesday afternoon. I put her on the train. She had a window seat. I dunno." He carefully turned his head and looked over to me as though to continue his doubts on my face. I didn't move. But Jakob lifted his eyes in rhythm with Cresspahl's, they came together again. "She didn't say anything" Jakob asked. Now Cresspahl also spoke for me to understand him better; still, that much I had picked up from his daughter. "She didn't say anything" Cresspahl said, more to himself, his words came out almost muffled, his voice was so hoarse and slow. "You know how she is. Just sits there and says she wants to go away. When? I ask. Tomorrow, she says. I ask: how so. But she just sits there and shakes her head." Cresspahl sat hunched between us, quietly rubbing his neck against the collar of his jacket, his eyes following each movement, strangely narrowed, unfocused, staring. The house stood in the night wind, deathly quiet, listening. Jakob said nothing. He sat bent forward, his hands between his knees, the edges of*

*the hands arching away from each other. Suddenly Cresspahl
seemed to wake up, in jolts his neck stiffened, his head turned
slightly, in an entirely different voice he asked, "Had anything to eat?" We both smiled (Jakob and I) at the tone of his
voice, he sounded so concerned, so affectionate. "No-o," said
Jakob, "and he?" he asked, "what about him?" "Tsk, tsk" said
Cresspahl slyly, already standing at the stove, lighting the gas,
with surprising rapidity he found a pan, poked lard from a
dish, "he telegraphed too late, so I had to get two different
kinds, schnitzl and cutlet, but it's for Jakob to choose." We
quietly remained in our respective places, watching him. He
stalked up and down the kitchen, loaded up the whole table,
the grease hissed and crackled and screamed, he was ham-
mering the meat soft with a wooden hammer, suddenly he
pushed the board toward me, because the grease had grown
calm with terror, a piece of meat went in the size of a hand,
and he had very large hands. His yellow-skinned, gout-
gnarled hands with hard veiny knots. He was talking incessantly: how he'd gone to Luise Arwt and told her: lots of
meat, and Luise Arwt had said such and so and a dog had
come strutting down the street "an' he gimme such a look
and then 'e said," soon I was laughing; Jakob sat leaning back,
friendly, watching. But his face looked frozen with absence.
Cresspahl was explaining to me how one goes about it:
schnitzl with salt and pepper. Fry good and through. A
breaded veal cutlet is different. You beat two eggs, here,
beat them. Then you dip the veal in the eggs. Another plate
with bread crumbs. Dip the veal in the bread crumbs. And
into the pan. There. How about another egg on top? Go
ahead, make it for yourself. He wiped the table clean and
sliced the bread and set plates down and knives and forks and
made us sit across from each other and took the narrow side
for himself. For a long time he looked at us from under the
hard bulge of his forehead. His eyebrows had a very gentle
sweep. His eyes were gray. The eyes were his age and his far-
away daughter and the thick wet darkness and his indigna-*

*tion and his concern. Jakob nodded. "Now eat," said Cress-
pahl.*


HERR ROHLFS

*A clear morning. I had my feet on the windowsill and was
thinking about many things when Hänschen finally came in.
He'd put away quite a few. "No, Chief," he said, "oh man!
That dame has more than one guy on her conscience, more
than one who's thought, take it easy, and all's well that ends
well. Stories I don't know any, only a few details here and
there, not easy to piece them together. All a long time ago,
not one of the victims stayed in Jerichow, what a town! or
he has no reason to shoot off his mouth. That's about the
drift of it. But I really made those people happy last night,
letting them pour out their memories. Oh, it was lots of fun,
Chief," he said, "too bad we won't set eyes on her." I thought
so too. But I didn't say it, so he piped down. Perhaps he'll
realize some day that we're not acting in a Western. I sent
him off to breakfast and thought about many things. I thought
this was actually my first serious assignment. Anybody can
play the detective, and with what result? at best a negative
gain, a positive loss. And a promotion. Or the contrary. If I
bring this thing to a respectable conclusion I'll be proud of
myself. If it goes wrong I'll have to quit; perhaps I won't. I
can't afford gloomy mornings. Let's find out something.
"Young man," I said to the assistant I'd called upstairs; the
fat one no longer likes me since last Thursday, sneaks out of
my way like a peevish rabbit. Maybe I should complain about
the heating? I'll send him out to buy some reels of tape to give
him a chance. He's one of those who can't stand anyone who
outranks him. So then, what about this one? young, conscientious, polite, trained to be versatile. I ask him: does my
calling him young man offend him perhaps? let him lay off
his damn mail. His boss can take care of that much better.
"Your lovely intelligent forehead," I say, "would you mind*

*giving the other track a rest while I tell you one of my fairy*
*tales? Now then. It is my pleasure to cast an eye upon two*
*deserving honorable men who have been visiting Mr. Cress-*
*pahl in Ziegeleistrasse since last night. Please don't bother*
*deducting anything! they're here for a bit of rest. How can*
*anyone listen to such trifling denunciations. Exact time. Fine.*
*In a little while those two will be going out. To the registrar*
*if I'm not mistaken, to a furniture dealer, they'll also stop for*
*a beer. That doesn't prove anything, don't be so hasty. Take*
*a little walk, get some air, always indoors. You might also have*
*a beer. Wait! sit down. Cigarette. You mean your education*
*cost a lot of money, let's not go into that now. We are no*
*police dogs! get that into your head. You must see everything.*
*You've already contracted the habit of seeing only the even-*
*tual guilt, you learn nothing that way. You know more about*
*a man if you find out how he treats his children and whether*
*he helps his friends so they'll help him in return, or whether*
*he just helps them, and how he stops to look at the houses*
*we build once in a while—we do; it's a fact: how he looks at*
*them from the architectural point of view, you understand.*
*You don't start out drawing a demarcation line between a*
*loyal and a subversive citizen beforehand. Everybody is a pos-*
*sibility. All right? We're now about to mention the purpose.*
*It isn't our purpose to put people behind bars. We need them,*
*that's why. And you're not sitting behind a window, nobody*
*depends on your services. You're supposed to take care of*
*people, to help everybody. What is a market place?" "For*
*everybody it's something different," he says. "Precisely" I say:*
*"Don't make a habit of the shortest way for you being straight*
*across that market place from the tobacconist to the post*
*office. Everybody's shortest way is different, important. Now*
*you may go." "May I permit myself a personal remark?" he*
*asks. Look, now he's short of breath. But I told him no and*
*sent him off. I expressed his innermost thoughts probably?*
*Oh, nonsense. I'd like to see the man who can put up with me*
*for more than three weeks.*

JONAS

*They let me sleep. I felt morose waking up in Cresspahl's living room under the low ceiling that had turned gray with age; but I had been (distraction is dangerous in sleep, how much more so at the moment of waking) rehearsing the previous day, changing into the Jerichow local and losing sight of Jakob, I was asking myself: what was I doing in Jerichow in her father's house? Would it restore the calm and clear thinking I had mislaid somehow in Berlin, I had set out on this trip with nothing but a hope, I was preparing myself for disappointment. Then the morning hit me, I looked at the sky standing hard and bright above the park around the Soviet headquarters; rising in a cheerful mood I thought everything could have turned out to be quite different (if not this, then not that either . . . ): I could have met Jakob dutifully in the course of a harmless courtesy call; he would have been a childhood friend of Gesine's, I would have said: ah, so this is Jakob, how do you do, so he works on the railroad, whereas. Whereas, now I had chosen him of my own volition, was watching him with avid excitement, the way one watches a cat (unselfishly, without formalities); suddenly I found myself welcoming all the obstacles and separations between us. Because he isn't easy to deal with, "good morning did you sleep well" has a different meaning with him: he establishes a specific attitude toward each person he comes in contact with, he shows himself reliable and means it. There is security in attitudes you acquire with him. When I entered the kitchen, Jakob was sitting at the table with a smile for me while he answered Cresspahl, who had asked "Can't you stay for good?" He was all alone in his house. He lifted the teapot off the stove, breakfast had begun. No one shook hands, each knew the other was there.*

— Then you went out. To the town clerk, to Messereit about the furniture, then you stopped off for a beer. It got around

UWE JOHNSON 67

fast, how he must have been showing you the town, you were standing before the war memorial . . .
— It was my first visit to Jerichow. He told me "this whole section used to be fenced off, Gesine once got lost in there, six Russians took her to headquarters, suspicion of espionage, she was thirteen at the time, for weeks her pockets were stuffed full of sunflower seeds," and "this is the school, that's the way to the beach," you know that type of landscape always makes me feel like vacation: because of the low houses, the cobblestone streets, horse carts coming in from the country, the country starts around the corner. And the people all have such quizzical faces (one of my friends says: backward, agriculturally retarded, due to overly prolonged feudal system, may he be right, these bright boys, we can't get along without them). I merely meant your sky is larger. You understand? It didn't rain. Yes. The war memorial: those huge rocks across from the cemetery wall, set up to glorify the German soldiers who died in the war of 1870/71, and toward the street, like the obverse of the others, the white plaster-coated brick columns with their hand-forged chains, to honor the dead of the Soviet Union's patriotic war.

HERR RÖHLFS
*Vetschnaya slava geroyam krashnoi armii pavscheem v borbe sa svabodoo i nessavissimosty nashey rodiny 1941–45 god*

*dlya dyela sotsialisma*

— Jakob told me how they had driven them through the town, from one end to the other, in open coffins. At the church, and I guess that made Jakob sort of happy:
— It didn't. He repeated it to me later, look: they might have told us something about that in school. But when we grow old and gray we listen to a newcomer with educated eyes; Jakob remembered every single word: Jerichow must have been quite a place in Saxon times, you can tell by the church:

you're supposed to have said. Originally it was Roman, you
can tell by the round arched frieze
— And the two round windows,
— That was the west nave, they added three Gothic windows
to it, right? and by the rough spots you can still tell that the
initial ground plan had the shape of a cross. No, seriously. He
finished growing up in Jerichow, you know. And then you
took in the convent, and by that time lots of people had seen
you. He didn't introduce you to many, still they thought you
were a bright boy the way you stood there and listened.

— *I hear your mother's left.*
— *so she has.*
— *selling all her stuff now, huh.*
— *always lots to do when this happens.*
— *good morning.*
— *but why? Something happen to her?*
— *I dunno. Not the faintest idea. I arrive at the house and she's*
*gone.*
— *some times we live in, man.*
— *you can say that again.*

— Maybe they thought I wanted to buy furniture from Cresspahl.
— No-o-oh. You're not the type. You don't look settled. You
didn't talk much in the street, only after you were through
with the town clerk.
— It was crowded, the town clerk's in the same room with the
interzone pass applications. I waited, leaning against a wall.
Since I didn't know why his mother had fled
— Gone away.
— gone away; it wasn't the only surprise in this cozy political
climate of ours. I had just come out of the very house she had
left, and when it was Jakob's turn and he said, "I wish to
report that Mrs. Abs is no longer living on Ziegeleistrasse. She
left word that she won't be coming back. That's my mother,"
they asked Was the escape arranged with a passport or

through Berlin? "Through Berlin," because he answered them
so calmly patiently as though it were nobody's fault, I was
furious, why doesn't he tell those uniforms off, I thought,
there are enough people standing around to hear him. "You're
angry?" he asked me in the middle of the market square, he
had a way of laughing softly with his eyes, I hadn't noticed at
first, laughing isn't the right word for it either. I told him yes
I was angry. "But it can't be helped at this point?" he asked.
"No" I said, I didn't want to give in just yet, "precisely"
I said "that's what you should file your complaint about."
He was looking at me, carefully, as though he had just
come to know me better, but not without irony, as though
the next move would have to come from me. It did, after all,
why was I standing (of my own volition) in this market
square? "Yes," I said. File a complaint with the proper authorities at the proper time, with the prospect of a definite improvement: that I could see, and I haven't forgotten about it
either. Now listen carefully: there are those gabled houses
around the market square, one of the oldest has the pharmacy
on the ground floor, next to the town hall. Don't laugh now.
He asks me—usually, if one asks questions like that, one acts
pensive and contemplates the pavement—he looks at me and
asks, "How did you stumble on Cresspahl?" I swallowed hard.
Answer a thing like that in one word. But I did want to tell
him, really funny how much I wanted him to know.
— Well, yes, I guess he liked you.
— You see? There, you see, something might have come of it.
— Yes. You arrive somewhere, you meet somebody, you have
to get along with him, or cooperate. You have to make friends
with him if it's to work out. That lasts as long as you need
him or until you go away again. Sometimes you're lucky, and
it can develop into something friendly with nothing but good
to it. But never the way you go about it, choosing, the way
you want to pin it down in time, not as the chance that it is,
but because of your own hopes and confidence. (Now don't
contradict. You saw each other three times, you don't know

what would have come of it. You realize that he probably saw you, really saw you, for the first time at the town hall.)


They were not yet used to walking side by side; they were conscious of the distance between them as they walked around the pharmacy to the back of the town hall. Herr Dr. Blach took the short cautious steps of city life; his shoulders were less broad than Jakob's, it made him look taller. With three approximate words he had established his acquaintance with Gesine, his credentials for entering Cresspahl's house; he might also have said, "I stopped her in the street," but Jakob hadn't wished to hear any confessions. He started to tell about Gesine, trying to find the memory of her, her nearness in Blach's polite attentive face, and he continued the occasional intent inspections of Blach's face as he continued to talk. He was holding his hands behind his back and from time to time he'd lift his head sideways with his fleeting smile; he said: "She must have been seventeen then." Also, one probably ought to take into account, he objected immediately: "a day is longer at that age (later, you get used to the clock; at your age perhaps, at mine, a day has three sections: before work, work, and after work; when you look up, another season has gone by)." And the young man who used to live over the pharmacy in those days, he had looked at her for a whole year deciding if she was the one, and then he found his opportunity and told her she was. In his opinion. "Then, for three more months, he saw her every day at school, and after that evening he'd blush every time, I mean: he couldn't look at her, wouldn't pronounce her name, wouldn't go to where she'd be (really blushed). Wouldn't ask about her." Then that whole summer she had sailed about the Baltic, it was a beautiful boat. And it was obviously incomprehensible how she could go on living without worrying about the real meaning of her life. "It is a terrible embarrassment for someone like that." It was all decided then? Sheer coincidence that she didn't sail to Denmark for good; could she have? Yes yes. No

coincidence, since it was a decision. "The boat didn't come
back, but he," (the one from the pharmacy, would Herr Dr.
Blach know what to do with him?) "understood only that she
had not gone away. During his vacation he went far up the
beach and thought he'd probably catch a glimpse of her
eventually." He was very unhappy. "One evening I walked
along the cliffs with her, shortly before her exams came up,
suddenly she stopped, pushed aside the brambles: do you
see him, she said, she shook her head. Hey! she called. It was
a windy day. You mustn't blush any more! she called. I don't
quite know how to explain it. From that day on he didn't
blush any more. I think they're still talking about that, because the whole town used to be upset about him or about
her, and what had she done to him all of a sudden to bring
him to reason, they imagined the wildest things." But she
simply told him to stop blushing. "She told me the whole
story after we came out of the water at the other end and
waited for the sun to dry us," Jakob said. He was no longer
telling a story, he was staring ahead of him as though he had
been remembering it for himself.

For a long time Jonas (Herr Dr. Blach) said nothing. After
lunch in the kitchen Cresspahl hung an apron around Blach's
neck, because of the good suit he said, and stood him next to
Jakob who was washing the dishes and declared about himself that one man who stands in the corner and rattles the
buckets is worth ten hard at work: as Gesine had said at
fifteen, over at the bucket stand, telling her father how to
balance the yoke when he went for water. But Herr Dr. Blach
didn't ask what that meant, although he noticed that Jakob
was chuckling to himself as he bent over the kitchen table:
thorough and absentminded he placed the dried dishes and
plates before Jakob and thought that this was the way things
were. He had forgotten when she had mentioned Jakob's
name, although it couldn't have been that casually; and so
one misses out on whole periods and connections between important events by not listening to a name, how often did I
fail to reach her with my words? How many years? five years,

maybe eight, she had walked on the cliffs with Jakob in the
evening, he imagined them skidding over the clay lumps into
the ice-cold light-heated water for a swim, and wading back
ashore against the slanting rays, and sitting side by side in
the sun-wind, and he heard her voice calling: Hey! and then,
less loudly, shall I tell you what kind of a guy that one was,
and he felt Jakob's tall calm figure listening beside her, looking at the water probably. Just once I'd like to see the two of
them together. After a while he became convinced that there
had been no ulterior motive to Jakob's story, and after he
managed to remember and compare Gesine's way of speaking
to the two quoted remarks, he was almost certain that he had
perhaps understood her. Then he fell to thinking about the
brothers of girls, the affectionate concern in what they told
about them; that way he probably missed several incidents
of the afternoon: although he worked until evening with his
two hosts in the deserted rooms on the other side of the hall.
The peaceful sight of a tablecloth unruffled in its place, of
closed cupboard doors and pictures still on the walls had
made them stand still at first, but in the room toward the
courtyard the beds had been dismantled and the wardrobes
were empty.

— And what was this thing with the envelopes?
— What envelopes?
— In the town cafe, when you'd stopped for a beer on your
way back from Messereit and Wallraff came up to your table,
the drunken brakeman, don't you remember, and gave Jakob
an envelope.
— From your mother, he said. A blank envelope. Jakob tore
it open and held the paper so that I could read it too. It turned
out to be a sales agreement for the furniture of one bedroom,
to be paid to and settled with my son Jakob within two
weeks.
— That's something new: that's good. What such an old
woman won't think up! And then there was something similar
with the salesgirl from the Consumers Store.

— Yes. Now I think Jakob took so much time walking through the town to let everybody who had anything to settle with him know that he was there. Yes. The girl had bought the sewing machine in advance. She was getting married at Christmas, she told Jakob, he knew the man, they came that same evening and took the machine away.

But before that came Herr Schneider from the town council, a small man, nimble as a mouse, he was from Breslau: he told the three men who stood leaning against the walls contemplating him politely, without curiosity, Cresspahl cleaned off a chair for him, the least one could do for a municipal official, because when he arrived in Jerichow from Breslau they had eventually put him in charge of the Desertion from the Republic Office, everybody got stuck with something: he said, yes, and these were his credentials, some also had red diagonal lines, so it was really true, he would promptly notify the housing committee. At this point Jakob spoke up for the first time: the rooms were registered in his name as official living quarters of the German State Railroad. "But you're moving out?" Herr Schneider asked, surprised. Because just then Messereit was pulling up with his dishevelled bad-humored pony, he bowed deeply to everyone with his melancholy moustache and began inspecting the furniture with grieving discourse and burst into pained protest when Jakob wanted to deprive him of the bedroom and the sewing machine; at which point Cresspahl called him to order. "Ten marks apiece," he said about the chairs. "Eighteen," Jakob repeated serenely. "That's their pre-war price," complained Herr Messereit, "post-war price," said Jakob and proceeded to annoy him with the detailed account of how he had bought the chairs and when: starting with a bottle of brandy for which you still had to pay eighteen marks today, Messereit was suffering, he wished he could go to the West, he said. Well, then he'd better hand in his application with the county council, and perhaps, if he had been domiciled in Hamburg before the war, they might let him go, said Jakob, but Herr

Schneider had just been explaining all these things to them a
few minutes earlier and Jonas understood from Cresspahl's
quiet mirth that this kind of behavior wasn't at all surprising
with Jakob. "But my bank account?" said Messereit in despair,
because he got many calls and the last three years had made
him rich (since the abandoned furniture was no longer sold
off at public auctions for the benefit of the State); it went
against his self-respect. They took the living room apart and
lined up the pieces and carried them out under Messereit's
old furniture blankets and hoisted them onto the wagon (the
air had become more humid toward evening, the pony was
shivering); and while the bedroom was being carted off, a
man came from the town police. Bony, slow-gestured, about
Jakob's age. Jakob called him by his first name: Hannes, and
smoked a cigarette with him at the window, Hannes just
wanted to make sure the transaction was legal, a mere for-
mality, they exchanged memories and greetings and asked
about common acquaintances. At nightfall, the rooms were
empty; all that Jakob kept was a small black hardwood chest
that Gesine had been permitted to give him for a birthday
present six years ago. They carried it over to Cresspahl's part
of the house. It wasn't heavy, only a little linen, Jakob's be-
longings in the furnished room might not even have filled it.
Since they had also sold or given away the lamps, they put
candles on the windowsills. The cold brittle-black glass darkness reflected broad flickering bands of light on the floor that
Jonas was sweeping. Before, they had talked while they
worked, brief instructions, occasional remarks about the various afternoon visitors. Now they were silent. In shirt sleeves,
smoking, Jakob leaned against the open door, watching Jonas
sweep the dust out of the darkness toward the lights, a delicate touching of the broom, wide circular strokes, the bristles
rustling on the bright splintery floor boards. From the kitchen,
Cresspahl could be heard at the stove.
"When did you see your mother for the last time?" Herr Rohlfs
had asked. "Two weeks ago in Jerichow," Jakob had anwered,
"then it can't have been yesterday afternoon?" Herr Rohlfs

had asked. That was last Thursday. "Perhaps Mrs. Abs tends
to suffer from nervousness," he had said, considerate, sym-
pathetic. Such politeness he had used for her, a leftover from
his wastefully good education. Actually, such respect was
totally inappropriate for the superfluous (so to speak) peasant
daughter who was becoming a cook on the Pomeranian estate
by the river: who had to repair her self-respect for quite a
while after the young master drove her into town once, in his
car, without any particular ulterior motives, merely as a favor.
Did she ever tell anyone about it? she told Gesine Cresspahl
as an example of incredible conceit. And one used to be
proud, hearing the guests praise the food through the open
dumbwaiter; don't let that make you proud of anything but
your cooking, Gesine, even if you're standing at the dumbwaiter in a white smock and the other kitchenmaids aren't
wearing one. These notions disappeared with the arrival of the
college-trained farmer Abs, and more so as she became ac-
quainted with his opinions about the unfair arrangement of
things in this world. Later she did move into and live in the
overseer's apartment, everybody had to honor and respect
her, although she'd probably never attached special importance to such precious treatment (and at that time she did
have her own eyes for young gentlemen of all kinds and the
overseer was seldom invited into the mansion with his wife).
As to her suffering from nervousness, her fluttering readiness
to fear, the apprehension of her present fifty-nine-year-long
life could surely not be compared to the hope and confidence
of younger years, of which she spent three waiting unfalter-
ingly for an angry young farmer from Mecklenburg who
wanted to try his and her luck in unknown far-away Brazil,
but in the end preferred to come back to the lie-infested
fatherland (without Herr Rohlfs' inscrutable knowledge
Jakob would not have recalled this attempted escape). Jakob no
longer remembered his father, in the meantime the uniform
had pushed to the top, in his memory, but he would more
or less assume that she had loved him very much (or was it
he himself who had been happy in the wide-stretching land

on the water on the big farm, with countless wagons standing side by side in the sun, with the smell of flowering lindens hanging dominant outside the cool rooms, above the limpid mirror of the morning river, in the submissive rustling of the reeds against the heavily moving boat?). Did the apprehension begin with the official note that his father had, most likely, died a hero's death? he remembered only the flight across the winter, over the broad crown of the treeless highway, under howling low-flying planes, the screams of the helplessly flailing horses, the blood on his mother's face, the groaning people under the tarpaulins next to contorted corpses that bounced at every hole in the road after the wagons got rolling once more toward the other side of this goddamn goddamn goddamn shitty war. She had gone on waiting, those first years in Cresspahl's house. But no Abs appeared on the lists of the Red Cross and the Red Crescent. She had grown quiet then probably, and avoided excitement, and feared the blood fluttering in her wrists, the irresistible never-ending anguish. "You have to be careful with her," Jakob had said and agreed with Herr Rohlfs about that peculiarly reserved concern of only sons; although he knew that circumstances have nothing to do with the person (whereas Herr Rohlfs seemed to think that a man's background or his biography explained him sufficiently, or at least understandably: as though the band of dust behind a wardrobe that's been pushed away, and a useless nail in a bare wall, and the silly intimacy of a flower pot in the window of a vacated room were still reliable indications). Jonas came back from the kitchen, gathered up the candles, stopped in front of Jakob. "It's not so terrible in the refugee camps," he said, it sounded as he intended it to sound: a factual information. He stood looking at him with attention; Jakob probably noticed. Although he shook his head. He couldn't retrieve that Thursday or Friday or Saturday for her, neither the time nor the events, thoughts about it were vague, intangible. He felt as though she had died.

— Here I sit like I'm myself, "I'm here too," "I'm somebody," and not just "anybody"; and the others "maybe don't realize who they're talking to."

— Everybody is somebody under his skin.

— And I drive a locomotive, not everybody can do that, I'm in line for a two-room apartment that's become vacant, I have my own opinions: all mine, untransferable, and they're not going to catch me for the army: nothing doing . . . so there. I can well imagine, I was a late child, see, I'm sure that's no coincidence and has something to do with the laws of dynamics of capitalism, my parents couldn't afford a child, but when they voluntarily put me into the world, they still couldn't afford it, actually. You understand? eleven years earlier, and I would have been one of the gangsters. Think a moment. You don't suppose it's improbable that I'd have killed every Jew just for the fun of it and had a good time in the war? that I'd have considered myself the master race and the rest of the world beneath me? Probably not improbable. And why not? because I'd have gone to school during that period, they would have taught me this and that and the other, "we are born to die for Germany," and the grown-ups are right for a pretty long time: until you can copy them in everything, then you feel you're right too. I go along with you in everything about the —what did you call it: the unique personality, and each his own blood stream, and Nobody Can Really Copy Your Smile, but is that the point? does that matter? Those are reasons for which one gets married, or they're useful some other way for your secret private life. But this—let's call it: personal uniqueness needs its opportunities, shows up only in exterior things; in what you do and not in how you feel. And the possibilities to do are only those that you find in the light of the world, what the know-betters, your educators, offer you. I've been lucky, that's all I mean to say. That is in so far as, seen from today, I'm glad I wasn't mixed up in the war. In so far as it suits me that I didn't have to get used to my father, he died in battle, the Jew butcher, the house burner. But I say they could have got to me just as well, and if somebody is op-

posed to it today, in his own most personal fashion, then he
needn't act conceited about it.
— Yes.
Don't take it to heart if I say yes. I don't know anything else,
it's pretty late.
Yes.


CRESSPAHL WAS STANDING in front of the cupboard with its
seven doors, leaning one heavy hand on the dark old wood;
you could tell by the hard, lighter ribs of the prominent carvings how very long it must have been in use. He had changed
from his corduroys into a gray suit and was wearing a tie; the
tweed bulged in thick folds across his broad bent neck. Rain
hung hard and even outside the black windows, pattered on
the stones under the drainpipe, chopped at the misty bridge
of light that rose from the desk lamp into the darkness outside. Jakob was lying far back in his leather armchair facing
the tanned scarred table top and watched Cresspahl place an
earthen jug and his bowl of pipes and the tobacco jar on the
table. In the middle of his occupations the old man lifted his
mighty, wild, embittered head and stared into the haze of
the room where Jonas was standing at the shelf leafing
through a book. His gaze became pensive, wandered to Jakob
who remained motionless, leaning on his shoulders. His eyelids were squeezed together as though he were trying to
picture something. Cresspahl crouched down to the bottom
door in the cupboard and brought three dented much handled
tin mugs to the table and dropped into the armchair beside
Jakob's, and after Cresspahl had poured from the earthen jug
into the clear brilliant hollow of the tin, Jonas came forth into
the light and only found the broad high-backed chair for himself at the opposite end of the table across from the other two.
After a while Jakob asked: "What do you do for a living?"
he had not budged. His pensive look merely seemed to have
been translated into speech. Cresspahl rubbed his shoulders

against the back of his chair and glanced with mock concern
at the young man who loved his daughter; when he realized
that this young man wasn't bristling, but was merely lost in
thoroughly absentminded reflections, he laughed with a faint
jerk of the head and raised the mug to his mouth and very
hesitantly moistened his lips. "My daughter sent me this
Dutch gin," he said in his hard careful voice, and after a
while Jonas began to talk in his refined Southern intonation;
he had just been studying Jakob's profile a moment longer,
now he was talking—to no one in particular, sure of himself,
practiced, breezy. He had sunk deep into his chair, on the
wooden arms his hands lay, quiet and relaxed like two auton-
omous intelligent experienced lethargic creatures.

All you need are a few medium-sized rooms in a building
that should, however, stand out—by the considerable dignity
of a metropolitan environment as well as by its own exterior
aspect—from the closely packed structures of profane purpose
(barracks, factories, apartment houses). Built of ordinary
Glindow brick like the others, but with a thick uneven orna-
mentation to portray somber durability (a war had been won
while it was being built). From the outside, the time-grayed
brick hypocrisy is, to this day, still staring into the desolate
tousled park; inside, marble-plated galleries inhibit human
speech and steps. One of the rooms houses the library, it col-
lects a maximum of books and magazines in this particular
field; in the next room sits the secretary between typewriter,
filing cabinet, potted evergreens; the director's office tries for
quiet dignity with outmoded furniture, bookspines and filing
boxes. Now you place the whole thing under glass, with its
auditoriums and conference rooms and assistants' cubicles,
prohibit entry to all unauthorized persons, and a few centuries later you take a look: and lo and behold: science has
not been harmed. "But scientists and students are included in
this appeal to be aware—in this grave hour—of the human-
istic duty of all fields of research. Premature and thoughtless
actions may now take on an importance that will boomerang
as heavy responsibility upon their authors. Before each deci-

sion we must ask ourselves Cui bono, for whose benefit. Does it benefit the State of Workers and Farmers?"

English philology concerns itself with the history of Anglo-Saxon language and literature. The specifically phonetics-oriented studies examine the language as such, its astonishing mutations from the earliest documents to the present; it is always somewhat embarrassed, because writers of the, say, eleventh century—not unlike those of the twentieth—may not have kept a precise, but a very approximate written record of their pronunciation, tradition in the form of habitual negligence, and there are no explanations for the apparently spontaneous transition from o to a, such occurrences prove merely that in human affairs things don't stay the way they were. All philology can do is describe the changes, either singly or in an assumed connection; there are rules though. From early via middle to modern English. In which direction, how far did the transition from o to a spread, here we may surmise either a peaceful or a war-waging movement of the language groups; the infiltration of French words into the English language offers us further irrefutable proof of the Norman conquest. Profitable to history itself with regard to periods that lie dim in the past. Whereas philology, philology deciphers discloses in early scrolls the long-since-forgotten words by way of better known quotations in other preserved writings; it compares dictionaries grammars maps excavations fauna and flora of the probable landscape. It retraces the order that ruled declensions and syntax; each dialect has its special dictionary with grammatical appendix. From the various versions of a text the seemingly most authentic (least corrupted) is set aside, which manuscript relates to which, comparison, chemical analysis of the paper, which water mark came from which paper mill (and is it really a water mark?), hadn't that paper mill already burned down at that time, the chase for the author, monastery chronicles, town records, family books, court files, tombstones. Then printing of the exhaustively researched text with annotations, inserts, elucidations, glossaries, elaborations, justification: and a one-year course to introduce the studying youth to the methods of analyzing Middle English texts. The words used in the text give precise information about the clothes, utensils, weapons, social structure, life expectations of the past human condition, profitable for the historical interest Man takes in himself. Language lives in the community that speaks it and perishes with it; whereas literature preserves for us one individual's relationship to the world, should one pay exclusive attention to the individual, consider the eighteenth century from the angle of its history of thought and the linguistic means it used to come to terms with and overcome the world? The change of images in English lyricism through the centuries. College libraries, scientific institutes, magazines and magazine editors of this particular field will be more than moderately interested in the revelations of the distinguished scholar—at last available in book form after painstakingly detailed research. Whereas, on the other hand, if history is a history of class struggles and literature a tangible illustration of Marxist theories, the benefit is undeniable, and who can seriously dispute the theory of the surplus value? And if one fine day each word that has been written with literary intention finds itself twisted around and around and our knowledge of Anglo-Saxon and all its related culture groups is complete, without a loophole, how do we face the present? An asset for the mutual understanding of nations, friendly co-existence. This fall, I'll be giving seminars supporting the Institute Director's lectures on "Literature in the Elizabethan Era," every Thursday afternoon from 2 to 4 P.M., Seminar Room Two, Dr. Blach, Assistant Professor.

Jonas Blach sat leaning against the back wall of the classroom in the midst of his students, listening to the irregular sound of the voice that climbed high with nervous accentuation, fell crumbling back, groped its brittle way toward a new paragraph. The young speaker's face was blond and fat, almost sucked empty with the effort of speaking to an audience, his overtired staring eyes jerked—unfocused, unseeing—from his paper to the bare wall beside his teacher's head; when he pointed to the blackboard, his hand halted in mid air, dropped listlessly to the edge of the lectern, gripped it tight. Ankle on knee, Herr Blach sat slanted against the wall, intent on the study of his fingernails, technical high school, he was thinking. The student's talk was patterned after the typical high-school structure of: introduction-main part-conclusion, the stitching together of the texts he had read was only too obvious, the assignment had been given and now it was being carried out, there was no chance for personal thinking. In Shakespeare's time the stage did not dispose of scenic means, therefore placards were used to indicate time and place, this explained why, at the beginning of almost every drama, the characters introduced themselves or each other to the audience; the back wall was vibrating with the presumptuous dignity of cobweb-thin organ music from the premises of the institute of musicology, papers rustled on the speaker's lectern, the students were slouched back in their chairs in an attitude of intent listening, induced by eighty minutes of immobility, two girls were taking notes, hunched forward between widespread elbows. The three high slender windows looked out into the courtyard of the fortress-like fog-gray quadrangle, the October day fell stale and pale into the cold dank air of the cube-shaped room. The exhausted voice found the assurance of the conclusion, formulated according to the director's habit which more or less meant that, now, one had perhaps learned something, or perhaps not (that all one could learn was assumptions and suppositions). And since Dr. Blach maintained the inexhaustible attentiveness of his gaze, the speaker added, disconcerted: that's it. Came out from behind the lectern, stuck his papers under his arm, stepped down from the platform onto the even plain of the floor and slumped, doubled over, into a vacant protective chair between two tables. But Dr. Blach had long since said "Ah yes," as though surprised, in his clipped easy careful enunciation, and added a hasty: "Thank you. Yes. Do sit down. Please," because Herr Blach was not only being polite while chair legs scraped and scratched across the tiles and the boys and girls

tilted their heads toward the back wall to tell the instructor
what they thought of the construction and content of the talk;
he sat motionless, his cool skeptical head against the cold,
music-pulsating wall and pictured in his mind how this talk
had been composed in overcrowded library rooms amidst in-
considerate conversations, during dejected walks and seemingly lucid nights in a furnished room between bed and
washstand, with pain and effort; he also exchanged friendly
nodding looks with the speaker whose face was gradually
calming down, the blush across his cheekbones fading with
every breath. So he turned in surprise when the young lady
beside him suddenly exclaimed that the leader of the seminar
was alone competent to express an opinion as one could see
from his distinguished weighty reserve; however, the reproof
became a joke because of her open laughter and Jonas objected appeasingly that he had not expressed any opinion at
all, when the others cried out: "Hey! Listen to that! Well!"
however, they were wrong. So he gathered their opinions and
remarks into a longish sentence, mentioned the words conscientious and effort and carefully laid out; although the young
lady had been right and sensed his discontent without looking at him, just from the way he sat there: this was effort,
the effort certified in the highschool diploma with nothing
more than an ability to use the mind without the exclusive
desire-determination-resolution-compulsion, therefore the boy's
thoughts had no independent feet to stand on and were mere
descendants of the traditional (model) trends of thought, as
though college were the continuation of school routine, even
science cannot bear the imitation of itself: he sat thinking,
had he anything better to suggest? perhaps not. He stood in
front of his students on the platform beside the lectern, handing out assignments for the following Thursday and included
the young lady's name on his list, in spite of her reticence,
what was her name, the first name? Gisela. As a favor to me:
he said laughingly, rebellious she let herself be reconciled
(the little girls). He announced the end of the class and
walked off, his papers under one arm, across the dull marble

tiles down the high somber corridors, while the seventeen
voices of the disciples of science echoed after him in total
confusion from the opened vacuum of the room, he did not
intend to educate them in his image—the image of a young
adult in a decent suit whose face had not become carefully
worried with the patient problems of over-intellection, but
looked downright adventurous, who was whistling—sharply,
on key—a tune from the nightly army broadcast for American
soldiers in Germany: so what . . .

Because for years now. For two years he had been looked
upon—in corridors and classrooms—as the gifted reliable
prompt assistant to the director, had given lectures, held
seminars, taken care of the business angle of the Institute
(ordering books, advising the students, dealings with the authorities, correspondence with related sciences of equal rank),
was considered secretive shrewd stubborn, "a bon vivant
when you got right down to it," some people and also the
director's secretary said, arrogant underneath. But long before, as far back as his finals, when the oral examination
ended for him with the question: would he be willing to assume this task in the service of science?—while the slanting
sun of a June morning beamed into the agelessly skeptical
barely kind old-man's face of the examiner, outlining it
sharply as he bent over the examination papers, while the
assessor sat in unfocused absence before the minutes he had
pushed away—the student Blach replied, yes, to the deceptive atmosphere of the situation (honors, excellence, can-
didacy, promotion) politely, full of good will, and felt secretly
afraid before the tenacious unwavering gaze of the old man
who was beginning the examination all over again—long
before the examination, he had grown tired of philology. At
that time his reputation consisted of a pleasant disposition,
erudition and three long lectures which had—along with
thorough, imaginative studies—hinted at something like
frivolity. Had he become educated now? the wisdom of the
Western era, of old men, had been passed on to him, he did
his job conscientiously and promptly and even observed all

the recognized rules in the hide-and-seek of personal contact
at work. Truly marvelous, this philological occupation: a far
remote occasional monument of strict interrelatedness (etc.);
not the profession, not the vessel to contain one's entire life,
after having been chosen as such, in ignorance and without
counsel, by a sixteen-year-old schoolboy in the out-of-the-way
oppressed narrowness of a hick town in Saxony, after a few
years it wasn't tangible enough for his eagerness to learn.
It kept one's thoughts in order, was neither sleepwalk routine
nor daydreaming; but could life be found in a text? he had
the impression it was passing him by. To use an imprecise
circumlocution, he couldn't find the proper word for it. The
card files and books for the acquisition of a teaching position
stood untouched on the shelf, neglected; he drifted aimlessly
through the two Berlins, many nights, with his self-assured
gentlemanly airs, looking for he knew not what. That's how
one finds nothing. Diligent and sarcastic he'd return to his
students the next day and know that they took his official
information and advice seriously, importantly, literally, because he was older than they and the old man's much-
esteemed assistant. Then they went their ways, with first
names like Gisela and a friendly, still young and pretty face
stuffed full with learning and taught English in a high school
of the Democratic Republic and forgot what they had learned
at the Institute because it had not been of vital significance
which was, moreover, none of the Institute's concern.
Whereas he, he would probably be addressed as *Dozent, Dr.
habil.*, next year, and associate professor, and full professor,
and be invested with the dignity of the service of science:
if he didn't do anything to prevent it.
Jakob was still lying on his arms (his hands seemed to be
pushed backwards into his belt) in the hollow of the
armchair, his head had slid sideways lazily with involuntary
movements of his chin, in the direction of the darkness.
Cresspahl poured himself a third mug, then he thrust himself
forward, seized Jonas' mug by the neck and forced it under
the tilted pitcher. As Jakob reached for his mug on the

table, his eyes came to Jonas and touched him in his thoughts, there was no question in his eyes, nor the dreaded, hasty: I understand. Can well imagine, because Jakob had been listening. He looked at him and fitted Jonas with the new traits of his talk and waited with? perhaps with patience for the outcome of it all. Outside the rain had stopped. After a while Cresspahl coughed into his foldy neck and said soothingly: "He stopped her in the street":

JONAS

*Yes. A street between gardens and low houses in a Berlin suburb one evening. The street lamps had not yet gone on. The headlights of waiting cars glowed dully, innumerable in the soft dusk, constantly gaining in color, when a lady came walking down the steps of a house, with two American officers and a heavy-set civilian, came to the gate in the garden fence, a young lady, a girl, when I saw her face I stopped dead*

*"Lissen" I said in English, nailed to the spot. There was nothing inside me except a clear cool fear that she might walk on. Another minute and I would have lost her.*

*She was wearing a light coat, the collar turned up, she twisted her neck without losing sight of me, I was standing exactly in her way, the peasant daughter fairy tale face, high steep cheek bones, deep-set Slavic eyes, her lips casually sure of themselves curled into a mocking expression: I explored her face hoping to be disappointed so all would end well, but her eyes set my—my circulation spinning around and around endlessly. "What film are we playing?" she asked politely with her voice.*

*What film: I thought obediently. I felt myself standing there, looked at from the back, I felt the trite accidental circumstances of this meeting, this street with its shapes of houses and gardens and parked cars could be anywhere and each word had the hollowness of lies, and, and it was like a film. I nodded with disappointment, a disappointment that was*

*other and worse than the indifference I had wished for a
second before, now I could see myself like a spectator in
the movies sees the romantic hero on the screen, grinning
all over my exposed face I said: "I apologize."*

*"You had better say you'll never live a refusal down," she
said, her voice singing with unchanged involuntary indifference. She still was not moving.*

*"No," I said: "I shall never live that down," now everything
was again as a few breaths ago. I felt my watch vibrate at
my wrist as I do now, and no longer understood its ticking.
One of her uniformed companions straightened up again at
the car after having bent down to get in, gay and lively he
asked what was the matter, let her call him over with a
movement of the chin, curious, with a sportsman's interest
she stood examining details in my face while she said: "It's
a friend of mine," sunny and friendly, the foreigner held out
his hand in a stream of words "Glad to meet you, name's
Conne. Any time? Plenty of room, come with us" but I sur-
mounted the introduction without stumbling or flustering
(even a trifle condescendingly), I said that I too was glad,
that my name was Blach, doctor of philology and so on, that
I could not go with them, unfortunately, sorry.*

*"What a scandal in a respectable film," I said after the other
two had climbed into the car, the door was open beside
me, she drove off in a terrible hurry in the huge lizard-long
car, although now, in my memory, there is no hurry, only
the way she stood there, lost to the world, waiting beside me
and not beside me. She had shoved her hands into her coat
pockets; she stood, lost, tired, looking down at the cobble
pavement beside her shoes, she was wearing her hair in a
bun at the neck that day, her hair is dark and thick. She
did not accept my stupid-clever retreat, she seemed to be
speaking for herself, until she suddenly picked up her eyes
in the middle of her question: "And what's supposed to be
the point of all this?"*

*What was the point?*
*I said I had no idea.*

*"Thank you for putting me in my place," she said in German, her German sang the same way. For the first time she smiled. The lights of the city on her face at night that spring, every evening the dust in the streets was perfumed with silent powdery rain drops*

"Yes," said Jonas Blach.

"Where did you find him?" Cresspahl had asked casually after some thought, when he came to meet his daughter in Berlin that summer and they were taking the subway back from Jonas at night across the border back to the hotel, Gesine laughed softly with surprise and said "in the street"; they said no more about it. "He stopped her in the street," Cresspahl said as though this had to be kept in mind tonight in view of present circumstances, and Jonas asked himself how that looked to Jakob. It happened every day, could happen almost to every man, it wasn't anything extraordinary; but he had not wanted to mention it just yet when he said "Yes," he had not mentioned it to any of his friends either. His friends were known at the Institute, they could easily be located in the surrounding buildings, they were enough to give him identity; he could already be recognized on the short walk from the assistant's office to the administration building; and couldn't he also be seen at the post office across the border asking for her letters? Sometimes, when the whole tidy nonsense of his professional existence seemed questionable to him and ridiculous, in general as well as in particular, he secretly regretted that he had not just looked at her and let her pass and remain a memory. But that he had dragged her into the instability and boredom of his daily routine as though she, too, were a well-known, well-defined, recognized, settled everyday occurrence.

But Jakob had no story to go with this. "And last Thursday?" he asked. Cresspahl looked up, wondering how Jonas would react. All three sat listening into the night to the sudden motor sound from the Soviet Headquarters, a heavy rapid weight was pushing into the puddles, thumping off on the road to the city. "Yes," Jonas said again with his brief toneless laughter of impatience,

the same laughter that had risen in his throat after the seminar last Thursday as he sat smoking amidst the furniture behind the more than man-tall ceremoniously armored door of his office, trying to defy his reputation which was, however, hovering nearby, ghostlike and important, proving with its large mute looming that his own life could not be recognized. And again he sat, now as then, not knowing what to do, staring across his clasped hands on the table after the smoke that was sucked up by the blackness outside, in Cresspahl's room:

ABOUT 5 P.M. THE SWITCHBOARD put a long-distance call through to the English Institute. The secretary—a delicate little woman, graceful, pretty, full-faced—took three steps back from the locker and wriggled her shoulders into her coat while answering with her name and the name of the Institute. The name at the other end was muffled but, from the intonation, she thought she recognized one of Herr Blach's friends (the tall one with the rimless glasses) who did, moreover, ask for Herr Blach. She said Dr. Blach had left. She didn't know where he could be reached. He had stayed late this afternoon and seemed to have an engagement for the evening. No. The Herr Professor had also left, was there a message? "No" said the other voice, and a longer pause strangely enforced the image of the tall friend with the glasses, until the call ended with thank you goodbye. The secretary contemplated the urgent and unproductive impression of the call for a stretch of her way, but when she met her husband as she did every night at the corner across from the subway station, she finally decided that she was not authorized to give out all kinds of information to anyone who happened to telephone.

But while, one hundred and thirty-three railroad miles

further south, Herr Bessiger was still bent over his telephone which he held encircled in both arms—with a disgruntled wrinkling of the nose he looked through his office window down into the street, stood up, long-legged in corduroy pants, bored with one careless finger in the starched shirt collar under the tie, Herr Bessiger, age twenty-six, editor of a publishing house and for several years a friend of Jonas Blach, due to his views and a few similarities: sociable, mentally alert, aggressive, verbal, fortunately for him married, a careful hesitant pipe smoker on the outside and fond of Jonas' "fickle adventurer's existence" which he sanctioned and worried about and yet he, himself, incapable of the unscrupulous flexibility he had wanted to recommend to Jonas for tonight and the next few days—Blach had

JONAS

*just arrived under the arches of the El train and was standing, halted in the motionless rainpowdered entwining crowd, which like me stood and watched the parade in the street: in military formation and uniform (blue denim overalls with wide leather belts and shoulder straps under dark-blue ski caps and a red arm band) silent men were marching beside the curb, eyes fixed straight ahead, disconcertingly soundless on the slightly wet rubber soles of their civilian city shoes: they were not singing, there was only the thin sporadic murmuring of spectators along the barriers. I was fighting a grin on my face, perhaps in order to establish security at least in that quarter, the compulsory enthusiasm of these paterfamilias marchers did seem funny. Because, by themselves, they had no meaning and had been pasted in like a stock photograph next to a long prepared caption, or the film stills of an event that, so far, had only existed in words, "the moment has come." But the quiet wet slurring of the rubber soles struck me as funny in itself. I turned my strenuously superior face away and pushed through the double doors of the restaurant; but the spectacle and the*

*discomfort stayed with me, the amazed lonely headshake*
*of a woman who had been watching beside me, who hugged*
*her shopping bag against her, mechanically, before I could*
*excuse myself for bumping into her and passing.*

"That was how it may have started. I walked through the
dining room, ostentatiously looking right and left, because
my walking through was to convey the impression to the
casual observer that I had an appointment, that I was looking for someone, in the open door at the other end I turned
once more, offering an expression of mild disappointment;
stingily lighted, stained tablecloths; it's all part of it. Straight
to the ticket windows of the El, few people, I paced the
platform from end to end, I did not turn back to look (error),
I disappeared with the aimfully hasty gait of a young man
(quantities of young men hang around this place every
night) through the side exit toward the Canal, through the
gray windy evening wetness, not the street . . . this was
really exaggerated I thought, I would have gone the same
way under most other circumstances, whereas today it had
all kinds of secret implications. I entered the parking lot
from the rear because I wanted to be able to read the license
plates without having to nose around among the cars, that
seems fishy. The meeting car looked like thousands of others
(we manufacture only three models), I climbed into the back
beside my boss and protector and said good evening to the
gentlemen in front. I had never seen them before, but they
looked so famous, they seemed immediately familiar. We
left the parking lot and drove rapidly north, and then things
like this: the man beside the driver was holding a piece of
onionskin up to his eyes, looked like the copy of a letter,
but the name had been snipped out (with manicure scissors)
and another strip was missing in the second paragraph, a
ridiculous possession, the man at the wheel grunted his
satisfaction, the paper disappeared: the kind of stuff no
movie dares show you any more it's so silly and they were
taking it seriously. And my boss at my side, one of those

old thought-worn faces, if you're around an old man like that every day and talk with him and do things for him, and you know that, years ago, he wouldn't give in, the fascists took away his chair at the university because of insubmission, then he starved a couple of years in America, now he's a little helpless and still full of ideals, all his life he has helped build pyramids of the mind—he is a venerable personality and you are the respected assistant. How can you be right with a man like that? Didn't I say to him: Your willingness to participate in these (let's call them) gatherings is important, but personal. Because these gatherings won't even end with barricades, only with martyrs behind bars; of course I'll be glad to go with you, and I think it's foolish—? There he sits beside me, friendly, his thin old legs pulled up, rapt with anticipation of improvements to come: I tried my best. When we got there, we were both in excellent spirits. I hoisted him up the stairs, at the door everybody bowed and whispered (he's the famous philologist, and in spite of his advanced age) . . . it was as though they had rented him for the occasion, a showpiece, a justification, like a potted palm from the cemetery florist. Because they didn't ask *him* had he been invited and on whose recommendation, as befits a respectable conspiracy; those who came after us were asked. When we had finally taken our seats in the third front row, he shook himself into position as he would otherwise do only during receptions for first-semester students, he was probably in the mood for a few earnest dignified words. Unlike me: although the people gathered here were not at all unimportant. All of them had accomplished something with their poems and scientific textbooks, for years they had kowtowed and let themselves be compromised for the sake of a reputation with national prizes, in newspapers, on television, solely to be able to meet that evening as the spiritual conscience of our country and discuss how it should be improved in the interest of a so-called human socialism."

### HERR ROHLFS

*They laughed as though they couldn't stop. Moldaw especially, the fat one, he was literally wallowing, yelling yeshtsho raz again and again, "yeshtsho raz: ee on skazal: Na sdarovye, Tovarishtsh, na sdarovye . . ." but I know lots of stories, quite a few people can testify to that, so why tell the same story more than once. "Glavnaya stantseeya Moskva. Angliskeeye ee Frantsooskeeye journalisty . . ." I began, when the orderly came into the room, clicked to attention: official business, the laughter and the liquor bottles on the table bothered me, and the unbuttoned collars, it's not good for the morale of the men, I felt so awkward that I walked out with him without a question and said good-bye a trifle too formally, they were in no condition to salute properly so they insisted on saluting all the more. I didn't think anything important had come. Perhaps another anonymous letter, so they have to run and call me right back from the so-called good time I'm having one evening a week. And the guard is standing at attention stiff as a ramrod, in the rain, impeccable discipline, one snap and the rifle is presented although I look like nothing in my civilian clothes, can't have seen me more than three times at most. They had given me the jeep because of the roads after the rain, now the air was quiet. "Pa-idiom," I said. We drove off. How do I know what they got whether it'll help? Cresspahl's house stood across the way, a black lump, two windows lighted. Let them talk. I wouldn't want to be sitting there in Jakob's place, next to the empty rooms. Ah, leave me alone! The message was from Berlin, "I thought I should at least let you know," said the young man who is beginning to please me, the paper is lying on my desk, all I have to do is sit down. Diligence for diligence, when I have no need to be nice. "Did you read it?" I ask. "Yes," he says, "you'll want to make a long-distance call." Very well! "Then connect me," I say. "You have observed me well enough by now to know with whom." He is grinning. Nice kid. I'll try to think of something.*

*Comrade! oh comrade. Dear Dr. Blach, dear comrade Blach, what was going on in that intelligent educated head of yours when you accompanied your professor to the end of the earth? First of all, meetings must be registered, that's a police regulation: as if you didn't know. But these holders of superior knowledge act as though the building belonged to them after they've held a couple of authorized meetings there. Misuse of authority by the janitor, he'd better watch out. I can well imagine: they probably managed to push us to the rear of their little club, to exclude us gently . . . no, actually I can't imagine. Now they brazenly meet in public, as though we were still part of it. I fail to understand: a newspaper wrote these discussions up! as though they knew enough to know better. And mail it to us, in case we'd like to join in the discussion. Correct time. They get up and talk about artificial respiration of socialist morality as though they were planning changes. As though they had a cabinet and an administrative staff, as though they had all the cabinets and my word had lost its power in every household. And they think it's a joke, playing hide and seek with us . . . boarding an airplane in the fall, with sunglasses, what sort of life do they think this is? Who are they to replace reality? I wouldn't lecture on the dissolution of backward agricultural cooperatives either if I knew nothing about agriculture: it all starts with a bad conscience, and why? because they are alone. We have accustomed them to ride through the streets, but the workers walk. We shall see. At any rate, one of them can't go on a trip, two days later I know all about it. And such a creature is now sitting in Jerichow right under my nose and bends decent people's ears as though I didn't exist. I'll take the case on because of affinities. Because I wanted to become a teacher once. The long-distance call. Thank you. Go to bed. Yes!*

*Twenty-six years old, profession: philology, promoted. The photograph on his application is exactly three years old, he was touchy then and conceited, who knows if I would have recognized him from that snapshot without bias? Couldn't they photograph him at the door! probably couldn't. What times we're living in when the State has to disguise itself and sneak into its own houses! It'll be his birthday soon, I think I'll give him a present. Father accountant mother doesn't go to work. I can picture it. Our son must have an education, become somebody, your family-my family and off with the poor child to college, and who pays for such silly ambitions? the State, yes, even if it has ulterior motives. As have the loyal, concerned parents who're out to cheat from the start. And afterwards the boy ought to go to the West. And then: "The boy never comes home any more, you ought to give him a good talking to"; but the boy won't let himself be talked to. Looks like a gifted career: college, exams, assistant, promotion. I know of a lady who also went to college, studied English philology. Was he in Halle for two years? No. Straight to Berlin. Fed up with his parents and small-town life, not nice of the boy. Dear Sir and molder of minds, I do hope this was the prank of an adolescent. Accompanying the professor is a pardonable mistake, you might have found some excuse; couldn't you dispense with that, with that contribution to the discussion? I hope at least that you met Cresspahl's daughter by accident, not in a villa in Berlin-Dahlem but in the street outside (but he's not the type). Otherwise the State is going to be angry, na sdarovye, you bookworm, it is already displeased. And now he is sitting in there, the bright boy, buttering Jakob up, "Lenin's theory of knowledge, you understand," and Tuesday I'm supposed to clean up all this mess without too much talk, Jakob isn't fond of speeches. He looked at me as though I were an opera singer, operas are out of fashion. And it's just as well: the harder I have to work at it, the better I come prepared and eliminate objections, and the better I'm prepared, the surer I am to have won you, Jakob. I'm sorry about that with your mother. Again I fail to understand: Every day in every city a militant group is on the march, one can't fail to notice it; if one of those makers of speeches is aware of such a march,*

*wouldn't he be seized by the notorious nausea of knowledge,*
*wouldn't you think?*


A man likes to be known by the name he gives himself. In
order to know John "The Magnanimous" we compare his
name to his deeds. On this premise—and adding that it does
not befit a man to name himself, that it is preferable if his
contemporaries (whether subordinate or not) bestow the
name—we compare the actions of the "good people, even the
best" to the quality they'd like to be known for. "Good" in
this case means "wanting better," their glory is the desire for
improvement through change. They are the only ones to
challenge the powers of evil (the manifest injustice of the
surplus value), therefore they defend the weak of the world.
What do they want? they don't want the widow's lamb
stolen. Justice is a not-wanting. (They do want: everybody
to keep his lamb, that there be no more quarreling over
lambs, that everybody own an equal number.) This decides
the future of humanity. What is necessary for the "good
people, even the best" to win a just victory? Solidarity against
the enemy. We now consider the conditions in a country in
which the revolution has come to a victorious end. (We refer
the question: Can a revolution end? to the subcommittees.)
What does this mean? Is life in such a State automatically
just? it is. (Why is it? Because, in that State, the happy future
has already begun.) Do the men in power do the right thing
all the time? it cannot be otherwise. What follows? As one
of the best said after the death of the Very Best (as we heard,
thanks to the lie-machine of the surplus profiteers—why? because they're trying to harm us): the Very Best in his bound-
less justice had his brothers-in-arms executed, countless num-
bers of them, because they were guilty of useful contradiction.
He stole land to build his power. He endangered the good
cause by calling himself competent to wage wars and was
not competent (and waged his wars on paper). All these
things we are told (as examples) after the good cause has

been saved by his death. This is called the cult of personality. End of introduction.

Where does the error lie? (Subquestions: are errors possible? can the good cause be bad? No. It is at least better.) Is the group of good people (as a group) impractically organized? There is a weak point: the individual. "The good are interested in something / that lies outside themselves." Is a person sublime who manages to disregard the self? Yes. Is such a person conceivable? Keep your nose out of my private life with your indiscreet questions. We're here to discuss the facts. What deprived the Catholic Church of veneration and respect? The dogma of personal infallibility. Is infallibility conceivable for a juster cause? Man is weak and prone to selfishness. The opportunity to be right makes self-righteousness. Anyone can make a mistake. But with a pilot, the mistake goes further than with children at play; when does a mistake begin to be a crime? Are mistakes punishable? The man in power punishes himself for misuse of power: that's a new proverb. I never heard it before. There are lots of good people, their leader must be all of them together with all their eyes. That ought to lower the error quota just plain statistically. Would not be desirable: leaders must respond to all the demands of their followers, they must be punishable for every mistake, if their harmfulness is proved, shouldn't we be able to send them back to the hard labor of daily life, overnight?

No. Because, what does the Best of the Best stand for, what does he represent, what is he invested with? The good cause. The good cause cannot be sent back. Does not each airing of errors harm the reputation of the good group? Does recognition of possible fallibility not render the good cause fallible as a whole, good only in its intentions and plans, not sacred, untouchable like What Is, but changeable even in that? Trying is laudable. But if the good cause is no more than an attempt (among other, equally good ones), it could be different. It is necessary that its fairness remain indis-

putable at all times. Freedom: acceptance of this necessity
... (What is necessary?)

"In every way unmistakably the meeting had the aspect of a
scientific gathering: there were minutes and an agenda, two
prepared speeches and a chairman who granted the floor,
each word was put on record: a conspiracy wouldn't think of
hiring stenographers. What am I saying 'had the aspect,' it
was a harmless discussion of various philosophical problems,
in the line of 'Reality and Proposition,' for over a month once
a week; it seems strange and not quite so official only to
someone who attends for the first time; the secret address
of the Successor was, of course, mentioned only in the introduction, generalized as 'Explanations,' they'd gone beyond
that long ago. On the other hand . . . last spring, we were
just coming back from our vacation, Gesine started to buy
her daily two and a half pounds of newspapers again that
morning, as far as Munich we just sat and read, we read
through the Italian, the Austrian, the West German custom
controls: secret address by the First Chairman of the Communist Party of the Soviet Union, you understand, and for
me it didn't all sound like din of battle in Turkey. But she
said right away: 'Now you probably think he's a regular
guy, honorable and what, no?' yes, I said: if a man is that
open he probably means it, what else? 'Now,' she says: 'in
his country,' she meant it was a political move of no importance. It sounds unjust, the things she says about us,
because she wants to have nothing to do with us . . ."
Or with the Americans either: Cresspahl said.
". . . or with anyone else, yes, if one wants to stay out of it
at any cost, one may be able to keep a clear head. But I had
to get off the train in Munich, exchange my clandestine
foreign-travel passport for the local exit permit, have the
newspapers confiscated by the border control and face the
slogans again the minute I arrived and back to the daily
socialist routine you understand, so I preferred to think he
was a regular guy and that things were improving. Democrat-

ization is progressing. I preferred to forget the newspapers in the passport office. When I read all the unread papers that had piled up at the Institute, I was curious to see what they'd make of it on our side, there was no mention of it. The XXth Congress had taken place, but there wasn't a line about the speech, it wasn't in any of the later papers either, and by and by I realized that it had not been meant for us. Well: there were newspapers on sale two hundred yards beyond the border, next to wooden booths with all the rubber bands in the world, and tomatoes, and Hollywood westerns that don't exist on our side either; the text of the speech was still around. I remember I analyzed it word by word: the syntax, its line of thought, to see if it could be genuine, since the government didn't refute it, it had to be genuine —as well as secret. You can't just shrug off the will of the State. And these people were gathered here as though it were otherwise, as though they were free again to ask questions: they acted a trifle too ceremoniously, too enthusiastic, not giving in, as though they were afraid that, each time one of them took the floor, it might have a bad end (that someone might say so out loud). Not so unreasonable I mean. Nobody got up to say: now let us bear in mind that our industrial production has slowed down and that the agricultural situation looks pretty precarious . . . oh no. They were thoroughly and objectively quarreling over ideas and sometimes they didn't show much consideration for the only ones that had been officially recognized so far: that was all. And if it was skepticism, then it wasn't so insignificant after all."


— Maybe so, but have you got militia teams on the railroad? — Difficult, with all those shifts: there isn't the time for all that exercising marching photo-taking. "People's Police Helpers" is the name for it (the traffic cops are breathing down our necks as it is), and it's not hard to talk yourself out of it, just open your trap a bit, or maybe you were a prisoner of the British: that makes you automatically unreliable see?

Armed to the teeth—sure thing: with a band around one arm. They distribute the rifles before the parade and then afterwards everybody obediently hands his in again. You don't think they'd trust us with weapons at this stage! after they've seen the kind of games you can play with them.

— And yet you're part of a solid organization, you march with and beside the others in the direction they tell you to, do you think a guy's got the guts to turn around all by himself?

— Yeah, and it has to be a guy with kids, or you can't take him seriously. Aw shut up.

HERR ROHLFS

*My leg is on the windowsill, stiff and cramped as though it didn't belong to me. The ankle keeps falling asleep, it's almost numb, anyhow, it doesn't occur to me that I might want to move it. No: not for this. And my hand wasn't banged up either so that a couple of bright boys could sit around discussing errors. The typewriter is in the car. If I want to make a few notes I'd have to call the assistant or Hänschen. Sometimes a man feels like making a few notes, is that so surprising. What the hell, go right ahead, I say. Okay with me. If a successor (to look at it from that angle) feels obliged to mention his predecessor's errors, dangerous though it be for the administration, he must know. I consider (I regard, I refute) the word "error," a lot of nonsense, what is it supposed to signify? the government has taken certain measures that didn't please everybody, as though that made them wrong! Nobody is in a position to judge whether they're necessary or not, except the party, except us. Me, in a way. They could have muddled on without weakness or losses, but since their prosperity and strength is supposed to grow in the eyes of the world, a little moral excitement is not wasted at the start. If unpopular methods are called errors, those affected manifest satisfaction agreement eagerness: that's the easiest. And they can afford to*

*kid us great mighty undefeated sayoos nerooshimy. sa-yoos
neroo-shimy, silence, the broadcast was over. I say to him
I remember perfectly, prominent dark angular eyebrows with
those loyal stupid desperate eyes deep underneath, otherwise nothing but snow. Frozen to the bone. I say: shoot in
the air at least. He says nothing. I bound out of the foxhole
into the snow, after ten yards he can't see me any more in
my snow coat. He shoots, the s.o.b. is shooting, the s.o.b.
shoots my leg dead. "Sons of bitches" they said after I got to
the other side and I all the time nemetski kamrad nemetski
kamrad surrender. Only later I noticed what had happened
to my hand. If I ever meet him, we'll play "defining errors"
together. I'll have a winter fabricated down to twenty-five
below and turn the years back to 1942 and take him back to
the furthest forward foxhole on the Russian front and then
we'll repeat the game of How do I act toward a comrade
who has decided to go over, do I shoot him in the . . . do
I mess up his hand. I wonder what time it is. I just blanked
out. Second time this week. This constant glare of the window
pane: you can't tell is it night or early morning or what time
of year. Accomplishments: all Soviet frontiers are safe and
solid, inside all they do is administrate. And what can we
afford (they needn't have let the speech leak out right into
the hands of the US State Department—what an expression:
appropriate perhaps. A private tip-off would have been
enough, then the Yu-Ess-Stait-Depatmint could have let out
one of its usual unreliable groping rumors: I'd have liked it
better. There aren't enough errors in the text). Because, what
can we afford? Every time you switch on the radio. Every
Western station hurls nasty comments at us across the border,
and dull-witted know-better talk and everybody is allowed
to travel where he wants to, in out as he pleases, and that is
supposed to work out in the long run? We started only ten
years ago. I bet they're standing by their rifles on the other
side, just waiting for the first stone to hit a window over
here, and me right on the nose as I sit here musing over the
good time I'm having on my one evening off. Can't afford*

*that. Not for this. I have a kink in my life, that needn't make
it an error. We can't let them discuss errors like that! With
me sitting here planning for a comfortable old age to ponder
my errors: as though my hand, my crippled smashed-up hand
didn't disgust my daughter, as though my leg were whole and
I didn't limp at all (when she grows older, she'll copy my
limp and what'll I do? I'll demonstrate. And I'll explain to
her how such things come about. I don't want any sons of
bitches to). If there have been any abuses anywhere, that's
our concern. We know all about it. Those who have no
business ought to shut up. And not sing any of their songs
either. I bet they're already singing.*

DURING THE NEXT two days the young man of the two Berlins
was almost continuously in Jakob's thoughts. It so happened
that the preparations for Tuesday evening could be accomplished with Jonas in mind; it made Jakob realize how automatically his own, his professional life, sped past from
morning to night. He had gone to bed around midnight, in
Jerichow. He remembered the shaking and swinging of the
bare black birch branches outside the window under which
he was sleeping; from time to time a branch clawed hard at
the glass, covering the monotonous murmur of the two voices
in the next room. The night was deep blue behind the head
of the tree (a pitch dark rebellious head around which the
wind wound long caressing strands of hair). They were still
asleep when he breakfasted in the kitchen beside the shabby
morning light; quietly he had closed the door behind him
and walked through the empty gray streets to the station. In
his furnished room that afternoon he found a note from
Sabine. Paper in hand he stood at the table, reading and re-
reading Sabine's letter which was as hasty and vehemently
urgent as her handwriting; his eyes caught the folder on the
bookshelf, he was about to fold the letter and put it with the
others, his fingers were already moving. But he smoothed out

the paper and laid it on the table; although he realized that he'd come back to it in the morning. Because he worked the third shift, Sunday, he had suddenly remembered that it was Sunday and that the man who was replacing him was married; actually he had intended to be busy.

Sabine called Peter Zahn on Monday, she merely wanted to ask which shifts Jakob was going to have, but the shift supervisor's office transferred her call to the locomotive office where her request for Abs was answered with a moderately surprised: no. He was, however, standing below the windows of the locomotive office, at the change-over point, talking to Kasch in front of his 41, explaining the no-passing method. The 41 is a freight locomotive model without tender. "With your 4073 you get stuck twice. You stand twice on the second track, eight minutes according to schedule. Passenger trains." "According to schedule," said Kasch. He was a man of forty. His small round head was densely grown with short matted hair, his two-day beard had a lighter color. There were thick greasy streaks at his temples from wiping his eyes. Some people thought he was crafty, because of his slanting eyelids; maybe they meant his reliable bitterness. Jakob had picked him first because it wasn't easy to get a promise out of him. He did have a violent temper. "Precisely," said Jakob. His coat and jacket were unbuttoned at the neck, it had gotten warm around noon. He felt the ashen taste of soot on his tongue, the heavy sooty air between the groaning engines. "Usually longer than that. And I have to take you out and put you back somewhere at the tail." Kasch had not nodded once. He had his fireman toss his cigarettes down, offered one to Jakob and gave him a light. "Somewhere at the tail": said Jakob bending over the flame: "because of passing. Always ends in a bottleneck. Can you run faster than schedule?" Kasch's hands were back in his pockets. "Look at the old grinder," he said and took the trouble to point his chin at the locomotive. "Yes," said Jakob, "no," he said. A habit he had picked up from Cresspahl. "You know the run, the slow spots, you know where you could afford to put on speed, if it served a purpose. If you didn't have to wait again afterwards." "Got to wait though," said Kasch, but his head was turned sideways and he seemed to be figuring. "You mean: if I got there ahead of schedule . . ." Jakob nodded. "I'd let you right through and you can get past while the passenger train makes its stop, since that's on schedule." "Can't do that all by myself," said Kasch. Jakob said he'd talk to Jöche and Ole Man Peters later and that he only wanted them to take a look at the run with his suggestion in mind. "As long as you're paid by the mile and not by stops, you needn't worry." Kasch was contemplating his legs, turned the toes outward and said "I get you. But not before Thursday. And only if I can really do it. And if it doesn't get into the papers." "We could call it the Kasch-Method," said Jakob, but he was joking. Kasch smiled briefly, and cordially said: shit. Jakob told him and his fireman to take it easy and stalked off across the tracks. Monday he worked the second shift. "Train's coming," they yelled to him at switch II, and the C-D said later Jakob had heard the train coming (it was coming around the bend toward the two double-cross tracks of an intersection, neither the clear, nor the slow-approach signal could be seen from the blind corner where he stood), he had happily grinned up to them and they had talked a moment longer—looking up, looking down—before Jakob crossed the tracks to his tower.

He had been careful to avoid anything that smacked of newspaper terminology, he didn't want to irritate Kasch. Certainly it would be "an important contribution" (if it worked) and a "severe blow to the monopoly capitalists," if this "thorn in their eyes" (the government under which Jakob lived) grew and prospered. He had been obliged to discuss running speeds with Kasch. And as little as Jakob could picture a meeting of scientists (a meeting simply, with changed participants and a different, less specific subject that did not immediately affect the day's routine or the distribution of labor), still, Jonas' story had somehow prompted him to mention the running speeds. This Jonas had a capacity for anger.

There were people he disliked in advance and right away
or whom he kept at arm's length with distrust: he had a low
opinion of them. And if, in the course of such a meeting (for
instance) "a well-fed and what do you call it? ingenuous
prophet gets to his feet—who's had a good sleep every night
of his life—and throws his sleepless fretting over 'freedom'
at the esteemed audience, he can't help it," then one gets
angry. Angry, because every man in the room knows that his
position, his title, his country house have been earned by
bowing to party opinion. Jakob's reaction would have been:
Leave me alone I want no part of you. Not more than that.
Perhaps his meetings were different. (And he had not forgotten that Jonas had asked about Gesine as though he hadn't
heard from her for some time. It was true, all last week,
every day, Herr Dr. Blach had taken the subway to the other
side of Berlin. The ride had long ceased to be a mere covering
of distance for him. It had become a mood of incessantly
changing light tones (the glare inside the station, the gradual
rising to street and bridge level) that tunnelled up into another
country: Stadtmitte Thälmannplatz (Kaiserhof) Potsdamer
Platz Gleisdreieck Bülowstrasse. But there was nothing for him
at the post office. And Gesine's short laconic letters only wanted
to prove how foolish it was trying to communicate in writing;
but he still had to find that out, so, every day, he invented a
new pretext for the ride. The only news from her, during the
last few weeks, was the nightly weather report for the North
Rhine and Westphalia areas over the West German radio
station, stressing the thought of her: perhaps it is raining outside her windows, but only because windows stay put and
don't change deliberately from one day to the next. It helped
him hold off writing to her himself: as though he couldn't
be sure that his letter of two days ago would reach her today; and also because sometimes he no longer understood
something he had seriously intended to do the day before.
But all this was Jakob's imagination; he merely thought that
a restlessness of this sort might possibly have increased Jonas'
anger until it pushed him to his feet and made him ask for

permission to reply to the previous speaker's freedom-loving opinions.) And as for Jonas' relationship with his professor-boss whom he had (you're free to imagine) asked in a soft whisper if he should take the floor, who (according to Jonas' description) had said "go fix him" grimly, humorously, but who could later be seen from the speaker's platform, sitting huddled and ill at ease, one hand against his chin, next to his assistant's empty chair—Cresspahl seemed to understand perfectly. Cresspahl whom Jakob placed on one side when he thought of his first two years in Jerichow, with himself the sixteen-year-old stranger placed on the other side, in comparison, this was perhaps similar: the old professor disliked all this talk of freedom, he had been rebellious once, like his assistant today who was now supposed to defend him against owners of country houses and "freedom" so that he needn't attack them himself? (Cresspahl had raged terribly about the requisition of the villa at the tile works while the refugees were still lying in the barns, he had not contradicted Jakob who compared these barns to others he had seen during his flight.) There were many possible reasons, possibly all of them intertwined, why Jonas spoke—not for five but for twenty minutes—and why his intended refutation became a series of suggestions. ("And yet all this struck me as supernonsense. I was one of the youngest in the audience according to the audience; according to myself I was already too old to credit myself with astounding future achievements; I'm not gifted above average. And I get up and make demands.") He could talk that way in front of Cresspahl (my father is a tower with short parted gray hair); but if you thought about it thirty hours later, with the loudspeakers babbling at you incessantly and you can only repeat what you have already repeated (Jakob shook his head, silently amused by the stubbornness of the next dispatcher who refused to accept his train, it was running too close to schedule), didn't such self-deprecatory confessions smack perhaps of impudence? Was it conceivable that he had stopped Gesine "in the street" with impudence? And what would Gesine say to such impudence:

You clown, she'd say, you undersized giant, how long have you been out of knee pants: she might have said. No: this guy meant what he said, and it wasn't a habit with him either. That was perhaps why he had started with this detour in an inconceivably distant city, and a meeting on an irretrievable Thursday on the other shore: Shouldn't one perhaps settle a question of semantics first? he had angrily asked the esteemed audience. Because of the definition? Conveys nothing to me: Jakob repeated to himself, amused as though he were thinking for the first time: "freedom" is a negative concept rather: it doesn't exist. Whoever enters this world addresses himself as "I," that's the most important to him, but he finds himself in the company of several other I's and has to readjust his self-importance; nobody is free enough for instance to step out of physics as far as he's concerned. As a social and natural being (I am a . . .) fixed to a considerable degree. The concept of the universe probably starts with "I"—"however, this cannot be understood as freedom as long as one considers Man (our human beings, the masses) as subject to the influence of the simplest causality, as is the government of a country," he might as well have spoken on agricultural conditions. Because he had stayed within the two-headed framework of State and Citizen (as he said) with his discrepancy. And the pivot of this discrepancy had better not be called freedom (Pavlov's theory of conditioned reflexes) but rather the obstinacy of consciousness: as well as its gestation. This is where he had started "making demands" as he put it. What was the meaning of "finality"? Yes: the individual pursues his own selfish purpose in all that he does, no matter how often it is called unselfish. And what is my purpose? Jakob thought with bemused mockery in front of his train sheet; his mood surprised him. Was it Jonas' purpose to enrich the world with his concepts of it? perhaps. It was not his profession to "make philosophic comments on the subject," it had suddenly come over him, hadn't it? and making this speech justified all the disgust and disappointments of years wasted in foolish waiting, huh? What if a man always bases his principles on his

most recent experiences? Jakob thought, but he wasn't thinking of Herr Rohlfs. He remembered that he had promised to
call Peter Zahn, and he felt uneasy planning to forget about
it. Moreover, he wasn't quite sure that Jonas paid as much
attention to himself as to the things he saw that didn't concern him. But what he had seen (what he had read: thought
Jakob, what he had said: he remembered Gesine's tales about
the libraries, about university life in general), he was happy
to have said and would vouch for and adjust his life accord-
ingly: and it did affect one's day and the effort one put into
one's job: as Jakob discovered to his surprise. Hadn't Jonas
left town immediately afterwards? after they asked him to put
his speech in writing and hand it in to the philosophy editor
at the end of the month, to be printed, but only to a trusted
member, not to breathe a word of this project and to be careful to avoid public appearances in the capital in the near
future. Well, if it could be arranged, and again he had probably sought the eye of his boss in the group that surrounded
them both at the wide-open (why wide-open?) door of the
meeting room. And the old man had nodded probably, lost
in other thoughts, with his cautious science-etched face: a
working vacation. Let's call it that. Let's call it that: and there
he sat in Cresspahl's house, in the front room (today. This
very minute) typing what he had in mind. And might perhaps, from time to time, remember—before Cresspahl—the
uneasy conscience he felt before his venerable boss whom he
had philologically deceived and who bid his assistant goodbye, friendly, extremely distracted (cordial: thought the on-
lookers) at the waiting cab. Because he did want to change
Cresspahl's opinion (to his own) about his daughter; who
had however gone far away. And Jonas had gone to Jerichow.
And my mother into the refugee barracks in West Berlin—by
train, and I make sure they all arrive safely and promptly
wherever they want to go.
That evening he discussed the no-passing method with Ole
Man Peters in the cafeteria. A morose old man from Mecklenburg with a walrus moustache and a thin high-pitched breath-

less chuckle of a laugh. He'd slant every conversation toward a chance to laugh like that. After half an hour he was poking Jakob in the ribs. All the chairs were taken at the table next to the food counter, thick clouds of laughter were bursting against the low wooden ceiling. A brief rain squall was drumming into the narrow slot of the cafeteria entrance. And Jakob? he was still around. When I got there, he had left. Probably went home in the meantime. Tuesday he worked the second shift again. In the afternoon he sat in on the chief dispatcher's operations meeting, he sat without noticeable distinction—a uniform among uniforms—at the long side of the big shiny table in the conference room. The many small panels of the four high windows painted the afternoon light in rainbow colors on the grain of the wood beside the notes under his quiet hands. He gave a report about his arrangements with Ole Man Peters and Kasch, and asked for permission to go through with the experiment and to cut down on schedule time as much as possible in the various individual divisions; he sat far back in his chair and spoke factually and concisely (no superfluous introduction, gave examples from the official timetable, described the conceivable advantage) as they had come to expect from his dependable thoughtful face. Perhaps he was a little more serious than usual; but this impression may have been conveyed by his curt "sure sure" when they pointed out that he would have to bear all the responsibility for the experiment, it may have sounded like impatience. About four in the afternoon he was in his room.

"JAKOV," SAID SABINE, because that was her name for him, with the accent on the second syllable. She had been pleading with him. He was standing, both hands clasped around the window latch in his rented room, staring out. From the back, his powerful closely cropped head was rigid with staring. Sabine sat on the hard wooden chair at the table, pulling at a cigarette. Hastily, clumsily, she leaned forward and tapped it out. Jakob turned. She wasn't sure she still knew his smile. One forgets so many things.

"I apologize," said Jakob. She had not come in her uniform. She was sitting before him strange sure most desirable. She had even changed her hairdo from the one she wore under her cap at work, now it was twisted into a bun at the back of her head. A single delicate curl was standing stiffly, gracefully, above the collar of her wool jacket.

"I'm sorry," she said. Her hands were in her pockets (making the jacket mount up gently over the skirt), she sat motionless, looking with careful lips into the gray walled-in back yard. Jakob no longer felt like looking at it. He leaned one hip against the washstand. It was a narrow room.

"I'm not allowed to talk with you about it," he said. There were wet cracks in the plaster on the house wall across from his window. On the clothesline outside the kitchen window baby clothes were swinging damp in the wind that was reaching down into the yard with shrill whistling thrusts.

"Nor I with you," she said.

"What do you think of him?" Jakob asked. She managed to stop looking at the yard. She turned her profile toward him and pursed her lips in the once beloved treasured disdainful pout. Jakob nodded. He pushed the cigarettes toward her and pulled the second chair to the table. "If I say at this point that it's asking too much, if I say that socialism in general . . ." he began. He took the burning match back from her. Lost in thought he went to get Sunday's note, folded it carefully and put it back in its place, the lighted cigarette rolled to the right corner of his mouth. Sabine watched him, silently. "You can't get even with me," she heard him say. She hadn't heard all he said.

"Yes," she said suddenly.

"No," said Jakob with something like patience, after he had waited a while. "You needn't take it back." "And you're even nursing my pride," she said, "so I don't have to degrade myself." But she had already stood up and scooped her coat up from the bed. She stood facing him with the coat over her arm. "We shouldn't have known each other any more after that," she said.

Jakob shook his head and helped her into her coat. "It's just because it doesn't help me to know what he asked you, and I don't want you to bend either," he said. They were facing each other. She turned a little in order to see Jakob's face reflected beside her own in the mirror above the washstand. She lifted the black wet-glistening hood over her hair, her arms held the position; she looked from herself to Jakob beside her, arms hanging, looking narrowed-eyed to one side, his face taut from the wrinkles between his gray eyebrows. Pensively, confirmingly, she said "ahem . . . hm . . . " to the mirror and Jakob woke up. He brushed a strand of hair in under her hood. "I didn't come here to fling myself into your arms," she said. Jakob nodded. His lips pushed forward, he nodded, smiled. They did not shake hands. At the front door outside in the hall they halted once more. She lifted her hands and brushed their backs over his temples. Then she was gone. And it was as though he had immediately forgotten her. In the evening he stood waiting for the bus in the market square. The colored neon letters of the savings bank were chasing each other in the deep black mirror of the wet pavement. In a narrow, less lighted sidestreet he could see the house in which Sabine had lived, before, in a room under the roof, standing out against the smooth gray sky. He still remembered the landlady's name. He made no special effort to look at the gable over which lights were dancing. He simply remembered. He felt distant.

— I've got to go now.
— Do you have an appointment with Cresspahl? might also give his daughter a call. I'll be at work at that hour.
— Yes. I could give her a call.

— Say hello to her from me.
— I will. I better go now, don't you think?
— Yes, you'd better. Goodbye.
— Keep well.
— You, too.

# III

Hello. I have a long distance call for you.

— This is Cresspahl. Who is calling?
— Blach. Gesine?
— Speaking.
— Do you know
— nothing. I know nothing. What am I supposed to know? Yes, sure I know. And he's always walked across the tracks . . .
— I don't think you could point a finger at anyone, at anyone in particular and say: you did it. It's your fault. You might as well say: he should have had a different job.
— Or better still if there had been no Second World War, then Germany would not have been chopped in two. And no one can imagine how well off he'd have been if he'd never been born . . .
— Do you mean to say you feel responsible merely because, two weeks ago on a certain Tuesday, you happened to run into him?
— Yes. That's what I mean. And if I could, I'd blame myself for that Tuesday:

GESINE

*I say, "Good afternoon. Is Herr Abs there?" and stand waiting at the half open door in the humid drafty hall. The woman looks at me. Her obnoxious eyes crawl over my face, make me look back at her. She is old. She is forty. Under the eyes and*

*around the mouth and at the temples and in the eyes her face
is spoiled with age; she appraises me, not knowing what to
think, while I focus on the thick artificial color on her lips.
Other people's lives. What do I care how many girls come
asking here? No. Anybody who doesn't live in this town has no
business caring. But Jakob has his name beside the door, I
bend half back to read it again. "No," she says. "Herr Abs
isn't home," she says. She is leaning against the door frame,
letting her cigarette smoke drift into my face, I say, "Thank
you. Goodbye," and turn and run down the narrow creaky
stairs, much too fast. Did she cast her eyes down? only fatigue
maybe? I don't know; if so I did something wrong. Made a
mistake somewhere. I'm standing in the street, contemplating
my reflection in the window of the tobacco shop: a young
woman in a trenchcoat who stands waiting, hands in her
pockets, collar turned up, surreptitiously thrusting her chin
out, is anything the matter (that's how I'm standing there)?
Am I afraid? She doesn't move. Did I do something wrong?
I shouldn't look like that. I look like some girl who's waiting
for the bus. The way I know myself I'll take the next bus
away from here: as though I wanted to go somewhere. "Thank
you," I say. "Twenty," I say. "Straight ahead?" he asks. I don't
know, what is straight ahead? "Yes," I say.*

*I really don't know what the mistake could be, I only know
what I wanted to do. But ever since I left the autobahn and
arrived in this city I feel as though I were speaking a foreign
language. Which I have forgotten and which no one here
remembers either. Or: This is the Elbe River. "Herr Abs isn't
home." I should have asked when he'd be back. I walked
down the wet street under the immense gray afternoon sky,
a streetcar was standing in the haze. The woman conductor
gave me back seven pieces of change, with a ticket for 20 and
another for 10: so, I thought, it costs twenty pfennigs to go
straight ahead (without the transfer). "Twenty," I was right.
Why am I surprised that Jakob wasn't home? did I think he'd
be sitting there waiting for me? I'll go back later. Here is the
railroad station. I'll stay here until it gets dark. Today's*

*weather report: light afternoon showers. There are still huts
in the main square. And the pavement I step on between the
cars used to be the ground floor of a house, with kitchen and
living room and foyer, I'm stepping over the frames of their
cellar windows (that's where their cellar used to be), they
have remained, stuck in the earth like tombstones. The whole
town has been wet-mopped, at three corners garbage pails are
hanging from dark green wooden poles, filled with hot dog
plates and brandy bottles, the small flat hip-pocket kind; I
imagine seeing fat drunken shadows alone and in groups
move away from the warmly lighted stands. They've just
switched the light on: I'd like to look in there, but the door
is made of frosted chickenwired glass, I know. I was in there
once with Jakob. We stood at the long brass counter beside
nothing but men with drooping trouser bottoms who looked
as though they had been standing there all day and were
never going to leave and Jakob said "Two large shots," and
they all looked at me in amazement and started talking to
Jakob and to me too, but he said "That's my sister," and they
all came over and shook my hand. That was three years ago,
I can't just walk in there after three years, although, who
knows, perhaps the same men are standing at the same counter and the pious greedy female pours them one consolation
after another, who knows what they'll say if Jakob isn't with
me, then I'll lose my temper and my father says: Gesine. One
can't let you go out alone anywhere. Yes, I say: on a fall day
like this, on an October night when all the houses are lighted,
everybody should be at home. It's no longer twilight. I'll go
window-shopping until everything is pitch black, then I'll eat
something somewhere and then take another streetcar ride
straight ahead and say, here I am: I'd like to wait until he
comes home.*

About 7 P.M. she was sitting alone at a table in the dining
room of the Elbe Hotel. Slowly, well-mannered, she cut into
the steak the waiter had brought her after half an hour. At

first she had sat, waiting, leaning against the back of the bench, smoking, watching the people at the bar. Three times young men, well dressed for the evening, came up and asked her for the opposite seat, she merely shook her head. She was wearing her blue suit with its cinched jacket and high collar; the blouse—of a coarse gray fabric—looked simpler but well thought out. It didn't make her look like a person who was traveling—light, carrying nothing but a student's briefcase folded in half and a thick brown trenchcoat; occasionally she'd glance up, let the picture of the head of this State and the excited voices at the bar filter into her thoughts, she did not give the impression of someone who ought to fear having her papers checked and who was going to pay for her dinner with money that had been exchanged on the other side of the border at an impudently low rate. Herr Rohlfs was sitting on one of the stools to the left in front of the bartender, regularly sipping at his two and a half ounces of vodka, he sat stiff and straight and never moved his right hand inside his pocket. Sometimes he'd glance up at the clock.

HERR ROHLFS
*Seven after seven. Eight more minutes. And Sabine wanted to tell him her impressions probably, then he could have answered: yes, isn't it the truth? and they might have got back together again: it would have made me happy for him. But then I also saw her come out of the house. One knows next to nothing actually. I'm not even sure he's going to show up. I merely think he will. How they talk, these people. I'd love to take the right person aside and whisper a few hints on the art of debating in his ear, all he can do is defend himself, communing with the masses, he calls it in his mind. Perhaps he is happy that they answer him (a good kick in the pants); before, they used to let him read his paper in peace; and they never read the papers. Why doesn't he kick them in the ass! this is wrong and that isn't right: before, the party used to say that, now it says this: they don't seem to*

*notice that things have changed from that to this. "Yes," he says, "yes." I feel like tearing off his party button. And I sit here playing the intelligent observing citizen after work and barter glances with unescorted young ladies as though I were not on the job. Nine after seven. I really don't find her pretty (although, what does pretty really mean? I don't know how I want my daughter to look when she grows up. Not like me); her face hasn't looked pleasant once, and never unchanging, so one might get used to it finally. I see. Her profile could bother me even. Stubborn. Narrow under the cheek bones, narrow at the temples. Capable of ignoring anybody. The way she wears her hair in a knot at the neck, a real bird's head. Those flickering eyes, I think she's laughing. Her lips casual, as though they weren't part of her. Is this seat taken? Perhaps I'll see who she's waiting for, not that it would add anything. She may wait for whom she pleases, she'll never sit otherwise, clear-headed careful intense for any spectator to notice for no one's good. That's just it. When she half-rises and searches through her coat pockets: she looks as though she were traveling. Much too thin: I feel nothing. I'd like to talk with her though. I'll go over to her and, in keeping with the rules of good behavior, I'll say "Rohlfs. May I?": there. I'm rather comfortable where I am. I shouldn't be so nasty to the waiter. I have a lot of nasty habits. I used to be a delicate child: and some evenings I have a useless memory. Eleven after seven.*

Good evening

**GESINE**

*I don't know what to make of it: said the frog as he looked in the mirror. The lordly curiosity of the man, and he is mounted on his barstool stiff and straight as though he wanted to ride it until midnight. Why won't he show his hand? Got too much in his pockets as it is. Is that how I am to imagine*

*the face of the ruling class? gloomy arrogant very wise? But
it's the other one next to him who is wearing the ruling-class
button and who's getting on his nerves, how angry he can be
all quietly by himself: without moving his back. He'll turn
around again soon enough. He inspects me as though he were
looking for a reason to make fun of me. If only I could say:
he looks like a professor of geology to me, like an airplane
pilot. He strikes me merely as a private person, but do they
have private persons here who act that way, openly, in keeping with their arrogance? Three years ago I still might have
taken him for somebody. The way he barks at the waiter. Like
a sick Great Dane who hasn't had enough sleep. Extremely
dignified. Doesn't like himself in the mirror. Has been living
like this for quite a while. We look at each other like two
strange beasts.*

Good evening. How are you?

HERR ROHLFS

*Jakob's coat is wet. "Is it raining again?" I say. He stands be-
side me, hands in his pockets, he looks at me. If I offer him a
drink he'll knock me off my chair. You see how attentive you
are, waiting here with your bottles, you lackey you. "I'll be
back," I say, Jakob won't like that either. Jakob examines me
with curiosity, as though my face had changed. You are looking at a conscientious civil servant who is having a hard time
fulfilling his essential missions on rainy evenings. As I turn
and push myself away from the edge of the bar I catch sight
of her again, I remember. She is holding her immobile face
toward me, as though she couldn't see beyond the region
around my barstool. "Take a look at that lady," I say to Jakob,
"That's how I picture Cresspahl's daughter. Am I very
wrong?" I ask. She has raised her coffee cup above the dinner
plate, her eyes slant past me lost in thought; before she wasn't*

*looking at me either. "Wouldn't say so," I hear Jakob say in his slow reliable voice, I lower myself from this stilted stool, there. "Wounded in the war," I say, I don't want him to think I'm showing off. We walk through the revolving door to the desk clerk, elevator, I say. He takes his time with the keys, stalks stiffly toward us, hands me mine, number 23. "I don't have much time," Jakob says. All right, all right.*

Good evening Jakob

GESINE

*Because one obviously obeys one's big brother without another word; do I expect a scolding? Jakob doesn't scold me. But he might say: you always think you know better, don't you?*
*— No. I'm wide awake, quiet like a sleeping fish.*
*— Did you see, did you understand?*
*— Yes. But do come back:*
*I noticed him only when he stopped beside the man across from me who was again bent over his vodka with quiet ease, he stopped and unbuttoned his coat while I thought: Oh Jakob, how well you dress in the evening fooling the people who think you work on the railroad, Jakob's peasant face above the narrow tab collar with a tie flowing obsequiously underneath. And I'd almost gotten up and taken the seven steps forward and stood before him and said*
*— Jakob!*
*— Gesine, hello there: I could hear him say, I saw his face remember me out of the corners of his eyes, he looks through the room and decides that they can all wait and turns back to me, laughing now with his mouth and says*
*— Now I'll take you wherever you want to go, how about that. I've missed you*
*and I stand before him, laughing because I'm happy. Where-*

*as: I didn't move from my chair, my coffee cup in one hand,
watching him address the man across from me, don't let that
one ask me how I am, let him finish with that one first. He
turns around and tries to slide from his stool, looks as though
he were groaning, suddenly he stiffens, hangs half to one side
and attacks me with his wild gray face and murmurs something (that makes Jakob notice me) without losing sight of
me with those suspicious longing lordly eyes, while Jakob
notices me, his eyebrows shift in a violent jerk like a whisper*
— Don't move
— I won't.
— Go outside until
*he replies to the big man's murmuring: his eyes so unfamiliar,
we can't recognize each other, until they both turned and
Jakob followed the long irregular steps of the other man out
into the lobby; but before he turned, Jakob smiled a quick
soft invisible smile of recognition before he disappeared into
the dark-paneled cave of the lobby . . .*
— later. I'll see you later, you understand?
— Yes. But do come back
*. . . which may lead to the staircase. They took the elevator
probably. The other man had trouble walking.*

"What kept you from going to the West in the meantime?"
asked Herr Rohlfs. The table stood with its long side before
the two covered beds under a low-hanging lamp, he had sat
down at it. He sat all the way back in the chair, his legs
stretched full-length away from him; he was still breathing
cautiously but his face had recovered its habitual outdoor
coloring. Jakob was sitting in the other upholstered chair
across from him. His hands were in his trouser pockets, he
was looking aside testily. His coat lay before him on the table,
shedding tiny drops on the plastic cloth. He was wearing his
dark blue suit, he seldom had occasion to wear it; in the cheap
rentable interchangeable environment of a hotel room under
the roof he looked like a man who has been stopped—ac-

cidentally if inescapably—on his way to a party. Actually one knows next to nothing. The previous occupants of the room (two of Herr Rohlfs' colleagues who had arranged for a first meeting here with a girl from the local nationalized sewing machine factory and who had tried to calm the usual shyness excitement fear from the start with regular reassuring: "Don't let the twin beds frighten you, we have no illicit intentions; we're here on official business") had left the lamp wrapped in an immaculate threadbare cloth. "I gave you reason enough," said Herr Rohlfs and Herr Fabian.


— If he had asked you that, Jonas
— I'd have said: I might as well have left seven years ago, and every day since then. Perhaps I waited too long.
— Whereas Jakob.
— That he had "reason enough" is the opposite of calling him a runaway from Jerichow and the Republic, and from their question: what had prompted his mother to leave?
— Rohlfs apologized for that.
— Did he?
— Yes. That's the kind of man he is. But Jakob told him to think up his own explanations.
— He might damn well have thought up something like socialism being a fine fresh start for young people after the war and you want a man to give all that up after eight years. And that, with regard to social progress for instance, the socialist concept of surplus value is much fairer and that a ticket to Berlin (and as far as I am concerned: the travel permit, the plane ticket) represents a historical retreat. Does that make any sense?
— But Rohlfs knew that Jakob had done something in the interest of socialism that very same day, an increase in the productivity of labor: acceleration after the Krivonov method.
— That's what I can't understand.
— Don't think I'm trying to sound superior. I don't care if the working day lasts eight hours, that's a lifetime. I'm not

trying to explain to you what meanings it might have beyond that. On your side. On your side: you're very chary of explanations.

— Yes. and Jakob

— Jakob, you see, maybe Jakob thought: if we do it differently for a change, Jöche (for example) gets home earlier; when he should get home. And the coal gets into the bunkers when it should, and we can start the new day. And if you (for example) want to take a trip, you are to arrive on time and not waste three hours sitting waiting on some siding. From his point of view it merely meant that he bore no grudge against Jöche and wanted him to enjoy his free time. If they did depend on him, he wanted them to be treated right. Now look, if a man has a certain wish.

— You misunderstand me. The basic conditions of any community system always get fulfilled: has nothing to do with the philosophy that's supposed to lie behind them. I didn't say Jakob was to decide how necessary someone's trip is. He didn't even refuse your wishes. Except that it never dawned on him that he, too, might have got on a train and no longer felt concerned with what we on our side call progress. Anywhere in the world they could have found a use for him, he wasn't indispensable here.

— Has nothing to do with it. I know because he told me. It astonished him. "How a man can ask a question like that," funny, he thought. He says: "If I don't hand in my resignation, simply stop showing up some day, Peter Zahn won't know where to find someone to replace me for the next two and a half minutes, he deserves better, wouldn't be nice of me. A lot can happen in five minutes on an eighty-mile stretch. And how could I resign!" because, in that case, he would have had to work three more weeks and what good would that have done him? Besides, first of all: he finishes what he has started and leaves his place tidy, in good order. And also, he had been asked something. Now he came up with the answer.

— No.

— Yes. Polite considerate dependable and what not. "They're

all human beings." I can just hear him, this one was a human being like the rest. He spent an evening with him. And though they had different opinions, it was still on the same subject.
— Yes. He wanted to make sure that you could decide for yourself and get out again if you wanted to. Because you were to be allowed to come on an official visit to Jerichow, if only to walk once across the street v voyennooyoo komandantooroo.
— The way you talk. Yes! As though I'd ever been in bad hands with Jakob. And not even because of me (out of concern for the tender child) he said, "I am not going to invite her."
— He wanted to make sure only as long as it was necessary. He may not have wanted to expose your father to all that coming and going.
— Yes, Jonas, your lack of trust. My lack of trust: yes. But we're not Jakob, you and I. All I know is the way he used to look for five-eight-eleven years, and the way I felt when he said "honeychild"—
— Gesine.
— and that's it. It seems to me more that: he did accept— let's call it hoping for a fresh new start—after the war, as far as he was concerned, he wanted to take it upon himself, as well as the decision it entailed. But the way he was on the road all night and would have liked to take the morning train right back: so that Martienssen (he's one of the dispatchers) could get to bed after his shift or do whatever else he was planning to do, without being bothered. He didn't want to involve anybody in a decision about these things, since it might become actual: yes. They could have nabbed me right then and there as a runaway from the Republic and a supporter of American imperialism: that, too, is a decision, and a perfectly appropriate one if you like; except that it could have ruined my life, Jakob may have thought: yes. But first this lack of trust.
— And what did Rohlfs say?

He got up and walked to the window. His hands in the side pockets of his jacket he stood, motionless, holding himself very straight, silent. His eyes followed the slant of the roof down into the darkness of the street. The station square lay deserted. Under the wooden awning over the ticket windows small blurred figures were leaning against the lighted wall. Toward the streetcorner, the bright yellow rectangle of the telephone booth protruded from under the roof. He couldn't tell his car from the cabs because Herr Seemann's driver wasn't reading just then. All that remained of the rain were thin watery paths sadly sliding down the glass. After a while he said: "I couldn't force your mother to stay. But I did want to explain to her that there were other possibilities. I'd much rather have let her get off the train at this station and sent her to you. The information reached me five hours too late. You understand."

Jakob had not moved. Now he leaned forward and placed both hands firmly on the rough wet cloth of his coat. He didn't turn his head to say: "Yes. You're saying that you don't meddle in other people's lives just for the fun of it." He was still leaning forward, staring motionless sideways down at his hands, in which the blood worked under the skin. "Can a man waste himself on a purpose," said his voice, detached, questioning, tenacious to the last sound.

Herr Seemann stood and listened, his head high. He felt his face freeze above the rigid neck and somewhere in the middle the hard grip of the teeth on his lips. He about-faced and marched out of the dimness into the haze of light at the table and stood in front of Jakob. Jakob leaned back and let the other man's eyes penetrate his misgivings. His temples moved. "Yes," Herr Rohlfs said gruffly.

"Like you," said Jakob. His hands turned over, the fingers open, loose.

"Or you, Jakob," he said.

"Yes," said Jakob. "But nobody who hasn't been asked."

Their eyes locked. Until Jakob noticed to his surprise that the other man had nodded suddenly, with closed lids. He got up. They said goodbye. They had an appointment for Thursday.


GESINE

*I stood waiting under the tree, head down, rebellious. Jakob
came up to me. I didn't move. He gripped my neck so hard,
I straightened up at once; he hadn't even wanted to look at
me. He stood alone beside me away from me sideways in the
darkness: as though he had only a hand to make sure I was
there. "If I didn't know your walk," I said. A car door slammed
in front of the hotel. I came out from behind the tree and the
headlights right in my eyes and I couldn't see and Jakob
pulled me back against the fence a two-yard leap across the
sidewalk. He was still holding on to my wrist*
*in his fingers I felt the soft warmth of grass in the woods and
the scent of trees and fir bark and Russian soldiers coming
toward us. Without a sound Jakob's head bent toward me,
his eyes told me to duck lower, his hand flattened my shoulders against the ground. He separated the leaves in front of
us to look through, we saw: uniforms, clattering messkits,
the tired necks of the horses, voices, the dull thudding of
hooves. As though the earth were hollow. The endless silence
above us, between the tree tops. Jakob's fingers stretched,
our arms were lying side by side, loosely*
*a car door slammed in front of the hotel. With hard wild
panther eyes it shot past us, all alone on the wide wet street,
wound around the deserted station square, leapt growling into
the darkness.*
*"When can you go back?"*
*"The day after tomorrow, early, by the autobahn."*
*"Don't feel sad. You think nobody wants you here?"*
*"No. May I take your arm?" I said.*


The cab driver said:
"I say: it'll cost you seventy marks, I'm on night rates

now. Means nothing to them. Of course it's an out-of-the-
way ride, but I get paid for driving not for arguing, right?
If they want to go to a different station I figure they don't
like the one they're at: just an idea, Mister. I mean: they
probably missed their connection. I didn't want to at first, out
on the highway in the middle of the night with this old bus,
nothing like that limousine of yours. Actually I did it for her.
He was the tall quiet type and at first I thought she was still
in her teens, but then she arranged it all with me, it was her
who had the money. Luggage they had none. Yeah, well I
guess he carried some kind of briefcase. Both dressed to go
dancing or something. Off I go. None of my business what
goes on behind me, once I've switched the light off; only with
drunks I watch out a little. Nice driving those two. Didn't
talk, no names that I could understand. I guess she fell asleep
after half an hour, with her head on his shoulder. He didn't
budge, just sat and smoked; handed me a couple of cigarettes
over the seat, plain ordinary ones from around here. In my
opinion those two have known each other for years. If they
were lovers, they might as well have been married. No rings
though. She was still awfully young; from a distance she
might've looked stuck-up but you can talk with her. Doesn't
let you forget she's a lady though. Even asked me when
that would get me to bed now, if it was just to say something
she could've found something else. I thought she was quite
cute. Maybe because of that sleepy look she had sitting up
when we got there. They both went into the station. No, not
arm in arm the way they'd walked up to me. She had her
hands in her pockets and walked leaning against him: as
though he was carrying her without holding her. As I was
saying."
Herr Fabian said:
"How much do you get for standing five minutes at night
rates? or for however long I have detained you. You're welcome. Talk to you again some time, and another windfall
like that one, huh? Maybe you'd have enough to get your
handbrake fixed."

HERR ROHLFS

*"Turn off that radio," I say. Do I have to play up to my own driver now? He switches off the light. In the middle of the night we're standing without light somewhere in this blasted black forest as though we had lost our way. "Man!" I say. He backs up like a maniac, one blind leap and we're across the ditch smack in between the trees. And only because some lights were coming toward us. A trailer-truck. If they were looking they've seen us anyway. "There was one of them long roosky sledges standing out by the crossing, halfway into the forest, with no lights on, but I saw them anyway, and it wasn't an accident or anything like that, the way they were sitting behind their windshield letting our headlights shine on them, probably tuned in to the wrong radio station by mistake." "Chief," says Hänschen, "do you think it's true?" That's not the point. What matters is how long the people around here have been sitting in front of their radios listening to that stuff, believing it the way they believe it's full moon tonight, according to the calendar. I don't see any moon. "While you were busy with the cab, I heard them talk about it at the stand, but they were all drunk. I only wanted to check," he says. All right. Jakob can't have known about that yet.*

*Jakob can't have known about it. This is something else. Where could he have put her? Bartsch is probably too jittery for him and Jöche is far away and the others can't keep their mouths shut. And he couldn't very well impose her on Sabine, Cresspahl's daughter of all people, and expect her to hide her from me: so he'd rather take care of it himself. Takes her to Jerichow as if I didn't mind a bit. I can just see him now on the express—which they caught, with the cab—his friendly smile, very well: I'll enter this situation, Herr Rohlfs, but don't expect me to take it seriously; he's making a game of it. Perhaps he doesn't give me credit for realizing who she is and right here on her own two feet and not somewhere else. I realize it much better now with her here. I bet they're not traveling straight through to Jerichow, I bet they get off somewhere before and take the bus in an entirely different direction,*

*and do the last stretch on foot. When he knows that all I have to
do is reach and I've got her. The birdie is no longer in the
bush. He's playing hide-and-seek with me as though I weren't
a killjoy, had given him my word of honor not to be one. Am
I a killjoy?*

*"Hänschen," I say. "If they recognize us now by some stupid
coincidence (the cab driver finally tunes in to the latest news
from the West and realizes what I looked like and this unusual
car: Pobyeda) and stop us, huh? and turn our car over—which
is entrusted to your personal care, Hänschen—and hold a
match to it so they have plenty of light to pick a suitable tree
to hang me from, without my pants and head down, and you,
Hänschen," I say. He's still feeling guilty about the radio and
for losing his head backing up that way. "Just nerves. I'm
sorry, Chief," he says. At last he's found his tongue again: "Of
course I'd defend you to my last breath," he says. I've gradually grown accustomed to the darkness. I can see his grin.
What now?*

*"Well, let's turn the lights back on and go pay a visit to those
dear relatives of ours," I say. "Will do," he says. The car
climbs through the ditch like a bear. One feels its power most
when it's still, when it stands with running motor quietly shivering, the headlights boring into the night, ready to pounce.
It can't be turned over that easily. While we're standing perhaps. But not while we're driving.*

— That's what I mean. I'm sure he's not one of those who tore
the buttons off their lapels three years ago, and sneaked
through the back doors while the laborers were out in the
streets and the hoodlums set fire to the pavilions of enlighten-
ment and nobody knew what it would come to. I'd like to
think he was strutting about with the same lordly airs and his
party button, that he didn't hide out and would have slapped
the face of anyone who'd try to lay a hand on him as a rep-
resentative of the State. He is proud, although not of himself.
— You mean: the news about the Hungarian revolution on the

radio that Tuesday evening had nothing to do with the fact that he let you catch the express? Still, the telephone lines he needed were blocked and the three men it would have taken to arrest you were standing guard somewhere else. Besides, this would mean the State had a personal relationship with Jakob and wanted to keep his esteem and be greeted by him. When the police refuses you a passport (whatever their reason), there's also an individual mouth that says, no, a person, but that person doesn't care how you feel about it, whether you keep your hands in your pockets and turn the other way when he walks by: it doesn't bother him because he has the right to be right. And in this case I rather think they didn't dare annoy Jakob too early if they were to pull off their mission.

— Yes. That too. I can't speak for your house, Jonas. From my side of the border, for me, those are illusions; and besides, I have nothing to do with your police permits. All I know is that I saw this particular one face to face. I saw him shake hands with Jakob. If that one had refused Jakob a travel permit he'd have wanted to discuss it with him. You don't understand that.

— I don't.

— And they could have been friends, if they hadn't stood at opposite poles, if the painful difference of their opinions hadn't been part of it. You want something, they keep it from you; he had no wishes like that. And when he tried to convince Jakob of the desirability of his wishes, he spoke to him as the State: personally. Now do you understand?

— They could have had pretty good times together.

— It's nice to think that, isn't it? I don't know: perhaps he did call for those three men he would have needed as you say; and the line was busy.

GESINE

*Oh how much I liked that cab. I was unsuspectingly walking to the station at Jakob's side, suddenly he stops in front of a fat old dinosaur on wheels, with clumsily protruding eyes for headlights and a broad furrowed leather bench in the back for people to sit on, and a five-spoke wheel to steer with, and all these different purposes were awkwardly harmlessly sitting side by side in a single car. "It'll cost you eighty-five," said the driver. He had switched the light on for us, but was leaning over the back of his seat, lethargic and undecided, looking at Jakob, but Jakob wasn't adding figures with his face, he lifted his chin, surprised, as though he had asked for the time and been told it was going to rain: which nobody can tell for sure anyway, and I burst out laughing and said, "as long as it's under ninety," whereupon the light went off. The car gathered its stiffly spread-out legs up under its belly and cleared its throat and started to cough and clattered back up the street we had just come down and glided arrogantly, nimbly, with old-age stubbornness past gleaming traffic lights toward the city limits between gabled brownstones and nineteenth-century warehouses, the headlights tore off strips of night while I thought of torches and plucked the clattering of metal apart until it sounded like the thudding of rapid hooves and thought If only he'd raise his arm and Jakob's arm climbed over my head and made a place for me against his shoulder, "Will you protect me, Jakob," I said and felt the soft tremble of laughter inside his chest and fell asleep and dreamed of trees knocking at the gates of the highway, bowing to us with white aprons around their waists*

*stiff and drunk with sleep I leaned against the ticket window beside Jakob, and at the tall end of the express and held on to the door handles and watched the rails rear up after our howling passage, the signals we left behind screamed: red, red, the forest ran away with them as though it had grown eyes all of a sudden, then came the large meadow with gray moonlight all over it and the sleeping bushes slid down toward the horizon with the gentle slopes of the night landscape, until the clouds drove together again and we shot black through the blackness in our narrow swaying tube, people were standing around us dense and somber and high like trees and said*

*nothing and I said nothing and Jakob said nothing and the
landscape closed evenly over the furrow of noise we had
ploughed and sank into silence. But Jakob was holding me by
one shoulder.*

*"Why are we getting off here, Jakob, do you have to change
somewhere else now?" I asked, stepping down with all the
others on the giant immobile platform island about midnight,
immediately seized by the large pale lamplight and the hoarse
barking of the loudspeakers LAST STOP    EVERYBODY
OFF   NEXT EXPRESS CONNECTIONS ON THE OTHER
SIDE OF THE PLATFORM IN FIVE HOURS   THE DIE-
SEL TO   and said: "But Jakob, that's West, Jerichow is to
the North." I've had to do with people who look at me with
smiling surprise, incredulous, when I think something in my
own head, they find that amusing, touching, feminine charm
taunting good manners; Jakob took me by the elbow and
lifted me up the iron steps and said "Where do you think you
are?" and right away wrinkles stalked across his forehead as
though he'd been unfair with me, that's when I noticed it
for the first time. And the second time when we were back
on the platform and he showed me his wrist with the shock-
proof watch and said: "Late"; standing still with his narrow
willfully calm eyes*

*like a child in school, all the mockery and teasing heaped on
the same one, it didn't make sense, it seemed so arbitrary: why
do they laugh at my nose and not at the red eyes over there,
for three long mornings I stood like a statue, thin-skinned,
driven into the desert, and went for Jakob with my fists when
he came to meet me in the garden and said Shall we fly your
kite today, and that wasn't supposed to infuriate me. I cowered and hammered at him blindly until he took my fists, very
gently, and held them apart and looked at me, Jakob is my
big brother (he's got hobnail boots) Today we'll climb the
Rehberge and fly your kite and you find that your big
brother is furious. And you can't come to his aid with hobnail
boots. And don't know what to say, except "It's none of our
business."*

*and it was as though I had taken him by the shoulders and*
*spun him around and he sees me standing there as insolent as*
*ever and surprises himself laughing, quietly, with his eyes.*
*"What do we need them for?" he said.*

— Close to midnight. The diesel conductor may have been
sitting in the stationmaster's booth, they were telling each
other the news, at that hour it didn't matter any more if you
left on time.
— But the track was clear, and for those seven minutes of
hearty man's talk, a freight train had to sit on the siding near
the big lakes and wait for our diesel to pass, and the whole
schedule was upset at the very start of the new day. We didn't
mind (when at last the motor started and the warm used-up
air began to drone with the gathering speed, the two of us
had long been absorbed in storytelling and we paid very little
attention to our departure, we had the whole night before
us), but the diesel was crowded with people who wanted to
get home after the theater or from the night shift to their
scanty sleep; I shouldn't have provoked Jakob with our su-
periority: it's none of our business, since we can't do anything
to improve it.
— You mean: for the first time he abandoned his principles
of punctuality and consideration. It marked a beginning. All
of a sudden it didn't matter any more if a man wasn't so
particular about his responsibility for other people's time.
— Perhaps. As long as nobody can get up and say: This is
how it was and no other way. It's this one's, it's that one's
fault. What if it were your fault, Jonas?

CRESSPAHL'S CAT HAD grayish-green fur. From the tip of her
tail black markings ran up her back toward the head, growing
paler and paler, under the nose she was suddenly white, a
white chest, a white belly, white all the way to the underside

of her tail. When Jonas entered his room Sunday afternoon, he found her seated in the hollow of the upholstered green chair at the table, so upright and dignified Jonas said a surprised Good afternoon. The cat didn't answer.

After lunch Jonas sat in the dead plum tree, sawing off the smaller branches with a bucksaw. Cresspahl stood in the gooseberry bushes below, saying this was a day of rest when nobody was supposed to work, but Jonas felt rather pleased with himself. Then they carried the long ladder over from the hallway and sawed off all the branches above the fork. Cresspahl was holding the ladder, pulling at a rope around the branch Jonas was working on. From time to time people would pass outside the garden fence and stop, because they were dressed like that, they had worked all week but this was Sunday, and they'd say something: Oh, the dead branches were being cut off, perhaps the whole tree was to come out? Yes: they said, because Jonas would lean down and put in a remark wherever it fitted between Cresspahl's answers: yes, that was it. A plum tree couldn't live over twenty years it seemed. That might be true, they said and walked on. When they had gone as far as the shed at the corner of the tile works and could no longer be heard but still be seen, Cresspahl would say something like he's a childhood friend of Gesine's, he's a veterinarian now. Oh, Jonas would say: how many cars does he own. Two, said Cresspahl: one for home and one for work. I see. Yes. And his father used to be a teacher, but in the end he too left for the West. After that they went on sawing, and when they had everything down, they sawed and broke the branches into handy pieces and carried them into the woodshed outside the workshop. The workshop stood up against the house at right angles and had large dusty windows. In the daytime Jakob's windows looked bright and inhabited. At nightfall they had almost finished digging up the stump. A few last strollers were taking the shortcut from the beach, passed the fence, stopped to ask: Were they cutting firewood? Yes, they said. It looked as though there might be enough to hold them for the winter.

Yes, it did look that way. Nice to have firewood grow right
in your own garden. Yes indeed, said Cresspahl. Jonas was
leaning on the axe, friendly, looking into the visitors' faces;
he wondered why nobody asked for news of Jakob's mother
or of Jakob. Perhaps they didn't know him well enough. Or
perhaps all this was less important to Jerichow than it seemed
in this garden. Or maybe Cresspahl didn't go in for conversations of that sort and therefore nobody ventured to ask about
it. Good night, they said. Good night, said Jonas and tried to
imagine that he had known these people for many years.
They carried the stump over to the house, filled in the hole,
then they ate dinner. Jonas felt very satisfied with his fatigue
and the thumblong strip of skin that was hanging from his
hand where the saw had chewed him. The skin would have
to grow harder there, eventually. He only wished that he,
too, had worked on something useful and tangible during the
week, then he could also have dressed up for Sunday and
walked along garden fences and stopped to talk to people; or
he could have gone to the Inn in the evening, after a few
hours of Sunday work, or simply sat with a good conscience
talking about what happened at the house and what the next
days might bring. Soon after dinner he went to the room
Cresspahl had given him (the little one, between kitchen and
workshop, with nothing in it except a wardrobe, the cot, and
a low table with wicker chairs). Cresspahl heard him pace
about and stand at the window and start typing finally; it
sounded busy and undisturbed.

Cresspahl was hardly accustomed to guests any more. All
evening he sat at his outsized table, leaning on his elbows,
smoking the same pipe, patiently, with long pauses. He didn't
turn the radio on. He could hear the subdued sound of the
typewriter, it was pleasant even, it made him think of dedication. He tried to recall how Frau Abs used to take care of
Gesine when she still came home from college on weekends.
She'd hardly ever announce her arrival, it wasn't a matter of
shopping beforehand, of setting a nice table for her. All in all,
he (Cresspahl) couldn't very well go to the pantry and de-

posit a plate of apples and pears outside Jonas' door, as
Jakob's mother would have done: on the other hand, it wasn't
enough to tell Jonas that the pantry door wasn't locked. Besides, Gesine had been at home here. Now Jakob had only
come on visits, how had it been during those years? Jakob had
simply lived from one day to the next; when Cresspahl heard
him out in the hall, they'd soon be getting together somewhere and talk the evening away: business deals, outwitted
authorities, local events. Once Jakob had sat astride the mailbox and, expounding on the intricacies of inlay, he harangued
his subjects of whom Jöche might have been one, although
in those days Jöche hadn't been able to take quite so much.
And Jakob wouldn't come down from the mailbox unless
Cresspahl, Minister of Inlay, replied to the cordial congratu-
lations of his dear colleague in office, from the same platform.
No, actually the subjects had consisted of Brüshaver, but he
was dead now. At one point both of them almost fell off the
mailbox. The thought of Jakob made Cresspahl smile, he felt
so present. Jakob never froze into an image of departure, he
stayed in one's memory as a reality of smiles and answers
and fun and life as a whole: like a gesture. Of course it didn't
matter that Jakob would just have broken off the branch
against which Jonas had struggled with both arms; Jonas had
enjoyed his effort; after all, why make comparisons? Gesine
was also living in the city now. Better not go into that perhaps. Or there'd never be an end to it. Jonas had come here to
let the world forget him for a while, he might just as well
have gone elsewhere that's why he had come to Gesine's
house. Yes? yes. It was instructive to see him outside his city
habits and circumstances, he hadn't even brought any books
along, the article he was writing over in the other room had to
come out of himself, all out of his own head, it was all Jonas,
interesting to watch. "Please don't think that I'm trying to
reform the world, recruiting people who share my opinions,"
he had said. "It is merely my chance to speak my mind,"
which did, after all, mean that he wanted a part in the world.
How reckless he was in his handling of words. Easily, fluently,

they poured from his mouth, sometimes Cresspahl had the impression of sorcery: as though someone were constantly drawing nasty cartoons of the world—an accurately calculated world, in spite of all the exaggerations and condensations, with nothing omitted; its truth looked unfamiliar. "We," he'd say, honestly referring to his friends and himself, but at the same time denying that such bullheaded controversial people could be grouped together: "But we are incorrigibly dedicated to the notion of progress." Cresspahl saw no reason to defend the notion of progress (what did it, after all, mean?), but the INCORRIGIBLY DEDICATED stopped him. INCORRIGIBLE was the term the socialist government used for its enemies, it implies quarrelsome superior foolish useless, whereas DEDICATED applied to the opposite side, to the international working class, UNERRINGLY convinced of the one and only path that led to socialism, to the indefatigably willing executors of party instructions, and what did INCORRIGIBLY DEDICATED mean (Cresspahl thought:) coming from Jonas? Obviously all his thoughts dealt with the establishment of the one-third Germany, incessantly concerned with what the one group—or the other, or a third, a ninth—called SOCIALISM, with respectively varied emphasis and interpretation, and since Jonas couldn't very well be thinking of anything but the government of his own country, he sometimes didn't see the forest for the trees, that's how intelligent he was: was that possible? thought Cresspahl, but he probably couldn't have noticed that yet. And would Jonas be able to hang on to his own opinions if he assumed a different name (for fun. For fun.) but kept the other one as well, passing himself off as anonymous in between the two? He said: it's in the interest of the government to abort ideological romanticism at its inception, and he'd rationalize it in such detail, so tangibly, one could only wonder at his previous antagonism, and he'd say that it was in the interest of the INCORRIGIBLY DEDICATED no longer to think by the book, and since all this was supposed to be glaringly obvious, there only remained the question of who was supposed to be right (truthfulness was out of the question, had been lost some-where in the discussion). Cresspahl felt unjust, thinking that way. He decided that Jonas amused him with his talk. There he sat, wondering about his daughter's life, not knowing what it was like. In the morning she'd come out of her house and climb into the streetcar and greet the doorman in English and type first one language and then another and act as go-between in a conversation as though she had a say in it; and who didn't? and if he did manage to imagine her under those circumstances, it hardly helped their correspondence; there-fore, why wonder about trying to please a visitor? It might have been Jonas' amusing, versatile way of thinking that had pleased her (and that he had stopped her on the sidewalk that spring, in spite of all his superior knowledge, just like in a movie); and that he sacrificed all customary means of communication with his twisted, triple-meaning insinuations, perhaps that pleased Cresspahl, too, after all. Although he had a hard time imagining it: a thing should be crystal-clear and handy. You'd like that, wouldn't you?

Before he prepared for bed, behind his table, he stood in the kitchen for a bit and munched on an apple, and when Jonas wandered in, tired and drained of thoughts, and started to eat from the apple plate without noticing what he was doing, Cresspahl stood beside him trying to coordinate his smile of pleasure with the motions required by apple-munching. "Good night," he said and turned his broad back on the kitchen, hands in his trouser pockets, swaying like a boat. He looked like comfort personified. "Yes. Good night," said Jonas. Back in his room the cat was lying on his chair like a castle wall: higher at the curve of the back, lower at the semicircle of neck and head and all four paws plus tail; her head was almost completely surrounded by the rest of herself. Jonas stood before her and thought: Why isn't she afraid? she doesn't know me, she ought to be afraid. . . . But she didn't move. He hung his jacket over the chair, carefully turning its back to screen off the draft from the window. As he walked away, he noticed that her eyes were open. Yellow, extremely

contemptuous. But of course: she was at home in Cresspahl's
house.

The next morning the cat wasn't around. Countless white
hairs were stuck to the wicker chair; Cresspahl had probably
brushed them off before he gave Jonas the room: as though
someone had not been living here all this time.

Jonas re-read the first few pages and noticed that there was
nothing beyond a surface design, with vertical and horizontal
threads, rendered incomprehensible by their very regularity.
He corrected the typing errors, the sentence structure; he
didn't feel up to re-thinking the contents. The words seemed
like supplies he had taken along and which had become useless at the end of the trip. The room didn't help either. The
heavy old furniture seemed to be making comparisons between himself and him, it didn't recall his purpose. He still
remembered Chapter Two was to conclude on conditional
definitions, but he didn't feel like it any more. That day he
wasn't yet particularly aware of his fatigue. He pushed back
the table with the typewriter and paced along the walls until
he came to the window and stopped and paced some more.
There were no pictures. Next to the door, alongside a white
strangely separate rectangular space, hung a seventeenth-
century map of the coast as far down as Lubeck. For no
reason. It had just been left hanging there. Why hadn't Cresspahl left the country? Because he had a house. What is the
meaning of a house? I'm sure I don't know, Jonas said to himself with satisfaction. He returned to the typewriter and cut
the last two pages down to one, and rewrote them. He had
seventeen lines left over, now it looked presumptuous.

Since morning Cresspahl had been sitting in his workshop
finishing inlays. It required paying strictest attention to his
fingers, no thinking beyond what they were doing. He went
in to see Jonas and stood behind him, rubbing the back of
one hand under his chin, staring into the distance beyond the
quarry outside the windows, finally he said in a trance-like
voice that: Catching fish is just as honest a trade as any, and
then there are the lilies in the valleys. . . something to that

effect, Gesine would probably know. Jonas knew by now that grinning was the wrong answer, he looked at her father and nodded innocently; for lunch they went out. But the entire town of Jerichow didn't come running to see them pass: as Jonas had expected. Lisbeth Papenbrock watched them placidly through the window of her shop, waited to nod to Cresspahl and walked into the back without any sign of surprise. Jonas had merely mentioned the official name for the transparent banners with slogans painted on them, but Cresspahl took the trouble of making a full stop and replied in thundering tones, confidentially leaning toward him: yes, indeed, the transparency of it all shines behind a good many people's eyes. . .! stood still, silent, bent over, his broad wrinkled face staring meaningfully at Jonas, then he turned away, resumed his stride, absentminded, heavily leaning on Jonas' shoulder: talking and breathing. Perhaps that was how he felt, thought Jonas. Still, he couldn't muster the patient serenity of the city policemen at the corner of the market square who watched Cresspahl march past, gesticulating with both arms, exclaiming, "Lisbeth Papenbrock's boy's been bothering Brüshaver's cat again, I have a good mind to. . . this good for nothing, constantly after the poor animal with his blasted harmonica; Brüshaver always used to sing when he washed, now the poor cat has a thing about music, and I have a good mind to. . ."; what could one say, one could only go on walking as steadily as possible, trying to balance one's shoulder under the powerful impact and smile wordless approval. He spoke with such intensity of the deceased Brüshaver and his cat that had been included in his will, his absentmindedness, his wonderful manners: as though the town and the times and the slight gentle windy rain were to blame for there being no more people of such stamina, that they had simply died out, "just one look at this kid and you know he's up to no good. That brat." When he clutched the edge of the table at the Ratskeller, and painfully, hugely let himself sink into the corner seat, and sat facing one in dejected silence in the late-morning half-light, one had a strangely pious shock noticing the cautious efforts of his breath, (*Jonas*) *when is he going to die, I thought.* He told the waiter at great length about the background and vicissitudes of the alcohol he was planning to drink before he ate his fish, Jonas might as well know he wouldn't find this poison in any other place, with distant eyes he described its bitterness—like quinine—and the inevitable pressure of the taste, going down, "because there are those that will let you by, but this one must be taken seriously!"; but when the waiter served them the stuff, he tilted his glass wordlessly first toward Jonas and then against his lips and sighed deeply and said no more until they had finished their lunch. He threw himself back against the seat, his fingers drummed an irregular pensive rhythm on the wood, his eyes looked so distant, so elsewhere, they protected him from the hellos of acquaintances who came up to the table, he bowed and sent them on their way with his distracted reserve. (*Jonas*) *I'll never be able to inhabit a whole town, I thought, not if I lived there for thirty years and accustomed waiters and tobacconists to my wishes and spent my money as though I were glad to pass it on. I thought of my friends and tried to remember what it was I liked about them and realized that they were spectators of life like myself, on the outside, apart, always ready to judge, and would rather not participate in coexistence within a system of rules and laws and habits, to defend solitude and aloneness (the so-called independence of the individual). There are those that will let you get by: I could get by anything. I recall the oily bitter leaden taste of the drink, I'll forget it. I'll leave cities that won't miss me. It must have started somewhere, somebody must have arranged for me to say on my deathbed: my presence among you is only in jest, don't take it seriously. And it won't even be the painful dignity, the grand gestures and motions Cresspahl uses for the little things, because the precious contents have been lost. When I say something like "incorrigibly dedicated," he gives me a meaningful nod and replies with an anecdote about two uniforms he once saw side by side; at first glance he had asked himself what a civilian was doing with a railroader (that was how he met Jöche): the same amusing shock, when words were subdivided into loyal and rebellious troops, separated and yet placed side by side like uniforms, but it had been Jöche, have you met him? Jakob, take him to meet Jöche one of these days, explain to him that he's not a railroader. Yes? That was Jakob's answer, after he had already stood up to go to bed, and we sat through the rest of the night with this kind of talk that I didn't understand.*

After lunch Jonas found the cat lying on his chair again. She arched her neck so delicately, gracefully above the broad sturdy haunches when a sudden small noise outside the windows stirred her eyes and ears, Jonas regretted that he couldn't speak of "withers" in her case. He bent over the chair and asked her if she planned to stay. She yawned and began washing herself nimbly with her white front paws across the neck and one ear. He cleared his papers off the other chair and sat down across from her and turned the typewriter around. He was afraid the harsh clatter of the keys would irritate her, but she lay still, head on front paws and purred, occasionally shaking her head, lost in idle but far-ranging thoughts. Reflecting on many things. All of a sudden she jumped down, and stalked along the walls until she came to the mat on the floor where she stopped and stretched, flexing each joint, anchored by her claws. Jonas' hands lay quietly on the keyboard, he watched her. She turned her head to his side. Immediately he got up and opened the window. She climbed through. He had guessed right: he had understood her. With stiff legs, slightly disgruntled, she strode through the wet garden into the fog.

In the evening Cresspahl came to sit with him. He had asked to read the finished pages, now he wanted to know the exact meaning of certain words. They had no light on. During a pause in the conversation Jonas heard her come in. Clearly the entering thud, then the soft padding of paws. He felt extremely pleased. He had begun to know her a little.

Cresspahl stood up to go to bed. He stopped at her chair and held a cupped palm close to her head. Her whole body stiffened. Rigid with petulance she raised a paw to the curved hand and tenderly batted the leathery hard skin. They exchanged no further greetings. When Jonas came back from the door she was squatting on her haunches, attentively indifferent as though nothing had happened.

He attached two sheets of paper to the lampshade so the glare would not disturb her. Then he switched on the light, took the other chair, and started to type beside her. She washed herself all over, sat up and examined him, motionless, with narrowed gleaming eyes. There were twenty-three hairs in her moustache. (*Jonas*) *Does it amuse you to write that kind of stuff, she said. One's got to live somehow, everybody is best, chto lootshe tshevo. You wouldn't happen to have a* little milk, would you ... ? ... See how my moustache quivers. *When I wanted to go to bed, she was lying on her flank, beside her outstretched legs. I crouched by her chair. Our heads were on the same level. She curved her neck and firmly posed a paw on my wrist, letting me feel the claws. My hand wandered to her shoulder and to the hard sturdy neck and pushed the skin up toward her jaw. Until, in a single shiver, she slid over on her back and rolled her head against the arm of the chair and squirmed and stretched against my hand, but never completely off-guard. All of a sudden she came to, extremely cool and awake, and pushed me away with incredible elasticity, curled herself into a castle wall and immediately disappeared into sleep. I felt bad. I should have noticed sooner: at the proper moment. For a second I had bothered her. A cat doesn't measure time in seconds.*

The next morning (that was Tuesday) Cresspahl found him crouching on the floor in his pyjamas playing with the cat. She was stalking around him with hunched back, softly bumping against his legs as she passed. She avoided his hands. Strode away in wide circles, turned, came back, brushed up against him. He asked Cresspahl what he should make of it. "She likes you," he said, repeated it even while he stood and watched. Jonas thought: it's probably early-morning sleepiness, stretching her muscles back in shape, perhaps she also likes the rough fabric of my pyjamas. Still, he waited until she'd had enough.

After breakfast she came back in from the garden. He had just stood up, rubbing his neck, distractedly, because he had got stuck in the paragraph about material and subjective consciousness. She had hardly sat down when he lifted her over his head and let her slide onto the windowsill, carefully in spite of his hurry, and started to type like a fiend. Then, shocked, he looked for her everywhere in the farthest corners of the room. She was perfectly contented, sitting against the windowpane, nibbling at her neck to perk herself up. After all, Jonas thought, I do consider this chair as having been placed at my disposal. Why won't she sit in the other one? We'll have to come to some agreement. (There was a cushion on one of the wicker seats.) After she had waited a while, he got up and carried her back to the chair and pushed the typewriter to the other side of the table and wrote until late in the afternoon. When he looked up it was getting dark, and since Cresspahl was not at home, he took her outside with him when he went out.

He went back to the Rathskeller to eat and stayed quite a long time, in spite of a loudspeaker next to him, one of the democratic stations playing afternoon dance music (at tea-time); at this hour many young couples had come for a beer and enjoyed the music, their enjoyment hung all over the room and communicated itself to him. While he thought of Cresspahl's daughter. And was surprised that missing her now didn't resemble the violent impatience he knew from certain habits of earlier days: asking about his mail three times a day, his curtailing of separations they had agreed upon, and all that. Now, his expectation was no longer unruly. The distance between them could be expressed in too many ways: in mileage on the East- and West-German railroads, in Foreign Ministers' Conferences (quantitatively), in party slogans and other tangibles. And he had no desire to believe that it was also raining where she was, or that she might be

climbing stairs, with her coat collar turned up at the neck
because the weather report for the North-Rhine and Westphalia areas was not reliable in this reference. He didn't think
she resembled her father. It seemed one couldn't deal—and
especially talk—with Cresspahl in all seriousness; perhaps
the inlays he kept defending—and whose heyday was past—
were symbols of the shameful span between the hopes and
the disappointments of his life. Cresspahl didn't seem to take
inlays seriously himself. He had avoided expressing any of
the thoughts that might have occurred to him in the meantime about Jakob's empty rooms. At most Gesine had the
cautious look, the mocking tone, the discretion she had
learned from him: learned from him. Yes? Speculations that
were as vague as the opportunity he now had to pad her
stories with Jerichow and her father's house. She was in his
memory like a feeling of an inexchangeable way of looking at
one, of climbing stairs, of startled halts: details could be dis-
missed, because the inexchangeability stemmed from all this
being real in itself, independent from any spectator or listener
or someone who was, strangely enough, sitting in the Jerichow Rathskeller thinking about her. In the end, one could
merely express one's gladness that such things existed in
the world. . . without reservations.
All evening the cat roamed. He had no idea what she could be
doing. Mouse-hunting was a human notion of utility; after all
she was no servant. She might be two years old. Cresspahl
said the mother also lived here (brought over by the notary
with best regards from Brüshaver, who was dead), but she
was becoming shyer and shyer with age. (*Gesine*) *My father
is esteemed by the world and respected, and cats run after
him.* He had not seen that one yet, with her aristocratic lack
of trust. The young one shared his room, although he wouldn't
exactly call her his guest. Cresspahl had not yet come home.
Toward midnight, he realized he wouldn't be able to sleep,
switched the light back on to read. The cat was crouching
under the typewriter, wild-eyed and awake, with raised

moustache (he saw only her head). He felt so calm, it made
him wonder. He was surprised he hadn't written to anyone.
Not even thought out any letters. It occurred to him that he
wouldn't know what to write to Jakob. He would have liked
to see him sit there, he pictured Jakob sitting there, in silence,
endlessly waiting like himself.

HERR ROHLFS KEPT a great number of sheets in a special
folder. They had gray print and crumpled soiled torn edges
and represented the topography of the former German Reich
cut up into handy pieces. The print was so old, the water
surfaces did not stand out in blue from the gray land, nor
was there any color distinction between the various surface
forms. Only an old-fashioned fly-speck handwriting had
drawn red-ink circles around localities islands forests and
pointed to geology and prehistory; an incompetent observer today might have had a hard time finding a use for these high-
school-teachers' maps with their over-precise drawings. Herr
Rohlfs did not remember his father out of spite and certainly
not intentionally, and when—past the circles and arrows and
exclamation marks—he retraced his own itinerary in search
for roads bridges hide-outs ambushes, his grimly ironic attention meant at most: that one might just as well look at it
from a prehistoric and geological point of view. Those times
also existed. And perhaps he refrained from adding his own
annotations (in black ink perhaps, or in green) with the same
stubbornness that considered half of his life an error: in order
to make the present look right. Also, one must not forget one's
working regulations.
He had been too late to see them come out of the third station; Hänschen had not driven as fast as the diesel. In the
shaded light with which the car was equipped for reading
maps he found the sheet that bordered on the Western edge
of the Jerichow region. In the middle of the Baltic Sea and

across the coast, the words "Rode-, Hagendörfer" had been
written in red ink; the ice came rolling down the Scandinavian
mountains over present-day Europe, the melting glaciers piled
up walls of earth and washed the stone into wide undulating
sand flats; at the end of the Mecklenburg Lake Plateau another glacier retreat constructed the tower of the Northern or
inner end moraine, end moraines are deposits at the edge of
the ice, ground moraines are deposits on the ice surface itself.
Thus, north of the end moraines and all the way to the coast
a layer secreted itself (in the course of millennia) consisting
of thaw-water sands, pebbles, drift loam, pebbles, marl, loess
and bands of clay, together with the remains of the water in
ditches moors swamps quarries, soon thickly grown with oaks,
red beeches, alders, the beasts of the forest and of the sea
lived here in peace, out of the transitory grew a fertile brown
forest soil. Some of the village names end in -hagen, and this
is the last we hear of the Germanic settlers who dug up these
woods at the beginning of the present millennium; hagen
meant forest; with reference to the water courses, it may be
added that the average level of the lake plateau measures
about thirty-five yards more than the Baltic Sea, the rivers
and streams had to force their way through the hills of the
end moraines into ground-moraine country and from there to
the sea. Sharp pointed check marks in darker, thinly-lined
fields indicate needle forests with wagon roads, round ones
leaf forests. The dotted, lighter surfaces are meadows. Thinner
lines stand for ditches, holes bored into the ground water by
circling icebergs. Leafy delicate roses with figures represent
undulating fields with indications of altitude. Parallel—sometimes thorny—lines are artificially constructed highways of
first and second class. Lines with bulges are roads on top of
dams. Localities were left in white with black cubes dug out
from the forest which they devoured. Anybody who passes
through this gracefully undulating landscape very rarely
realizes what may, after all, be part of a good overall education, the information that local folklore books or walking-tour

guides are supposed to convey to the tourist or vacationer when he finds himself in a landscape that has neither high mountain ranges nor open plains, and does not know what name to give to what he sees beneath the spanning sky.

No. Too late now to change the traces of the German settlers, the coin findings from Roman times, the migrations, the Slavic settlers, the moats, another German penetration, round graves, long graves, conic graves. Anyone who passes through this landscape at night, for the enjoyment and relaxation of it (not on official business and not on his way home from work and not for the good of the world in whatever possible imaginable sense, but solely looking for a land that glows from afar as we are told) should at any rate realize that we're not going to ask questions about the surface structure of the landscape during the ice age or about the homeland of recollections, but whether somebody has possibly different notions with respect to the obvious improvements in human life. Is capitalism supposed to return to agriculture? (The fields of the expelled landowners have been divided among day laborers and refugees, deeds are no longer valid, castles have been turned into old-age homes, schools, houses of culture, recreation hotels.) Who will then be allowed to bathe in the Baltic? The regular shimmering structure of the castle that rises from the forest in the night and draws the onlooker's eyes along the lanes of its park is not architecture or petrified history, but a memorial to exploitation. Whoever is not for us is against us, and unjust with regard to progress. Who is for us: will be the question; and not: how do you like the night with the dark villages between the curves of the soil under the huge cloudy sky.

Because, only equipped with this knowledge of ways to ask and answer, a man, any man, can take the proper attitude toward the last bus that had been waiting for the diesel passengers in the square outside the station; a Pobyeda turned into the street and stopped in front of the pole with the bus schedule, and if Hänschen managed to read correctly with his flashlight, and if the schedule was not just a leftover from summer vacation days, they had taken the bus a few minutes ago and were now sitting on the decrepit seats, their knees pressed against the seat backs in front of them, their hands holding on to the rod, silent, side by side, extremely strange among the weary passengers, beside their shaky reflections in the night-misted window, because the bus saved them five miles on foot; but Hänschen straightened up once more beside the car door and went back to the rusty metal box with its many layers of pasted-over schedules and threw the flashlight on it and bounced, stomach first, back into the car and pointed his chin toward the reclining mass of Herr Rohlfs and said: "Chief . . . , you know that bus goes right up to the border, the one with the lake where the shore is still ours and the water is Western . . . " and Jakob had negligently walked past the line of waiting people at the still-closed door of the bus, when the driver came out of the station restaurant, flanked by the two control policemen, into the light of the single lantern above the steps, and Gesine paid no attention whatsoever to the waiting bus, her rapid irregular steps beside Jakob's steady slow ones came out of the narrow street with the low houses into the town, it had the sound of going home to those who stayed behind, because they also hadn't gone to the local police station (thought Herr Rohlfs:) and Jakob stood at the window in front of Gesine who sat waiting on a bench near the door, reading a paper even, or paced along the walls, hands on her back, examining the posters with childish curiosity, I'd like to apply for an entry permit into the restricted border zone, your identity card please, are you traveling alone? and what reason do you wish to give for your trip? Actually we only want to take the bus as far as the second stop, And does your present relationship to our State entitle you to this application? besides, the permit office wasn't even open on an ordinary Tuesday after dark, for which purpose one ought to be able to rely on other departments for a change, Herr Rohlfs didn't feel like following the bus and picking up two arrested individuals from the border control of still another division, because one can do that just as well by telephone, and perhaps they had already started to walk from here, nineteen miles in the windy moonless night. When Hänschen returned from the station restaurant with hot dogs on paper plates and mustard, Herr Rohlfs switched off the map light. While they ate, he merely remarked in an astonishingly nagging tone that even West German water was too cold for bathing in this season.

GESINE

*And today I still can't say more than how we walked, and tell you which village names I forgot again since then. Even if we had seen anything, I couldn't tell you about it. Because we talked about the points of the compass, and the roads, and the lights we saw, it was impossible to go by the stars that night. For a while we took our direction from the wind.*

JONAS

*No they hardly talked about the birdie in the hand that gets plucked and roasted, as well she knows, and because it felt so odd to be walking and not driving along a highway, and they couldn't see the villages before they were smack between the houses, because of the night and the fog and the drizzle: rooki vvergh! she shouted in her head every time an un-expected tree loomed up before her, because you must be first to shout it. They didn't know the way, neither had been here before. I've always marveled how the peasants know the remotest villages in the vicinity although they've never been there, only heard stories about the farms and the quality of the soil and jailings and pranks, and then, one day, they take the horse out and drive straight to it without stopping, as though the willow dam and the fallow stretch and the piece of forest had been contained in the stories, together with the shortcut that saves you a corner; she won't have been able to stand at the station and act the foreigner in Sicily and in-*

*quire with perplexed curiosity Where do I catch the bus for
Taormina Would you have the kindness to. With Jakob she
probably walked as though they knew all about the bend in
the road at the pebble quarry straight through the village
past the broken-down barn, the edge of forest, exactly north-
east. That must have been about two and a half hours past
midnight. Stop: said Jakob. As they came up to where the
logs might be lying across the little brook, because the path
through the fields had stopped at a ditch; with her back to
him, half a step ahead, she stopped and waited and finally
tried to see him over her shoulder. Because he, too, was standing still and didn't walk ahead toward the clearing in the
bushes on the shore and didn't look anywhere, only at her,
and she tried to shake the chill out of her shoulders and stared
past him toward the road, her eyes following the constantly
interrupted searchlights above the fog and said I feel grumpy,
Jakob, helpless, disappointed, consciously incorrigible: all these
unfamiliar places. The deserted farmhouse, the roof timbers
black and nude, the dishevelled thatch, the new consumers'
stores and the castle renovated in white, the school for col-
lective farmers, the cardboard roofs of Poll And Purchase,
machines rusting in the farmyards and those crappy war
memorials: and the whole world is fighting over this and she
(Gesine) has no idea what it's all about: homecoming had
been a failure, and only three hours after midnight, while I
was wide awake, lay with open eyes in Cresspahl's dark room
and thought Goddammit, the world is full of opinions about
freedom, it hasn't been waiting just for me, I act as though
I had something to contribute that nobody knows, as though
everybody would perish without this revelation out of my
brain, do I want to be indispensable? Can't even make a fire
with it. And Jakob was holding his hand out to her from the
other side of the brook so she wouldn't skid on the smooth
slimy gnarled logs and she said, so, on her toes bent forward
for balance and, no, Jakob said. Even if they had seen something, it couldn't be told.*

— No. But I didn't ask you because I'd like to think it was I
and not Jakob who brought you to Jerichow from the autobahn.

— Then why did you ask


GESINE

*We stopped in the hallway in front of the Count's forge. Jakob
was leaning against the door post, smoking. Every now and
then the wind slapped around the corner, lighting up his face.
I was pacing up and down the splintery worn-out floorboards
in my stocking feet, beating my shoes against each other. He
watched me tear the drenched kerchief from my hair and pull
it through the ring at which we had tied the horses the day
he took me along to have them shod, and it was more than
just Do you remember you were stepping from one foot to
the other while we were cutting the roan's hoof, you thought
it hurt him, it was Jakob who had been left for me. Who
took me by the arm and it all became real. (I know the horses
are dead.) Now we'll go to my father's city and see how different it has become from my memory. But I felt gay. I rebuttoned my coat at the neck and stood over him, the way he
was sitting inside his massive body, all scruples and attention,
on a broken three-forked plough in the Count's forge in the
middle of the night on an ordinary Wednesday, and I put my
hands on my hips and looked at him sternly, until he said:
"I guess we'll manage without an umbrella," because I had
told him about the umbrellas they kept holding over my head
in Taormina because of tourist trade and tips. I propped myself against his shoulder and put my shoes back on. He knew
my feet hurt. He didn't say anything. I finished his cigarette
and we walked into the Countess' forest. It was about three
in the morning and we wanted to avoid meeting anybody on
the road so close to Jerichow. I couldn't even find the polar
star. By myself I'm sure I would have lost my way. All the
many little paths. I would have strayed into the typhoid*

*cemetery and stood at the edge of the open pit, like the
summer after the war when I always ran down to the village
from Jerichow to see Jakob and the third time he accompanied
me to the road and asked me about the tree nursery and the
ant heap and from then on I knew the way. Fear was still in
the vicinity, but no longer came to meet me. Still, the open
graves and the chickens that kept running over from their yard,
and the fat, tree-streaked rough cold cube of the castle and the
corpses on the hay wagons like sheaves of wheat and I saw
the naked foot of a girl slide out stiffly from under the dirty
tarpaulin and closed my eyes and heard the heavy thud under
me throbbing against my lids: drugged with heat I lay in the
brown grass of the forest, half in the shade of a fir, while Jakob
pulled the horses evenly, even as eternity, across the fresh
stubble and we sat side by side on the soft crusty plow and
ate our afternoon snack, and something from inside me suddenly asked Is it true Jakob about the concentration camps?
days I've never been able to think of as: yesterday, and tomorrow it will have been the day before yesterday, or: that
was ten years ago; in the meantime, I've learned much more
about monopoly capitalism as a form of imperialism and can
look at the past with the eyes of today. Those days never pass.
Every minute I'm thirteen years old before Jakob's wide-
spaced motionless face with the half-closed lids, and I hear
him say Yes it's true. Impossible to live with that. It's useless.
How can you answer for that? How does it fit with the wet
rustling beech leaves under our feet, with the swaying circling
fir tops overhead against the gray night sky, with my wretched
life, with Jakob whom I can't see in this black high-walled
ravine, he shouldn't walk so fast, is this how I wanted it?
that's how I wanted it. That's what is worth wishing. What
had it to do with Jerichow that was lying at our feet as we
emerged from the thicket on top of the hill and halted, Jakob
and I standing silently side by side: a somber lump in the
hollow, its church tower pointing and a light on in my father's
house: what did I want in my father's house?*

— Can't we finally stop, then you pay and go home
— And where would you want to go, Gesine

JONAS

*they had run across the street, diagonally down the dam, and
were standing behind the alders on the log bridge in the
quarry when the heavy roaring came racing down the street,
in the curve the headlights seemed to spring right at them.
Jakob stopped dead. The light carefully traveled over their
faces and paused at each detail. She fell against him, shocked
with fright, and stood stiffly, her face pressed into his shoulder, with infinite slowness, like eternity, Jakob's hand pushed
her neck down, away from the cone of light, until the searchlights were switched off, on the road, and the car disappeared
behind the trees and they were kissing each other, after how
many years? After eleven years. Perhaps. No. She bit her lips
watching his face in the light that the shadow of branches
was pushing out of his eyes and from his forehead and showed
her what a trip to Jerichow was worth. There are trains and
entry permits and extra ration cards for the West German
visitor, and since she had already discovered that freedom
does not mean: being able—but forced—to do otherwise, she
now understood that Jakob could not have been left over
from those days as the big brother: a security and solver of
all problems. She didn't put her arms around him before he
stood at the door and wanted to leave again right away, when
we could see it with our eyes and she no longer needed to tell
anybody: something has changed. (Because it can't be told.)
And when I came into the kitchen she planted her teeth on
her lips where she had bitten them before and Jakob was
just preparing to say something, before Cresspahl and I noticed her. And Jakob? And Jakob?*

When Jonas came into the kitchen, Jakob was standing at the
table facing Gesine, his hands pushed backward against the
cold colored tiles, when Jakob looked at her face again, she

had hardly realized that anyone had come in. Her lips did not move. "There are riots in Budapest . . . " Jonas said, hesitating more and more, looking from one to the other as though undecided about the sentence he had begun. He was barefoot, but seemed not to have slept. His shirt stood wide open at the neck. New thoughts distracted his smile, once again he said: "Budapest, riots . . . " as though he, too, had no more use for his sentence and merely wanted to ask for the hearty astonishment of those present. Suddenly Gesine stepped out of the blinding lamp light and lifted her elbows until the back of her hands could rub her eyes. She was toppling with fatigue. Jakob half turned to Jonas, his face began to radiate as if he couldn't see out of his eyes for mirth. "Crazy, what . . . ?" he said.

HERR ROHLFS

*What the hell is this? was all I thought. Is my room a hotel? What is he saying? this completely drunk young punk. "Commandant reports to Comrade Stalin, regiment ready for inspection. Suddenly: hachoo. Sneezing. Comrade Stalin asks: who sneezed? Step forward. No one moves. First squad: SHOOT THEM! Fire! They're mowed down. Who sneezed? No one moves. Second squad: SHOOT THEM! Fire. Who sneezed? Nobody. Fire. Third squad: SHOOT THEM! SHOOT THEM! Three squads flat out on the ground, mowed down. Fourth squad still standing. Well, who sneezed? Man in front rank takes three steps forward, snaps to statue attention. I, by your leave, little father, I sneezed. Stalin nods vehemently, says cordially: Na sdarovye, tovarishtsh! Bless you, Comrade!" he says. "Would the gentlemen care to introduce themselves?" I say. They get to their feet as though they'd been arrested. Each face is awry. They have to pinch the fat one in the corner to keep him from falling into my arms. "The orderly," I say. This milksop. This promising young man. On whom I have wasted two hours of my time.*

*Now he sits there and tells my jokes and is on duty. "Informal
little gathering," he stammers, looks to the others, all his
seniors in rank, no one comes to his aid. He introduces them
to me, one by one. Each in turn stands at attention, not particularly straight. Never mind. I can well imagine. Sitting
here half the night listening to the AMERICAN FORCES
NETWORK and RADIO LIBERATION and NORDWEST-
DEUTSCHER RUNDFUNK, and now the news and toward
morning they start drinking. In uniform. All right. "And the
dignity of our State?" I ask. "Don't you even understand
enough to know that the proper joke must be told in the
proper circumstances? Are we circus employees?" No answer.
Who sneezed? "The gentlemen will hear from me through
the proper channels." I can't very well call them comrades.
"Please leave my room. Typewriter," that's when Hänschen
appeared in the door. He grinned at the sight of those dejected backs. "Yessir, Chief," he said. They all turned. He had
already vanished. I simply waved them away. The orderly.
"Restriction to quarters. Key." Now he can properly stand at
attention. "Clear your orgy off my desk." Always the cheapest
vodka. What do they get their salaries for? He comes back,
one arm full of bottles, glasses in the other hand. Now how
about a salute. Why isn't he saying Please Apologies now?
How does he know I couldn't take any more at this point?
Hänschen is standing behind him, loaded with our things and
thinks I'm unjust, I'm only taking it out on others. Yes I am
unjust. Out of self-esteem. The young puppy was on the verge
of tears, swallowed, trembling with blushing and nervousness
and said in his touching unsure voice after several attempts,
we stood calmly in front of him, waiting for him to get it out:
"Why don't you have the whole bunch shot? Why doesn't the
Red Army make mince meat of the lot of them?" I turned
away and inspected my desk. Everything was back in its
place. There was a stain on my pad and one of my penholders
had been stuck into the flower pot. That's what I ask myself
too. Paguibshi za tchestj ee zlava nashee rodini. I don't know.*

"But it's you," said Jonas, now he was surprised. He had accepted Jakob's reprimand and immediately forgotten it. "It
makes perfect sense to me. I like your father's house, you
know," he said. She hung her head sideways and examined
him from underneath, curious, expectant. She seemed to have
nothing to say. Jakob pushed himself away from the table.
His face quivered involuntarily. He gave both of them an attentive look and carried this look (as from a conversation interrupted for a moment in one office and brought into the
next), with him into the room Jonas had come out of. They
understood he was going to stay a little longer. "Good morning, Jonas," she said. Again she was tearing the kerchief from
her hair, one hand pushed the hair up at the temples. It
wasn't so terribly wet.

GESINE

*Holy Cresspahl, what is it? I thought. Did I forget some-
thing? Wait: the street was smelling of drizzle and dust and
my fatigue, I was looking ahead of me at the fence around
the garden, at the waiting car, and in this view I foresaw the
hotel room and the last cigarette and being able to go to
sleep provided I climbed the stairs blamelessly straight and
lady-like and now nine steps more: and someone was jerking
me out of my half-sleep, a complete stranger, he said something impolite, rude, then I remembered the sound of his
voice and realized I had made a mistake and looked him in
the face and was about to ask, almost, WHAT IS IT YOU
WANT I AM A STRANGER HERE MYSELF. I was still
standing on the sidewalk. I knew the university was three
blocks away, I looked for the university in his face, but apparently the stranger had forgotten to keep his face in check,
to make it look the way he wanted it seen, he was staring at
me in a way one doesn't look at a human being, the borderline
had disappeared for him, and I noticed the spring. Realized
the spring, and looked around for the moon and the stars and
asked him what movie it was we were playing in. I have for-*

gotten. He understood, and his adroit, practiced, shameless understanding of what I meant made my sleepwalking (the
movie) complete. It may have pleased me, how do I know, I
have forgotten. I remembered that I had spoken English, the
joke began to amuse me, and it was a little like the expectation
one feels turning to the cartoon page in the family magazine,
with the probability of flat disappointment afterwards, when
the cleverly invented jokes are over, and so I said in the King's
English, my father would have been downright pleased with
me: that he probably wouldn't be able to live it down if I
should now open my mouth to a big yawn and turn over and
go to sleep as I deserve after four hours of probability conference or whatever subjunctives I'd been translating. He answered, and this I do know: I forgot his words at once, not
to lose their meaning, here as everywhere else was the tenacious purposefulness one musters in a wish-dream, but something is lacking, the wishing is not complete, something inside
rejects reality and wipes it out like a sponge wiping chalk
from a blackboard, and then the dream returns where it
began, and one's contentment mounts like a jet at its second
spurt before the sound barrier and withdraws again before
one's incapacity, and a third time, more and more threadbare,
the sleepwalking starts with climbing the stairs and a voice
says LISSEN YOU, and my voice says Which movie are we
playing (I know: something was lacking here before, as negli-
gible as a little sand between two loose fingers)? and the
voice says I shall never live that down and the dream breaks
off like a strand of glass, with cramped trembling of emotion
which I remember from a documentary, the three intent jolts
of the jet fighter model in the wind tunnel the moment it
breaks through the sound barrier, and now the dream was
complete as it can be when one is half asleep close to morning
and waking up one knows clearly that one's self-deception was
intentional. Shall we stop now? I thought. But I had let myself
in for it, now there was no breaking off, because, when someone has gone as far as saying my name is Conne MAY I IN-
TRODUCE THIS IS, then everything runs automatically, on

*the tracks of bourgeois behavior, then comes the invitation to*
*tea, and then the theater restaurant, and then this, and then*
*that, and all the things that were invented to help us persuade*
*ourselves that we are not lonely, that we do—after all, be*
*reasonable, admit the obvious—have quite a lot in common*
*shouldn't we raise a family? He was standing across from me*
*in my father's house and was as real beside me as Jakob and*
*I didn't know what to say and said GOOD MORNING and*
*felt ashamed of myself and ordered my memory to remember:*
*this is Jonas who loves me. All right.*

Jakob was sitting in front of the open stove on the floor, a
piece of wood in each hand, blowing into the remains of the
fire. Already once he had raked the coals (surprised, midnight
early morning coals), the red turned white at the edges,
dimmed to gray, again he pulled across the crust and blew.
Threw on shavings he had brought in from the workshop.
They jiggled. They smoked. A sudden bang, a hissing, and
the flame burst through. He placed the first piece on top, with
each new piece his hand appeared reddish translucent at the
door of the stove. He slammed the damper shut, the crackling
grew hollow and muffled. The draft began to moan. "We need
more wood," he said to Jonas who had come in. "Put some
water on to boil." They left the room in different directions.
Jonas nodded cheerfully after him; Jakob was already in the
garden; still quietly amused, Jonas stood at the kitchen
window and watched Jakob over at the shed gather an arm-
ful of branches in the kitchen light. His movements were
dancing back and forth between the rigid shadow crosses of
the window grating. Jonas went back. "She is with Cresspahl,"
he said. Jakob straightened up at the stove. There was so
much surprised amusement in his eyes, only now did Jonas
remember Jakob's total immobility at their arrival. But now
he looked cheerful, sinking into the chair before the typewriter, his chin high as he noosed his tie back into place. He
brushed his hand softly across the keys of the typewriter, it

looked as though he were taking a liking to it. "But you stopped in the middle of a sentence," he said. Jonas nodded. There were only three words written on the page. They had been there since midnight when Cresspahl came home and said: "Here you sit and write . . ." But it was different with Jakob brushing across the pile of finished pages, he didn't lean forward, he said, "Boy! You sure have been writing here, huh? We saw your light from far off." They smiled at each other. Jakob shifted against the back of the chair to see Jonas more comfortably. "Go ahead, man, tell me," said Jonas.

She sat in front of Cresspahl on the edge of the table, letting her wet scarf dangle before his eyes. "Today you'd have needed more'n a scarf, daughter," he said. He was sitting in his armchair, fully dressed in the middle of the night, examining her out of the corners of his eyes, begrudgingly. She flung the scarf away. "But she must have had a reason," she said vehemently. The radio was not turned on. There was nothing on the table except the bumpy pocket watch that could not be heard when Gesine spoke. "Get yourself a housekeeper. It's not right for you to be sitting here alone in your chair and . . . " she broke off, hesitantly. She was not shocked. Cresspahl looked at her politely out of his wrinkles and slowly, unhesitatingly, finished the sentence between the ticking: "that I might die one night with no one to see me sit here." "Yes," she said, shocked.

Jakob split the air with the blade of his hand and didn't answer. It had grown quiet behind the door of Cresspahl's room. Under the dome of the lamp, balls of light were unraveling threads of smoke, nothing else seemed awake in the house. You couldn't yet see the dawn. "There's only one thing we know for sure," Jakob said. He lifted his eyes to Jonas. "Yes," said Jonas. Worried, he slid off the windowsill and began to pace. "If they catch her now, she's come to Jerichow to start a revolution. She must not leave the house. All right, Jonas?" He had slid down all the way between the chair arms. His legs were dangling. The trousers were soiled and ruined from the wet roads. "Has she her camera with her?" asked Jonas.

"Tiny. Not longer than a finger. A toy." "Christ!" said Jakob. Jonas felt him slide away into other thoughts, but Jakob asked unexpectedly: "Can you drive?" Jonas shook his head. "She can. Why? Must you go back to work now?" Jakob rocked back in surprise. He stared at him, drifting off into his thoughts. "Christ, yes . . . " he growled distractedly. In the mirror at the door, Jonas watched Jakob's eyes recognize the figure that was stretched out in the chair. His incredulous smile tugged at the corners of his mouth until it widened to an open grin. Jonas realized they had not understood each other.

Cresspahl was standing at the stove, mixing rum with boiling water. His pipe dug rigid folds at one corner of his mouth. Jonas asked about Jakob's mother. Cresspahl held a glass to the light, tilted the bottle over it until the grog was practically overflowing. She hadn't arrived at the reorientation camp yet. Gesine had sent her a money order. But the quarantine lasted three weeks.

The room with the typewriter had three doors: one to the kitchen, one to Cresspahl's room, and the third through an alcove into the workshop. It had been Gesine's room. They carried Jonas' sheets, typewriter, papers over to the workshop where they made up a bed for him with a down quilt they found in the alcove. That's where the tied-up packages stood that Jakob's mother had left to be mailed.

Jakob stood before the open closet, pulling a fresh white case over one of his blankets. Gesine peeled off her coat and started rearranging the chairs around the table. But soon she gave up, walked over to Jakob, stood beside him. Again she saw his forehead wrinkle, he was absorbed in his work. He held the case up high, shaking the blanket into the low corners. Threw the whole thing over one shoulder and began fastening the buttons. Finally he tossed the blanket on the cot, smoothed the sheet once more, turned away without another glance at the finished work. He took Gesine by the shoulders. She was so tired, her face looked shrunken, but the eyes held their own above the cheekbones, cool and clear

from the wind. "Must you go?" she said. He nodded with a
narrow, distant look. He let go of her, picked up her bag
and held it out to her. "Empty out," he said.
"Is it still raining?" asked Cresspahl. He reached for Jonas'
wrist and looked at the watch. Jakob had to be at the station
in twenty minutes. Jonas went to the window and opened it
a crack. At the stove Cresspahl was moving his lips as though
tasting the chilly windy air. "It is quiet now," said Jonas.
Her things were lying spread out all over the blanket. Jakob
picked them up piece by piece. "Are you out of your mind?"
he exclaimed in a low voice. He came up and held his hand
out to her. The two metal objects were lying side by side,
lengthwise, delicate and shiny; there was a muffled clatter as
he closed his hand around them. He slipped them into the side
pocket of his jacket, took them out again, put the camera
away. "Show me the safety catch" he said. She reached over
and let her index finger slide slowly down from one point of
the barrel until it stopped at the release. Jakob put everything
away in his inside pockets. Amused, shaking his head, he went
over to his chest under the mirror. "Wet as an otter," he said
and tossed her a pullover and a pair of coveralls. Then he went
to the stove and felt the tiles; she could tell they were getting
warm by the distracted way he bowed his head. She was still
standing at the bed, the clothes he had thrown to her in her
arms. He smoothed her hair and asked gravely: "Yes?" She let
him peel her out of her jacket. Then she said: "Fine." He
waited until he saw her face; then he went to the kitchen.
"Now you can go sailing," said Cresspahl when she appeared
in the kitchen door in Jakob's clothes. She looked gaily from
one to the other, the light was in her eyes. She accepted the
glass that had been standing in hot water. "My father may
speak," she said with her voice. She sat down at the table.
(*Jonas*) *And we did not say it. May we live happily in our
old age.* Everybody got up when Jakob did. Gesine climbed
over her stool, and walked around the table and stood in front
of him. She lifted her arms to his neck, his hands brushed her
shoulders. Their lips touched. (*Jonas*) *And it would have*

*surprised me if she hadn't kissed him.* "Come back," she said.
Jonas was standing behind her. He nodded. Cresspahl bent
his head to one side for the smoke to rise freely. "I feel that
way, too," said Jakob. He turned away. They heard the front
door click.

### HERR ROHLFS

*This playing hide-and-seek is my own fault. The State speaks
ominously of the gravity of the hour, hoping the people get
the hint; the people do get the hint, but think it somehow . . .
Somewhat tactless to take it to the police chief during office
hours. If I had my way we'd still be going in circles, looking
past each other, never meeting. Is that Jakob sitting there in
front of me? Wouldn't be surprised if he dozed off, leaning
back as though he had all the time in the world. He does
have a lot of overtime. Yes. It's Jakob all right. Why don't
you drink, Jakob? (How do I know he doesn't?) If only I had
accustomed him at the right moment to trust me. Now I
could hand him my credentials, my revolver, the salvation of
my soul, he'll think I have duplicates and keep a spare just
in case. The fact is I own nothing that can't be replaced. He
might have had his jacket pressed while we were at it. He's
got something in his jacket. Who hasn't? One of us must say
something. Now.*
"Promise," said Jakob. *I felt taken by surprise. It was the
easiest. An atmosphere of trust, based on the principle of
mutual advantage. When Hänschen came back from downstairs with Jakob's clothes dried and pressed, I officially informed him this assignment was finished. Hänschen swung
around and looked at Jakob as though he had made a mistake
about him, as though there were something new in his face.
Jakob was standing behind the chair, putting his clothes
back on. Hänschen didn't know what to think.* "From four-
forty on, you're at his orders," *I said. It was past five o'clock.
Hänschen snapped to attention, blandly, he acted offended,
refrained a little too visibly from thinking.* "Aye aye, Sir," *he*

*said. He didn't even have the consolation that I'd tell him all
about it later. I didn't have that consolation either. "Ah yes,"
I said, "this is Hänschen. This is Jakob." They shook hands.
"Are you very tired?" Jakob asked him. No. Nobody was tired.
"I'll give you an order. I'd like something to drink." A fine
start, Jakob, I thought. Only one conversation is possible at this
point. Is Hänschen perhaps supposed to say Yes so I see. He
isn't sending him away. And why should he goddammit?*

The dawn had turned white. The cat jumped on Jakob's
trunk with a dull thud. She lifted her head, catching her
reflection in the mirror. In the mirror one saw Gesine's shoulder under her hair. She moved. The cat hissed at her. Then
yawning overtook her again. Stiffly, deep in thought, she
stalked to the window, climbed up, her greenish fur squeezed
piece by piece through the slit and out into the fog, the tip
of her tail dipped suddenly and disappeared.

When Gesine entered the kitchen she found Jakob sitting at
the table, his head lying across his wide-spread arms. He was
asleep, like an animal, soundless and patient. She stepped
back. Her clothes were dry, crusty and crumpled with mud.
She climbed into Jakob's black brakeman's coveralls and began
to make the bed. In Cresspahl's room all was quiet. She lifted
her head and listened. The fog was rustling. She went to the
window and pushed it open. Hunched, uncomfortable, the cat
was standing in the wet grass, lifting her feet. She walked
a few steps, without stretching her back, stopped again,
hesitated.

Jakob slowly sat up. He felt looked at. "Are you hungry?"
whispered Gesine. He shook his head. "Get into my bed," she
said. He got up. He pulled a pack of cigarettes half out of a
pocket, made a face as though tasting too much tobacco on
his tongue, put them down. Head bowed, with irregular steps,
he walked past her. Kept his hands in his pockets, pushed the
door open with his back and was gone. Gesine began clearing
off the table.

He was stretched out under the cover as though he didn't want to move. He did not turn his eyes to the door. Gesine sat down at the edge of the bed. She looked at him questioningly. "At noon," he said. But his eyes kept their rigid direction toward something invisibly distant, he was only looking at it, no longer thinking about it. (His eyes weren't moving.) Finally one arm came out and pulled her head down beside him, he closed his eyes. She lay motionless, quietly, eyes open, until he fell asleep.

The cat sat on the smooth rickety workshop steps. Her eyes were narrowed slits, crankily she looked from side to side. Gesine stopped before her, but did not set the milk saucer down right away. The sky had begun to radiate above the mossy gutter, the white was growing harder and harder. The frost fringe was beginning to glitter. (*Gesine*) *"Don't be so grouchy": I said. She blinked crankily and lowered herself, paw after paw, down the steps. I lowered the saucer to her. Before she began lapping she pushed her head back into her neck and looked at me, round-eyed. I crouched beside her, watching. The air felt like noon warmth. I felt as though I had perhaps come home after all.*

Jonas stood at the front door waiting for Cresspahl to come back from town with a string bag full of rolls. Swaying he stepped over the puddles with swinging arms, his head high on his neck. He grimaced and stared at Jonas, exaggerating the face Lisbeth Papenbrock had made, that was how she had looked at him. She had been too surprised counting all those rolls, she couldn't even ask him any questions. The old magpie. He should have brought her along, then you'd really get all the news. "I see you squinting at the paper. There's nothing in it. But Lisbeth would tell you: the rebels have already occupied the Jerichow station!" Jonas shook his head. He had no desire to look at the paper. Cresspahl frowned at him. In silent surprise he walked ahead into the kitchen. "Daughter . . . " he began, gesticulating.

Over breakfast Gesine was telling about a trip she'd taken. IN TUTTO IL MONDO PALMOLIVE IN TUTTO IL

MONDO PALMOL: she said, but Münchner Hofbräu also
recommended itself to the woman who was settling down for
the night on top of the central heating in the subway; the
homeless lay in silence, a criticism of the social reform theories
that were being thought up unscrupulously at the IMPE-
RIAL PALACE hotel (il nuovo grande albergo) that was also
flickering its neon praise over the faces in the subway. Cresspahl had pushed back his breakfast things and pondered dark
thoughts. Jonas sat attentively, hand to his chin, asking her
questions. And she told of donkeys in the rain, eighteen propo-
sitions between Roma Termini and Villa San Giovanni "may I
carry your suitcase," the things landladies won't do for money,
Lei Communista—? Si, si. Cresspahl came up against the back
of his chair. Had she perhaps tried grappa? No. That was
somebody else. "But I never drank anything so cool and clean
as a DRY MARTINI in an altezza su livello del mare metri
cinquecento cinquanta. But when it rained it had looked
exactly like the Rehberge, if Father would disregard the boy
who walked her back to the pension under a giant umbrella
and who murmured contemptuously when passing children
teased him and asked "una Inglese," because he wasn't sure
what she was. And the 25 lire left over from the last tip had
been brought back for Jonas who might, however, pass them
on to a venerable old father who was always so short of
matches. Of which also a few remained, only no more PHIL-
LIP MORRIS. Because Phillip Morris really HAS IT. Scusi.
She couldn't stay more than two days, and such subterfuges
don't help. Cresspahl put the stuffed pipe in his pocket and
went outside. They saw him stand still in the yard. Bent over
the burning match he climbed the steps, ducked under the
door and disappeared. "What made you go there?" asked
Jonas. Jakob had not asked that question. "I was unhappy,
Jonas." Her smile grew more and more ironical, finally he
reached for one of Jakob's cigarettes, just to be able to look
away for a while. He thought of the week he had spent with
her in the same region last spring. He understood: she had

gone back in the fall to find out if the week was holding up. It was asking too much.

— You were telling us about it as though you wanted to make us understand something, and I asked you to help you express it. But you didn't want to express it.
— No. I don't remember us ever having talked quite so un- fairly to each other as today.
— Yes.

Cresspahl did not look up when she came into the workshop. She stood behind him, watching his hands. He had a veneer- ing disk in front of him and was etching grooves into it, one close to the other, she didn't know what for. She needn't stand there as though she'd come for a well-deserved scold- ing, he grunted. "But you didn't even turn your head." He could feel it from the back, and "I must say it's not right the way you live. I can't even help my own daughter, can't take care of her, has nothing to do with the house. Only, you're so far away, I bump my head against the walls more often. Ge-sine! People always say owls hatch owls, they'll never grow up to be quail, if your great-aunt could see you now. What you can't do with words, and I like how you puzzle it all out in your educated head with a moderate dose of conceit and the accurate little letters you write me. Always straightforward and beside the point. A shame I don't under- stand right away what it says between the lines. A man can do a lot of guessing, also that there's something wrong maybe, probably on purpose. And I haven't much to say. Perhaps I can tell about Brüshaver's cat, and how the sky gets very blue at night, and drip drip ever so evenly all through the day, and the pavement has a bluish shimmer when I know it's black, and the lights look yellow at twilight. That's the kind of nonsense I put down on paper for you, and you still have no idea of what my life is like these days. Or you write to me 'everything is so crystal clear, the branches in the park stand sharp and long against the big blueness, the gables look black from behind as though they were cut-outs, but in front where the streetcar passes they are gray in the yellow light, the scaffoldings are like match sticks, thin and delicate, and slowly, very slowly, the big blueness grows darker until all the lights look white and the fog lifts,' yes and it may be the same fog that's outside my window, much later, when I get up in the middle of the night and look out, because I wonder why I can't see the birch. Then I see the fog outside and the birch is still there. Only: I can't see it. Because of the fog. Your loving father. Those are facts we won't have to argue about, they don't need explaining, but beyond that I see nothing, in everything else you're no longer at home here, so don't wonder if I think it's not right the way you live. Jerichow can't help you," he hoped that wasn't what she had come for. She might also realize that this was going to be another day with a big blue sky and shiny branches; on such days you could see that the workshop windows needed cleaning. The kind of weather that always made him feel a little sorry she wasn't here any more. He stopped as abruptly as he had begun. He was now dovetailing extremely small pieces of wood, holding them close to his eyes, sanding them smooth. All the time he felt her presence behind him, but when he turned around she had left. Jonas saw her stand outside the shop on the steps. Shading her eyes, trying to look into the sun probably. Jonas started cleaning her other shoe. When he leaned out of the kitchen window to put the spotless dull leather in the sunshine, he saw her squat on the steps. Jakob's pullover came up to her chin. Her legs were dangling from the wide baggy pants and the polished thin wooden sandals were swinging on her narrow feet. She seemed cheerful, blinking into the light

JONAS

*and we rummaged through the linen closet, the three of us, trying to locate the damask tablecloth Jakob said we had, Cresspahl was shaking his head, he didn't understand, totally*

*helpless he came back from his room. She's sleeping, he said.
We looked at each other in amazement and tiptoed after him,
from the sun-warm half of the house into the gray clear chill
of Cresspahl's room where she was lying on the couch in front
of the bookcase, under the yellow cover, sleeping. She looked
as though she had fallen asleep the moment she rolled over,
one shoulder drawn up, her hair had come undone, her stubborn face heaved with each breath, her arms around her head
as though she intended to lie there for ever. Cresspahl crept
closer and covered her feet and crept back again. They both
looked at me and smiled because I wasn't moving. And then
the worried expression reappeared on their faces because
neither knew what to do. Then Jakob came over and put his
hands under her shoulders and neck and lifted her carefully,
when she opened her eyes she couldn't see anyone but him,
and she locked her arms around his neck and said with surprise she had dreamed, "Jakob, how broad you've grown!"
and Jakob smiled out of the corners of his eyes, looking over
to us to see if we were going to tease him. She sank back and
looked at me and at Cresspahl and smiled; her eyes wandered
back to Jakob and examined him gravely. "Come," he said.
and the way she sat in her room that afternoon, across from
me with the typewriter on her knees and pulled out the last
sheet and handed it to me with absent eyes, her hands on the
keys, looking nowhere in the striped sunlight that filtered in
through the blinds, she put the typewriter away and arranged
the typed copies into a neat pile and walked over to the mirror
once and turned and stood before me. I could tell from her
voice that she thought of something that pleased her and that
she looked at me when she said: Jonas, I want to tell you. I
happen to love Jakob. She was sitting on the table across
from me, out of reach, distant with serenity, her eyes were
narrow with thinking, irony, curiosity. Her thrifty taciturn
face that changes when she turns it toward the window with
the sun sitting in the corners, growing paler and paler as the
sky clouds over
Jakob passed through the room and did not stop at our*

*silence, embraced us in one single glance as though he were
happy to see us silent side by side in the sunny studious room.
He passed through and said, "You can go to the beach now.
It'll soon be dark. Be back by evening" and disappeared behind Cresspahl's door. We heard Cresspahl's step on the
floorboards. We saw the narrow curved brass handle bow to
the old wood and felt the door strain against the tongue of the
lock as it slid softly, sharply into the wall.*

— I expected you to get up and walk to the door and close it
behind you, hasty and dignified, like a young man of readily
offended responsibilities. And I felt ashamed for having asked
you to help me with this too, *(Gesine) but he didn't move.
He stared at me as though hoping to peel all kinds of estrange-
ments off me, layer by layer, until he shrugged and turned
away and slid down horizontally between the chair arms,
hands in his pockets, pensive, and immediately his eyes came
back to me, without their curiosity. "I have tried, how should
I conduct myself, I don't know," he said with an embarrassed
laugh*

— The basic rules for decent conduct, you see. . . they must
be reinvented according to the situation *(Jonas) I would have
taken the next train if only I could have turned my eyes away
from her for a second. It was as inconceivable as the possibility of staying. "I don't know," I said, "you tell me what I
must do." "Come," she said. "Let's go to the beach." I remembered that the door had been locked and immediately
forgot about it again until later that evening. I know that the
sky was completely white when we came out of the house.
Soon it started to rain. The sky grew denser, more compact,
weighing on the narrow strips of land. I know the hard wind
that leaped up from the sea and into our eyes, and her hands
clutching my shoulders, and her head beside me, wet from
the rain, motionless, staring down into the waves that broke
under us over the steel jetty and froze, foamy, spraying, be-*

*fore they crashed and turned over and wriggled through the*
*heavy pilings and unrolled full length, lazy and irresistible,*
*onto the sand. "On the crest of the waves," said her voice, yes*
*on the foamy crests—before they break.*


— SO YOU BLAME YOURSELF for having crossed the border no
matter how. That means: no going back. Which means for
me: one can't afford to cross it in the opposite direction either.
— Please come.
— I don't know what keeps me here. Perhaps I've started
something and want to see how it works out. Your father
would say: you can't run away from your own life. Do you
want to annul the fact that we found a gentleman sitting beside Jakob in your father's house when we emerged from the
rain three hours after sundown, a gentleman who introduced
himself as Rohlfs, who bowed and shook your hand and
voiced his pleasure at making your acquaintance? And a
young man on the other side whom they introduced to us as
a garage mechanic. You went up to him and thought you liked
him, and neither Cresspahl nor Jakob knew how to get you
out of the house, away from between those two men?
— But that didn't depend on me. I hadn't set it in motion. It
had been running long before I came into the picture. I'm
sure Jakob knew how to get me back to the autobahn. That's
not it. Not all of it.


"A friend of Jakob's," said Cresspahl. He got up for her to
sit in his chair. He remained standing behind her, leaning on
the back. Jakob was sitting at the other side of the table, near
the window, next to Herr Rohlfs in the other chair. Herr
Rohlfs' face didn't look quite so gray that evening. He had
been sleeping all day. He looked friendly and wide awake
under his dark blond crew cut, and when he lifted his heavy
eyelids toward Gesine he smiled warmly. Good evening. He

could see at her mouth that she, too, remembered the evening
at the Elbe Hotel. Then it was over. His face tightened, grew
angular at the temples, the eyes lost their soft indecision, became sure of their grasp. He seldom moved, except to turn his
head toward Jakob. Hänschen sat beside Jonas on the couch,
Jonas far back, his head on the pillow, Hänschen at the edge,
hands between knees, head forward. He was watching Cresspahl's lips move. The shutters were open. From the street one
could easily have counted the people in the room in the warm
yellow light that stood behind the rain.

"Perhaps we ought to start all over again," Herr Rohlfs murmured hesitantly. Jakob leaned back. He seemed to be studying Cresspahl with loving concern. Cresspahl shook his head.
Gesine looked up and around, but her father was standing
quietly, her eyes wandered back to Jakob. The windows were
black as night. The light touched only the thin streaks of
water which the wind was pressing against the glass, pre-
venting them from running down.

"Your father said," said Jakob, "the way they're pushing people around, look what happens to a person, and all that is still
going to happen, and you can't rely on anything. One fellow
complains they don't let him keep his secrets; the other says
they don't let him speak his mind. Why should they? All that
rubbish about human rights. No one can speak of dignity and
human needs and order in the world, no one can, unless he's
Reverend Brüshaver. Which I'm not. Which you're not. But
the way they're pushing people around."

"Mr. Cresspahl is referring to the State," said Herr Rohlfs.
"We started out with the natural need for human coexistence.
I affirmed that the progress of a community can be measured
by the fair and reasonable balance of individual interests, by
the satisfaction of the egoisms. Your father called that: one
man keeping the other contentedly alive. Forcibly, living
conditions must become more and more pleasant as socialist
production improves and expands. The basic condition for
such logic," said Herr Rohlfs.

JONAS

*is the abolition of capitalism. The founding of a proletarian State. The building of a socialist economy. One man keeping the other contentedly alive. She lifted her face and held her chin to one side. Her eyes wandered to Jakob, halted at the window*

"It doesn't depend on us, but on the administrators of the socialist surplus value. We live according to the use they make of the progress potential," said Jonas. Hänschen pulled his upper lip between his teeth. His fingers caught each other and held on.

— You were magnificent, you two.
— We were magnificent.
— What is a progress potential? The railroad: for happy traveling. It is also a potential for mobilization of the armed forces of socialism. How many men or horses per boxcar? Technology in general. Guided auxiliary or supernatural witchcraft. Those unreliable witch doctors. Those reliable experts. A definite future. An indefinite future. The moral outcome of applied natural sciences. Man's desire for happiness directed toward free participation in the machines for automatic living. They have strikes in West Germany. On strikes. The State, liberally founded by nineteenth-century capitalism. Not quite that liberally. Its basic structure could not be changed by the new orientation. Has been changed radically when the proletariat took over. Is such a government still selfish? No. Possibly because each government official submits completely to the demands of the government. Stands or falls with it? Don't take that tone. Aha! Who is the reactionary here? Do you believe in Man's moral potential, do you believe selfishness can be transformed into brotherly love? Let me say it this way: I prefer the railroad potential. You're telling me! But the Soviet Union liberated Hungary from the

fascists. They could have remained liberators only if they had left after it was done. Revolts are an historical error. They are a reality. One must not interpret reality on the strength of one's personal experiences alone. One must look for the continuous lines of evolution: anatomy of progress at every present moment. What is progress? Intellectual. Social. German furniture thesis: Only at my table does one sit on the proper chair.

— Did it really last two hours? We've been discussing these things for the last ten years.

— Yes. Really two hours. You knew each other the minute you met. You simply had to agree that you could not come to any agreement. When you reached that point, you identified yourselves and each other. Then you noticed that we had been listening. You were extremely surprised. I found Cresspahl standing behind me, Hänschen had long stretched out and didn't say a word, neither did Jakob. And in the sudden silence I thought of the many trains that had been running all over the earth in the meantime.

"That's asking too much of a man. . ." Jakob said finally. He didn't smile. He didn't look up. Since he had to have his hands free at work, he had developed the habit of holding his cigarette in one corner of his mouth. His right eye was always half closed when he sat smoking, head down.
"And that is precisely what is being asked," said Herr Rohlfs. Jonas had wanted to reach for a cigarette. His gesture froze halfway across.

— I almost realized, at that point. I wanted to get up, started to get up when I noticed that nobody else in the room was moving. Everybody sensed that I was about to move, although not one of you was looking. Not even Jakob:

"Stay where you are," said Jakob. Jonas' head shot up, trying to look Jakob in the eye.

Jakob's shrug coincided with an annoyed nod from Herr Rohlfs that expressed what Jakob said when he turned his head halfway toward him, without looking at him. Because that instant Jakob may have realized how it looked to Cresspahl. Throughout the conversation Cresspahl stood motionless, bent over the back of the chair against which his daughter's head was leaning, one of his hands was closed around the wrist of the other in a strange clasp: two wide-spread fingers touched the sleeve as though they only had to bend a little to pull a longish object out from under the cuff into the hollow palm; his head was bowed. He seemed to be looking at Gesine's hands in her lap. But Jakob kept expecting Cresspahl to raise his head and focus on no one but Herr Rohlfs: that's how it looked to Cresspahl. (And why had Jakob sent Gesine and Jonas to the beach and asked Cresspahl to lock the door behind them and said "listen, Cresspahl. . ." and started to tell him everything since last Thursday? or rather: he didn't say anything, he laid the revolver on the table and let Cresspahl take a look at it and conclude that the situation (the "toims") had reached the point of this precious metal object, this masterpiece of French craftsmanship than which progress could go no further and which could not be avoided, after that Jakob's sole explanation was that Herr Rohlfs had, however, shaken hands with him. Did he want to share his secret with someone finally, and not assume all the responsibility with his lonely judgment? Or did he think his opinion was not solely competent?) Cresspahl had been lying beside him, gigantic, all to one side, he let the thing spin turn dangle between thumb and forefinger: "yes," he said after Jakob had finished explaining. "Yes" in his careful hardworking way that looked at each piece of news from all angles and set it aside in its place as though he were filing the events, piece by piece, in the drawers of his seven-door cupboard. But when Jakob went on talking, Cresspahl looked up at him with blurred melancholy eyes, thinking all kinds of thoughts, suddenly he sank back on the couch with a sigh: "The way they push people around," he said. Jakob looked at Cresspahl lying there, arms crossed over his chest, staring up at the ceiling, breathing bitterly to himself. Outside, the window was getting dark. They were silent. That hadn't been the point. When Herr Rohlfs promised safe-conduct and free decision, Jakob's answer was solely concerned with the question of supper ("Would you like to come for supper? What's your favorite brandy?"), this meant to both of them that seven armed strollers would be enough to guard the corners of Cresspahl's house. That one gesture of Herr Rohlfs could switch off the light. That, at the first thud of furniture falling and bodies being thrown, the front door would crack and break from its hinges and that the floodlights would swing across the street, away from the gate of the Soviet Headquarters and focus on the long low façade of the house in which, that instant, the two windows beside the door had suddenly grown dark: Herr Rohlfs was standing before the mirror, fastening the tie to go with his good suit, he grimaced at the sight of his worried face, freedom is accepting what is necessary. "That's no help," said Jakob. (Jonas would have said the same thing. Jonas would have left the revolver lying on the table. That's why he didn't stop and let Gesine sit on the table across from him and smiled indulgent surprised approval of other people's well-being for which he had no time.) "It does help," said Cresspahl. "He got what he wants," said Jakob. "He's the one I'm talking about," said Cresspahl. And this may have been what Jakob realized that hour before midnight: no matter how much power a man had in the world and had changed and accomplished enough to live beyond contempt and sympathy: like Herr Rohlfs, Cresspahl was still able to refuse him shelter assistance food with the words "You are not a good man," although a judgment of this sort must strike any reasonable citizen as pure madness. At first Jakob had interpreted Cresspahl's plan as vengeance according to the old books where guilt need not be irrefutably proved; but in reality Cresspahl was making a distinction between the *socialist cause for which each and every one must make sacrifices in view of the important future* and the in-

dividual who had carried this cause all the way into Cresspahl's house with great effort and total dedication of his person (Cresspahl insisted that this was so, with violent nodding
and narrowed eyes. He sat up and stared at Jakob with his
wild face under the tousled gray hair until Jakob finally said:
"Yes. He has made it his cause."), this individual had started
the whole thing and was interested in its favorable outcome
(which nobody except him could fully consider the accom-
plishment of an effort), and Cresspahl wanted to frustrate
this presumably completely one-sided sensation of achievement, because he considered the effort "bad" without looking
at the reality of it (because the other reality was his daughter
Gesine. He could not save her from sitting under the lamps
of human interrogation, but he didn't want the man whose
proud personal achievement had brought her there, to sit
behind those lamps, in comfortable shadow). To Jakob the
shrugged consent at the end may have seemed like the feeling
that applauds the incomprehensible beauty of ancient temples, is patient with Sunday churchgoers who uplift their
lives with incomprehensible singing and unfounded words
and holy organ music and are as real as the sight of two lovers
embracing in a doorway at night whom one passes with a
shocked smile because this is completely out of reach, and
not desirable even.

Jakob looked away from Cresspahl's hand closed around the
revolver and said to Herr Rohlfs with unshakable indifference:

— He said: I'll shoot you down like a mad dog if. . . And
remember: immediately afterwards they toasted everlasting
friendship.

— And when did they tell you? Right at the outset? (*Jonas*)
*I saw her for the last time in the floodlights of the Soviet
Kommandatura. She nodded to me and took a step back
beside Cresspahl who towered in the driveway sprayed with
drizzle, "Tie a scarf around your neck," he said. The night-
black rainy trees in the wind, the harsh floodlights, the over-*

*loud loudspeaker with the blurred windswept autumn-hoarse
national anthem sayoos nerooshimy, the immobile blank face
of the driver who opened the door for her, the cone of light
over her eyes (she didn't turn again, stared straight ahead
into the darkness) above her cool narrow eyes and the jolt
that pulled the long nimble beast of a car forward into the
rain which the motor noise and the red taillights and the
shadow swallowed up immediately.* You couldn't have expected him to drive you innocently back to the autobahn.
— He did though. I heard Jakob talk to him behind me and
simply fell asleep. Then we stopped for gasoline and we
changed seats, Jakob hung backwards over his seat and began
telling me, it didn't take more than three words. I said what
one says: I'll think it over, and we fixed an appointment for
the tenth of November in Berlin. That was all. Who is afraid
of a business situation? The last forty miles they let me drive.
Now I know all about Russian gear shift, can you imagine?
Did you expect struggling and wild shooting from the speed-
ing car? But I want you to know one thing: I really intended
to think it over.
— That is tomorrow.
— Yes, that is tomorrow. I'm telling you that was not it. We
stood for seventeen minutes in the parking lot, you know,
those circles behind a row of trees, it was early morning, the
rain had become light gray, when Jakob saw them coming,
he recognized them by the yellow plate. They hardly put the
brakes on. I climbed in and drove off. That was all. For a
while I still saw the car behind us in which I had come. I
thought: Jakob is sitting in there. I couldn't remember how
we had said goodbye. Then it disappeared in the cutoff after
the Elbe bridge. My visit was over. Only: we all lived calmly
through it and simply go on living as if it had not affected
us exactly as much as it did Jakob. Hänschen, the chauffeur,
had come outside with me and flagged them. During the ride
he said to me: "You know, he's okay, after all," he meant
Jakob, "but he won't get away with this," that's what I meant.
And tomorrow, you see. . .

Is your party still on the line
— I've been cut off
I'm very sorry. Technical difficulties. That's all I know myself.
I cannot reconnect you.
— Long-distance operator please. This is local operator:
seven – five – one – one – seven. The charges, please.

# IV

Herr Dr. Blach took the first early-morning train out of Jerichow back to the two Berlins.

Cresspahl's daughter stood in the first post office behind the border, filling a telegram form with words for her father.

Herr Rohlfs had returned from the autobahn via the southern suburb and the big bridge. He was sitting before the report sheets of the last two days. He learned that Jakob had been missing from the city since Tuesday night. Shortly after he was informed by telephone that Jakob had been seen twenty minutes ago getting out of a Pobyeda at the corner of the street on which he lived; he had not been wearing his uniform. The Jerichow branch reported Herr Dr. Blach had boarded the first morning train with a Berlin ticket. Then came the text of the telegram.

The secretary of the English Institute said:
"The director didn't come in, but he called. The assistant professors wanted to know if the seminar was canceled although I tacked a note on the door. Two inside calls, more from outside, but always the same voice. I said Herr Doctor is away on business: that's all I knew myself. If only I had known! So I merely asked Did you have a good trip? when he appeared, shortly after lunch. He had come directly from the station, you know how he is, he stood at the door and said: So there you are! that's what he always says, but today he sounded surprised. And for a long time he wasn't all there. He sat down beside me without taking his coat off, as though he

didn't know if he were coming or going: as though he weren't
at home here; he kept staring ahead of him, not thinking anything, you can tell whether a man is thinking or not, after a
couple of years, usually he turns his head and does think of
something until it makes him grin, he's all set to say it, but
now he looked as though he had stumbled on something that
cannot be thought: more like a feeling. He stared at the cigarettes and didn't know what they were, I kept holding them
out to him, finally he took one, felt for a ten-pfennig piece
in his pocket and put it in the box beside the typewriter, but
I fished it out again and gave it back to him and said no no
weren't we old friends? You don't see that do you? Because I
always said he was arrogant quietly inside himself, huh? And
not because nothing mattered any more at this point, and not
out of pity either (because something had happened to him,
what's that one like I wondered, what's she like), but because
it had happened to him too, arrogance protects one from
everything, from this it hadn't been able to protect him. I
told him about all the calls for him and that there'd been one
with a funny name, that made him look at his watch, I could
see that was the name all right (I won't repeat it to you, then
you needn't forget it again). Something had to come out right
today. To the others at the Institute he merely said he'd forgotten to pay his union dues, that was as arrogant as ever,
but he didn't care how neatly he'd put it. He might have
gone into the old man's office to make his call, but he didn't.
He pulled my phone over and dialed. No answer. No answer.
When he tried for the seventh time I thought I'd hit the ceiling. The old man had said he'd be at home all day waiting for
his call, and now he isn't there. Where is everybody today?
Blach asked and looked around the office. Usually they crowd
in here and want to know what's new and wait around for the
old man and buy cigarettes from me, and now we've sat completely undisturbed for six full minutes. You'll find out soon
enough. Well and then, as I told you before, then the old man
comes in, you know what he looks like, you saw him the other
day, remember, he looks like a hedgehog, a short touching

little man, his head all the way back on his neck, he holds both hands out to Blach: So there you are. He meant it however. It was odd to see him empty-handed, usually the cab driver has to carry two heavy briefcases with books after him and he keeps looking over his shoulder to make sure they're there. The hedgehog, we call him. He can shave all he wants, he still looks like a hedgehog. He puts a finger in his collar, rubs, looks at Blach, is delighted to see him, I'd like to. . . I'd like you to. . . well you know: Speak to you in my office. Blach cradles his shoulders trying to look not quite so much taller than the old man, he's always done that only I never noticed before today. He nods to me, follows him out. I was so nervous, I picked up his cigarette, I paced about the office, I locked the door: I thought they'd start yelling any moment, the others needn't hear that. But not a sound. And they'd left the outer door half open. I walked over and closed it. Then the housephone rings. I rush over, it's the old man. Completely friendly and serene: please come in for dictation. I take a deep breath and in I go. It was as though they'd settled the whole thing in three words. The old man is in his arm-chair, Blach at the window, his shirt looked as though he had washed it himself, all day on the train and not enough sleep, but now he had waked up, I mean: as though for a while he'd got rid of whatever had been bothering him before, he wasn't arrogant or nervous or anything, just stood beside the old man, how often I've seen them standing like that side by side, I thought, and how much easier things had been since Blach came to the Institute, because he knew how to handle the old man, the old man likes him and, you know, when there was real trouble, I never had anything to do with it. Because Blach would take care of it and dictate to me and I'd take it in to the old man and he'd raise his eyebrows as high as they would go and look around for Blach and Blach would look back at him just as surprised and then the old man would sign. And then they'd stand side by side: another job well done. (As though I knew what was coming.) In view of the fact. . . , the old man began. I already had it down on my pad. He leaned sideways,

took Blach by the wrist, helplessly shook his head. Blach
shrugged, it really wasn't easy to put that in words. They
started all over again. Professor, says Blach, a shame I don't
remember every word of it, well, something like this: it was
most kind to have counseled him, but he cannot tolerate being
told which assistant to keep and which to let go, that's the gist
of it. Yes, the old man says: that's interference. It is absurd to
judge scientific pronouncements from a political point of view,
it is totally . . . I told you I can't remember. But it had an air
of importance about it and if I'd taken it across the border we'd
be hearing it on the radio right now and I'd be two hundred
West marks richer and we could go and buy that coat, never
mind, I'm only saying. Blach made it all sound very formal.
Very administrative which was better still. According to personnel regulations they had no right to resign; still less: both
of them at once. We were sure nobody could find fault with
it. And they did it only for each other. I don't know, it was
the spirit of the thing, I can't go on sitting there all by myself
as though I'd been left behind, they'll think I squealed on
them at the Institute. Or something. I'd had enough. So, after
they walked out, I sat down and typed my own resignation
and put it with the other two, you can scold me now if you
want but not more than five minutes. I realize: it's silly, completely ridiculous honor and self-sacrifice, but at that moment
it was the right thing to do, believe me. I just couldn't stand
them being so alone. Somebody telephoned for Blach, I looked
at him, he shook his head arrogantly (yes: arrogantly. I like
it now), amused, and I said: Herr Dr. Blach is not in. Then
it was over. Each took the other's arm and out they went. One
thing I'd like to know though: the old man is well-fixed, with
a bank account, he is home now on his couch and listening
to music, but Blach, what is Blach going to do now?" Where
did you put your resignation, on the table? Yes. Then you'll
go early tomorrow morning before the charwoman comes in
and take it back. No. Yes. If you want to be that particular
you can't work anywhere any more these days, and where's
the money to come from?

HERR ROHLFS

*What are you reading, lad, let me see, I'm interested. Thought Structure and Its Desired Effects, Questions of Style and Expression (I used to have good marks in that, perhaps I can help you). And will you open your mouth for everyone to lip read your thoughts as in Cresspahl's house? (Cresspahl feels like a piece of my own life somehow, although he's only one of countless acquaintances.) You hardly typed those sheets for people like Jakob, did you? What do you think. I said: we must see to it that the following gets around: that a man cannot, after all, simply get up and say whatever comes into his head. If they panic at the sight of the empty Institute and show themselves weak, I say: don't yield or we'll hide in the basement. We'll bring the old one back once his assistant has escaped our scientific potential, across the border. He may have some forty marks left, has no idea where to go tomorrow, stands outside as though he were already in the West. Stop and think a moment: that isn't all. After you've been kicked out it is more than possible that I might find myself in the same cafe two tables away from you, waiting to be served. It is conceivable that we'll come closer together than last night. That's what I say. But he is reading and re-reading those sheets as though his own writing astonished him. Let me have a look. "Put it down. I'll pay now." Too hot. (Didn't we meet somewhere before, why yes, weren't you) he'll put it in his coat pocket and finish his coffee and his cigarette, that's how one does these things. I'd have to get up walk through the cafe to the coat rack, put his coat on instead of mine, leave mine hanging for him on the hook, and out into the street: the waiter. I've already paid. Then he knows what's up. But he won't know if I take his wallet with the article, some of the money: that's a plausible motive, the article is accidental. But he can't afford to buy himself another coat. I'll take it to the lost and found. He'll go there and say: a gray coat, gray shetland. Is this the one? Yes. Is anything missing? Only money. The next day the papers will run a little piece on the gentleman-crook who shared the money and escaped after leaving*

*overcoat at lost and found. The papers are full of things these days.*
*I don't get it. He's sitting here as though he were planning to stay. I've given him reason enough. The rest is no concern of mine. Let him take his article wherever he wants. That's a different division. Picking pockets is not my line.*

— And you felt as though the threads had slipped through your fingers.
— I don't feel I'm running a puppet show. I admit the outcome wasn't what I had bargained for. I had been working with different situations too long, you might call it the atmospheric aftereffects of Jerichow.
— That's no reason to let everything run haywire. You had to ask me what Dr. Blach had been doing in the meantime. I told you all I know of Jakob. And instead of watching out for the results of what you started, you. . .
— Yes. I did some technical advising on armaments for a TV show. Laugh if you like.
— Why didn't you feel like speaking with Jakob?
— About what? He lived on for a while.

"Know something?" said Jakob's seventeen-year-old clerk who was sitting outside the examination room with another girl and was eager to talk about something else: "He's a scream. You wouldn't think so would you? I don't really know either what makes him so funny. But just the way he comes in and shakes your hand and looks about the room as though he couldn't remember, and stands with one hand to his head, finally he sits down and says: Let's go. As though it were all child's play, taking a walk and picking flowers, when you've got to be so fast and accurate. When traffic is slow, he switches all the loudspeakers on and lets them talk, he knows everybody, the things you get to hear: where they were last night, who's had trouble with his wife and Mary's having a baby but she's still not sure who the father is. . . really! Of course, I can't tell you about that. I only happen to sit there as a trainee, they're not talking to me. Then it all begins: I start taking notes. And then something like this: all the lines are busy and we've got to get through, so I listen in: Haven't seen you in ages, what are you doing tonight?; I blush when I hear stuff like that. He gets up, takes the receiver away from me, listens in for a while real friendly, but only until they've made their date, he doesn't let them start all over again, he disconnects them and switches us in, I mean: he could have made fun of me. But he doesn't. He goes back to his chair and on with his work so dead serious that I burst out laughing, and then he looks over with eyes like slits and nods in agreement. See what I mean? At first when I started with him I expected God knows what, because of that girl from the Head Office, you know the one I mean, the one who's so progressive he dropped her, they say. And then I heard all those other things, you know, about the Linden-krug where the women conductors dance on the tables at midnight, and all that. Well, you know how people talk. But what I'm saying is that when you work with him he's nothing but nice and calm. So calm: when there's a meeting at the chief dispatcher's some get all excited and scream and yell at everybody that their systems don't work and all that; but he just does it. And when it doesn't work he looks over at me and waits to see if I want to say something, and we discuss it calmly and nobody gets excited and everybody gets taken care of. You learn a lot from him. Or when one of his friends comes in and talks about marriage, he doesn't joke or anything and even if I go out and stay out for a while he's still sitting there same as before, merely asks the other guy whether he needs some money, see? And he soon found out how jittery I felt about the exam, so he went over the whole thing with me, from start to finish. And I didn't even realize, he did it so casually. Train's coming in, he says to me. I take

it down, clock time, train A passing train B, we telephone and
coax the chief dispatcher to let it through. He refuses. He
must. What's an interlocking? he asks. An arrangement of
signals and signal appliances so interconnected that their
movements must succeed each other in proper sequence. Is
that correct? yes. He shows it to me on the chart. There are
three tracks. When the chief dispatcher gives the all-clear on
track 1. . . he lets me explain. The chief dispatcher closes
signal transmitter $A^2$, thus closing siding $A^2$ (signal receiver),
the signal turns white. Now the chief dispatcher has closed
all opposing signal transmitters, down on the tracks the yard-
men close the switches and set the electric semaphores on the
siding, this unblocks the chief dispatcher's sector $a^1$, $^2$. Now
all is ready for the operators in the towers to open block $A^2$:
the train may enter. Of course he interrupted me, but when
you realize the way it works—which you can't in class and
not from the books either, but here I saw it, the way the
switches go back and forth and that there's somebody sitting
at every block station and all that. And always a little something else besides. When I was absolutely certain that the
train could come in, he asks me: and now explain to me please
why it isn't coming in. You can't explain that of course, so
you laugh. But I was quite right to look it up in the freight
traffic manual; it said: for all trains, reason: siding not signal-
controlled. He starts all over again, coaxes the chief dispatcher
like a sick horse, don't make such a fuss he says to him. . .
that's what I mean by funny. And you can learn a lot. Because other dispatchers just sit before their mikes and give
instructions and when you ask them about interlocking then
it's somebody else's business and they don't know too well
themselves. But he has everything in his head and never gets
stumped; and once when I showed him with my hand above
the table how high the books of regulations had piled up, he
merely looked to see if I had got the proper height and
nodded and said: Doctors also have a lot of things to learn.
That's what I mean."

— You know that they've seen each other since then, don't you?

— Of course. I know everything more or less, but it doesn't help much. Because the machinery went on running, I couldn't stop the reports or I might have lacked proof. . . Or I might have imagined that I had lost my overall perspective because one tiny three minutes was missing somewhere, what had happened in that lapse? Yes I know Herr Dr. Blach paid Jakob a visit on the following Tuesday, that was October 30th, and on the 31st Jakob took a train to the West. They spent the evening. . . what am I to do with that kind of information? Three-twenty P.M.

— He took the number 11 streetcar from the station. He asked the woman conductor where to get off for the Railroad Head Office. Two trainees were standing in the door. He asked them for Herr Abs. They're wearing the same uniform, he thought, they'd probably know who he is. They'd never heard of him. They stared at the stranger with something like suspicion and Jonas immediately thought of riots and red slogans warning: WATCH OUT FOR AGENTS, and he was quite wrong. The boys simply thought if a stranger comes here we ought at least to know him by sight. They noticed the stranger was relaxed and confident and expected to be helped (Jonas was still accustomed to seeing everything function) so they called the watchman out and the watchman couldn't utter one friendly sound for hoarseness and high blood pressure, or so it seemed, actually he was delighted with the interruption and started pointing vaguely somewhere into the haze where whistles were leaping up around a foggy monster, and then he told him—or perhaps he had no time to tell him because that was when Sabine arrived

— Up to this point everything sounds right. But that's not when Sabine arrived. They met, yes, but the meeting itself was unobserved and I don't believe they met at the gate this way, because she didn't know him. Does one go out of one's way to give a complete stranger directions for six minutes? Not Sabine, because Jakob could have interpreted such a long

time as intentional remembering and Sabine wouldn't have
wanted that—
— All right. Then Jonas found the way by himself as far as
the guards outside the iron-grilled door.
— as far as the guards
— whom he didn't ask for information, had the good sense not
to ask, being a stranger. He walked past them as though he
knew where he was going with some official business in his
briefcase. And before he walked in, his eyes traveled up the
crisp clean brick wall and he felt as though he were in a
cellar out there in the hall in front of the watchman's booth,
because of all that structure rising up from the ground floor.
He said good afternoon, reached into his jacket with the
casualness you learn only in Berlin and held his identity card
open through the window and said: Herr Abs please. It's a
joke the way those guards are nothing but part of the setting,
sheer ornaments.
— No not quite. Their job is not too strictly defined. For a
while the police also did the watchman's work which meant:
nobody passed. That's fine theoretically, but since they
couldn't know all the administrative intricacies and functions,
the railroad found its service hampered by overconscientious
adherence to its own regulations. At that point they put a real
watchman back into the watchman's booth, a man who knew
when to make an exception and let a person through in spite
of everything, and the guards outside did a sort of pre-
policing. And if Blach had been obliged to show his identity
card to them (as I assume) his previous impression was
probably intensified as he went inside, yes, go ahead:
— yes: as though an innocent stroller had suddenly been
whisked into the subterranean vaults of some general staff.
Outside the sun had been shining, but in reality there was a
war on. Because Jenning (if it was Jenning) probably didn't
bother looking at the identity card, immediately he said: No.
And then proceeded to explain with much gusto how inaccessible the fifth floor was to a stranger and why, because you
miss one word and the brakeman down in the yard holds

the wrong flag up to the engineer (because Jenning used to be a brakeman, he knew what he was talking about, although it was a somewhat far-fetched way of refusing a pass, watchmen enjoy doing that). I don't see how Jonas can have got past such reasonable weighty brakeman objections, if not finally at that point
— at that point more likely
— Sabine had stepped out of the elevator and heard an unknown young man ask for Jakob (And at what time is Herr Abs through with his shift?), so she took him in tow and went back to the elevator instead of out into the street and across to her office, and while they waited for the cage to come down they told each other their names, while Jenning
— turned away with a disgruntled grin and took the receiver off the hook and dialed Jakob's number, more or less trying to excuse himself by announcing the visitor. Sabine was extremely pretty.
— And in the narrow rising cage he probably explained to her with amusement and animation how a man feels like a Boy Scout under such surveillance, or like an angry grain of sand in a machine, or altogether like a useless human being, without revealing to what extent he was telling the truth about himself: socially speaking, jobless, without prospects, cast out, he was nothing but himself, a young man devoid of qualifications, because what can be expressed in the number of marks left over from the previous and last payday is not much, just enough to go dancing.
— I see another possibility. First, as you said, Sabine took him upstairs and through all the amusement and unaccustomed civilized thoroughly intelligent talk she either: realized all over again how far Jakob had grown away from her. Here was a friend of his whom she knew nothing about, had never met, had no idea where to fit him in, and if Jakob had this kind of friend he must have changed unreachably. Or: she thought he had been sent by me. Because he probably acted friendly innocence so much, it didn't seem believable. He might have come with a message, instructions, a tip for

Jakob (or for her), that's why she didn't take him to Jakob's
door but sat him down in the culture corner in one of the two
armchairs with a table between them and the Railroaders
Journal and the Union Magazine and a flag pinned to the wall
to underline the portraits of the heads of the State (I'm de-
scribing it the way it must have looked to Blach, these culture
corners are all the same, there is probably one just like it at
the Institute). And obviously he started leafing through the
papers on the table and when Jakob's clerk stood before him
and said his name he had almost forgotten that Sabine had
walked past him and back to the elevator because she did
not wish to be thanked, because she was offended that he had
given her no hint as to who he was. Actually Blach was the
only one who knew nothing before yesterday morning.

— So what then?

— As I was saying.

— She must have had a knock signal for Jakob's door. And
she simply said Jonas' name through the slit and went back
and thought now Jakob would be able to talk to her, if this
unknown young man had been sent by Herr Rohlfs. It could
not be gone into for several reasons. I'm not vouching for
this. I'm merely expressing my explanation of why nobody
understood her behavior yesterday. You needn't hesitate. This
far you may still agree with me.

— Very well. Let us agree that nobody consists of the opinions people have of him. But now my question is: what did
Blach want to see Jakob for? Here you may have a few chrono-
logical gaps . . . he had delivered his manuscript to the editor.
It had been accepted for publication provided the political
developments of the next few days did not prevent it. In that
they were right.

— Still, your driver left your car standing outside the TV
studios to ride across the border to West Berlin every day and
come back with all the latest magazines whose on-the-spot
photo coverage of the Budapest events was worth as much
as a prince's wedding in the old days; you won't bother to

deny that. He didn't shove them right under your nose at least, did he?

— Yes. So Blach had nothing but private chores to take care of, he may have tried to expand the draft to a book, just for the fun of it. Indifferent, attentive he sat in his room near the Pankow church for a couple of days, his rent was paid. Tips on jobs could only have come through his friends who would have tried to find a place for him out from under my watchful eyes. Instead he went to see Jakob. After all, Dresden is a beautiful city, too. What was it he wanted from him?

— But we have a detailed report on everything they did that evening. And we don't know which of these details corresponded to Jonas' wishes, something he had been looking forward to during the trip,

— and we don't know which things were purposely brought about by Jakob and which just happened by accident, we assume therefore

— First: a visit with the reasonable justifiable practical side of life:

Jakob's back could be seen through the open door. He was sitting at his slanting table, hands in his lap, gazing up at the loudspeakers which said: "Can you take train four-five-one I repeat can you take train four-five-one" and they answered each other: "Train four-five-one okay after one-three-one clears I repeat"; Jakob leaned forward, switched his mike in, and said, "Taking four-five-one immediately on track one, clear track two for one-three-one"; the clerk was back in her chair, bent over her report sheet, writing. The loudspeaker repeated. Jakob held his right hand over his shoulder without turning around. His gesture had something extremely courteous and cordial, Jonas realized one didn't stint on handshakes here. After he let go of Jakob's fingers, the face appeared over one shoulder. He gave his visitor a friendly look, but his left hand was already busy again flipping switches, it seemed as though he could receive his visitor only with his eyes, not waste any thoughts on him; but this might have been something peculiar to Jakob. "In twenty minutes," he said. Jonas went to a stool at the window. It was open. A light drizzle drifted in. Outside in the street the sky had been a deathly October blue; now everything was a radiant white in the West and solid, the filtered sunlight came pushing through under the rain making each drop stand out. There'd be choppy clouds this evening. Suddenly Jakob had come to the window, had placed a soap dish on the sill and left his cigarettes and gone back soundlessly, miming with lengthened lips and upturned eyes in the direction of his clerk: She's very nice, very young as you can see . . . we'll talk later. Again he was sitting against the springy back of his swivel chair, resigned, hands in his lap, conducting conversations as though he had been stopped in the hallway of his apartment house and let a neighbor tell him about his day, without interest or impatience, just sitting there. "Have to think of it first," he was saying. "Really. You don't say. No. It's not a rat race. Okay. Three minutes distance. I'll do the lead-ins. Okay okay. Send her in. We'll take her," and Jonas suddenly felt a craving for this type of work. These were tangible durable objects, boxcars, locomotives, coaches; the movement of each completing all others, interdependent, all tied and gathered into a single high-up overall perspective; every occurrence in Jakob's head corresponded to a reality, something really did happen, shouldn't that make a man feel he was singlehandedly supplying half the day and the area of a small duchy with universal events? "They have three buttons there," Jakob said, bent forward while he wrote, Jonas turned to face him, "you know, a three-way squawk box. One for reception. One for transmission. And one for them to switch me off without my knowing it." He looked around to see if Jonas was smiling. He was. "But one of these days," said Jakob tilting his chair, gravely staring at the girl at the other end of the table, she lifted her head and waited just as gravely—what gay eyes she had— "one of these days every inch of this track, all ninety-eight miles will be automatic, the rails will be illuminated glass

rods, different colors, little lighted bugs will crawl forward
when I make way for them or stop when I block them, everything will be electrical, all controlled from one station, no
brakemen, relay throttles, stereosound, think of all the man-
power it would save and how much cheaper it would be . . . ?"
Jonas sank back. Once more he had the impression of not
understanding, felt ashamed of his smile which had been
sheer politeness. "And what if a fuse burns out?" he asked.
"Yes-no," said Jakob, "then I'll be an electrician, a checker of
contacts, anyway." He stood up, restlessly paced the room.
Then he remembered that he had been in a good mood before, came over to the window, made a friendly face, looked
down at Jonas. His hands were hard and wide, long-fingered,
but he couldn't flatten them out the way Jonas did, the post-
war labor was still in the joints.
"But that is technical progress and something else entirely,"
Jonas said. Two telephones started buzzing. Jakob walked
over and took one receiver out of the girl's hand. He listened,
the conversation on her phone was over, Jonas could see she
was preparing to say something, with appropriate modesty.
How old could she be? Seventeen maybe. And so polite. Jakob
raised his hand questingly, caught the flying cigarette, twirled
it into his mouth, carelessly lighted it. His eyes were scanning
the floor in rhythm with the cigarette rolling around his
mouth. He switched on the loudspeakers. "Going out. I repeat.
What the hell are you people doing?" asked a voice. Jakob
squinted toward the bridge down across the river. "She's on
her way" he said. But it seemed of no use now.
Because it was a long time before they could go home. When
Bartsch unlocked the door, Jakob had just cut a generous
helping of time out of the night with light and heavy express
freight and commuter trains and long distance connections
that would all have to wait until tomorrow in a twisted tangled
pile, all you could do now was wrap it up and tie a neat
string around it and throw it away, he said. He had drawn
a large horizontal line across his train sheet and all traffic had
to stop where that line touched. The loudspeakers were yelling

their heads off: how were they supposed to work that, the side tracks weren't infinite, for how long were the lines supposed to stay free, couldn't at least the express traffic be squeezed through before, we're busy too, please take one more express, please: but the orders said otherwise. The line had to stay free, but what for, you'll find out soon enough, all this time Jakob had the connection with Dispatcher North cradled against his ear, there wasn't a sound in the receiver and then Bartsch came in and stood in the middle of the room and said with absentminded reverence: "Those idiots. Those stupid . . ." and at this point Jakob turned to the window without looking at Jonas and said: "All this is secret you understand, and if you'd rather go out," but Jonas shook his head although Jakob didn't see, his eyes were fixed on the train sheet. The four of them said nothing, waited, the room became hollower and hollower with voices and light, and somewhere near the big meadow sat a freight train with tanks and jeeps and light field pieces in front of an immobile semaphore, the first to bar their way, the soldiers had jumped from the cars and stood in small smoking groups and wondered why so many passengers trains were going past them while they stood waiting, and when Jakob cleared his throat into the mouthpiece, the North Dispatcher said: "They won't give it to me." Jakob sat in silence and smoked, suddenly his arm flew up and hit the table and he was yelling: "Take down the name of that guy! Has he an opinion about the Russians to hold them up? Does he think other people have no opinions! We also know where they're going and this guy holds them up. As though ten minutes made a difference. Tell him that his goddamn honor is driving us nuts down here, we can't keep the lines free forever. We have trains waiting. People who want to get home. They too have opinions about the Russians, but they don't bother other people with them," two minutes later North was talking, the military train moved south, would come through in twenty minutes, the name of the honor monger could not be found out, "fine," said Jakob.

They went on waiting, on all the sidings commuter trains and diesels and freight stood stock still, wondering why nothing absolutely nothing moved on the clear main track. In the stations employees were stepping up to the blackboards, wiping off figures writing higher figures in their places: probable delay thirty minutes. Forty minutes. One hour. Indefinite. For by then they had certainly heard the fast heavy train with its windswept songs thump through the fog under the tower. It had no lights on and from up there it looked like a monstrous red-eyed worm that was creeping backwards, it thundered across the bridge and was gone, but: but the second one (closed boxcars with forty men per car) had gotten stuck somewhere, as soon as this announcement came over the loudspeakers Wolfgang's clerk (an elderly woman with a tender dreamy face who had intended to finish the sweater for her grandson that night) had to put away her knitting, because Jakob got up from the dispatcher's chair and sat down beside Bartsch as though they had to stick this out together, fists began pounding on the door, Jakob leaned over and lifted one screaming telephone after the other from its hook, helplessly chirping they lay side by side on the table, the loudspeakers echoed announcements of passing war material, countless passenger trains were being proposed and refused by Jakob whose "no" sounded less impatient but just as final as Bartsch's, they no longer bothered to explain that things were just as hectic for them. They were in constant communication with Dispatcher North, with the chief dispatcher, with the freightcar pool, with the traffic police (central command), traffic police had appeared in great haste and blocked all streets that led to the station, all over the city radio-cars were receiving instructions from the station and stopped and turned and aligned themselves along a street with no houses and high wet trees, and for some time that was that, then Dispatcher North announced the soldiers' train, but the station dispatcher wasn't listening, the brakemen's radio sounded unsure down there in the darkness, then the loudspeakers

began their self-righteous vigilant braying, long strings of boxcars were assembled and pushed out of the way, and the
freight pool dispatcher dropped his telephones and came rushing in, where in God's name was he to find all those cars?
Bartsch (perfectly calm now, bent forward, smoking, one hand
to his forehead) pointed out that there would also be a need
for heavy freight, that a certain empty train from the south
couldn't be expected for another twenty minutes—if she made
it at all, through the tangled maze—okay then! and now the
second train was pulling in from the north, stopped gasping
between the platforms of the passenger station, the soldiers
leaned out between the doors, friendly, eager for a bit of
conversation with the overtired irritated crowd that stood
waiting among suitcases and Mitropa booths, immobile like
the freight trains on the sidings, because the brakemen were
pulling switches everywhere, not only toward the south, and
the loading ramp had not even been cleared. Meanwhile, the
city garrison was opening its gates, army trucks began flood-
ing the street with their headlights, kept in contact with red
light signals, motorcycles raced ahead to the crossings, sprung
horizontally to block the lanes, waved trolleys and trucks and
private cars and pedestrians to a halt with crossed, uncrossed,
crossed arms, formation after formation filed past the traffic
lights and the eyes of the waiting people who watched the
mysterious white circle reappear at regular intervals with its
Cyrillic letters: OUTCHEBNAYA (driving school). As soon
as the empty train came across the bridge, before it entered
the station, brakemen rushed at it and tore it and plucked it
apart (the soldiers were still leaning out over the platform, the
south and north trains weren't moving, the tracks were empty,
unused) finally the shock of cars against the hump, the clear-
track signal, the second military train got under way, we're
rid of that one, now the third: tanks with their drivers sticking
out to the hips, directing turns with circling arms, clumsy
adroit monsters climbing up the loading ramp, brakemen
creeping under cars, closing air hoses, squad after squad pouring from the trucks and up the narrow stairs into the cars.

Megaphones cackled, motors howled, wood splintered delicately under the caterpillar treads, the siding locomotive
hissed away. Now a quick call to the locomotive office, has the
S still not come in, what in the hell are you doing, got to
notify the chief dispatcher that the train is ready, chief dispatcher wants to know can she pull out, okay, go. And now
let's see what we have accomplished. There is a big empty
square on the train sheet between time and space, instead of
the usual neat tight ingenious crochet work, and what runs
horizontally through all this emptiness? three lines and a half.
We're going now. If the waiting traffic has not become hopelessly entangled you'll be caught up by midnight. Of course
you'll have new delays by then. The Russians? The army high
command? Give them my regards. Take it easy now. Take it
easy, Jakob. Yes, take it easy. Say, Jakob . . .
"Yes?" said Jakob.
"What if we had played along with him?" Wolfgang asked.
Jakob asked no further. They knew the guy's name. What if
they had blocked the through tracks like section North? What
if they had shoved the army transports on some siding and let
the regular traffic through as usual?
"They'd still have made it by tomorrow morning," said Jakob,
"and I'm not thinking of the three of us . . . honor monger.
He says he's positively miffed! And you and I would get ourselves arrested. I mean: like playing stupid just for the fun
of it."
Herr Dr. Blach rose to his feet and came into the light. The
clerk sat waiting. Jonas cleared his throat and said: "And
you would have acted according to your convictions."
"That's what I mean by playing stupid," said Jakob with a
smile. He bent toward the woman and shook her hand. "Good
luck, Herr Abs," she said. "I'm not miserable," he said. They
all smiled.
Today Bartsch says he'd already felt something funny that
night. The way Jakob had stood there, with his coat over his
arm, as though he didn't know where to go now.

— And second: finding a safe place for a manuscript. Blach
had taken a room at the Elbe Hotel

late that evening he sat with Jakob a table away from where,
a few days earlier, Cresspahl's daughter had gained an un-
favorable impression of the local service. The waiter was clearing away the plates; Jakob said—his speech had never
sounded so Pomeranian to Jonas—"Isn't it awful?" It was not
a question. He was not asking Jonas. His heavy overtired face
hung lonely oblique, supported by one hand. The eyes were
half-closed, inaccessible: and once again Jonas wondered how
he could come to understand Jakob. Because Cresspahl was
so far away, and his mother had disappeared, and Gesine's
mad visit, all that didn't help, all these people had their own
actions that did not explain one another. Impossible to know
if Jakob had been thinking of a certain peculiarity of democratic highschool politics. Perhaps fatigue had pushed the
words on his lips, the same way it had resurrected the long-
drowned tender intonation of his childhood by the river because, without transition or change of breath or facial expression, Jakob turned and signaled the waiter with two raised
fingers and said "sto gram," and now his conduct even
matched the quietly pleased face of the waiter. Jakob leaned
forward and began, concerned, eager: "Jonas,"
how would he like to become a brakeman, he asked him.
Everybody could find work there. They were forever short
of brakemen. Whereupon Jonas remained true to character
and asked, how so? Why didn't people want that job?
Yes-yes, said Jakob. It doesn't pay well. Looks simple: just
running back and forth with the wheel chocks, jumping on
a train, watching for the signals, locking the couplings, con-
necting the air hoses, but that's already quite a lot. Besides,
it's dangerous. With all that running, everything is greasy and
you slip and an engine rams you; did you watch all that business at the hump? And exhausting: a man who'd work on two
tracks before now has to take care of four sometimes, so he
often has to climb through the cars to get to the other track,

and something comes rolling along there, now the signal is usually vertical, that means quickly you push it down. And, Jonas, there is a shortage everywhere, many have gone to the West or into the army, the others find better jobs for themselves, that's only natural. But for you it would be interesting, so much new, constant exercise, lots of fresh air.

Constant contact with people: thought Jonas. "Sure, sure," he said. He'd think about it. And then he added in the same breath: "No, certainly not."

"That a man can always pick what he likes and vouch for: you call that freedom?" asked Jakob. Jonas listened for irony in his seriousness. "Da sdrastvooyet tvaya slava," Jakob said seriously. Da sdrastvooyet tvaya slava. And good health. And a long life. Yes.

"You know I don't understand," Jakob began again. "Why don't you go to the West? Since you have Gesine there and they'd let you work again in your field. . .?"

"That is no reason for running out on the Republic," said Jonas politely. "It's enough for being met at the station, hello, so there you are, it's enough for room and board and help you get a new start; but I would have to live there," said Jonas. He realized that Jakob didn't understand his reasons nor did he want to probe them just now, he merely wanted to hear them. The bottomless emptiness of fatigue, of being fed up, when a man is too tired to replenish himself, is forced to live off other people's realities, accepts them without judgment. You know, I don't understand. Jonas shook his head and took it all back. "She happens to love somebody else."

"My little sister," said Jakob surprised, smiling an astonished smile. "Tchelovyek! Sto gram!" he called. He leaned back, happy, he had the heavy resilient expanded intonation of the Russians when he said: "And now let's drink to her health."


JONAS
*She didn't tell him, I thought. She'll never tell him, I thought. I searched for exterior self-affirmations, something to set me*

*apart and give me a position: I was impeccably dressed, somewhere overhead was a hotel room with two briefcases, for the moment I was here, inconspicuous, sitting at a table, tomorrow I'd be gone. I was passing through. That was the attitude I tried to convey, facing him with the threadbare availability of a definitely limited visit, polite, and all the while it came welling up inside me again and again like now: can't you see that they renounced. . . that she was thirteen and he eighteen when he was given to her, unexpectedly, a gift from fathomless foreign skies, how he must have stayed out of her way with his love affairs, substitutes all of them, one's sister is always too young for that kind of confidence, and then she was eighteen and couldn't stand keeping anything secret from him, they discussed everything with the detached reserve sympathy advice of brother and sister: which they were forced to remain to each other if it were to be at all bearable. I know how it was for me; but nobody will ever know how it must have been for both of them. Perhaps I would see her again after a long time (after six-eight-ten years, not even that depends on me) and I would recognize the intent watchful movement of her eyes, her mockery expressed by hands folded under the chin, her distant unreachable silence as she sits far back in her chair surrounded by people who are all talking to her with tense animation, as ignorant as I of this unique non-interchangeable life of hers. By then I, too, would have become filled with various outward traits: almost with the quick forceful capable movements of a brakeman who jumps across between two cars an instant before the bumpers hit, and straightens up, and tightens the coupling with a few casual pushes, bends and vanishes like a shadow into the steam haze between the wet greasy rails, I'm waiting for the car, placidly, the wheel chocks in one hand, not a second too soon I bow down, bring the screeching wheels to a sliding, a grinding, a final halt. . . and all the other things one sees brakemen do from the pedestrian crossing above the station. But all these weighty concrete contents occupations expressions of life will not keep me from watching myself to the minutest detail. At the height of fear and haste I'll still see myself run like an "indistinct shadow into the steam haze, between the wet greasy. . ." I'll never learn to live her way. I'll always say: And what comes next? What is the social judgment of my conduct? What prompted me to change my way of living, away from the security of habit? I wouldn't believe anything I'd say or think while she'd be slipping into her coat, blindly sure of herself, and walk out without a twinge of doubt, as right as a young horse that's being harnessed for the first time, it tries to scrape the halter off his head with his forefeet, some manage to get them off, who hasn't seen the slender nimble colts in the sunny meadows from the window of a passing express— incidentally equipped with radio and restaurant facilities, claiming your attention with concerts and coffee trays even if you happen to look out the window: I'll be leaving tomorrow morning: With the memory of the barman's shabby familiarity, of the photographed heads of State on the wall above the brandy bottles, retouched to make them look two-dimensional, of bits of conversation and dreadful music and hot sultry crowded flesh on the dance floor under the noisy loudspeakers Hottest hottest desert sand—far from my beloved land: years and years of dire strife—work work work, my bitter life: day in day out no luck no home—far away and so alone. The couples who are dancing to that must have some thoughts: which ought to prove that I may be right at least in this. A neat scientific assumption.*

Sometimes an early October morning will look like June in certain closely defined areas (a square of pavement, a view from a window, a housefront, gardens with high fences around them), the same dense hard radiant light of about ten in the morning in June. It needn't be a clear day. Often it is no more than a thick petal-white eye in the midst of gray choppy clouds that gleams like bright hot summer. But if one opens the window and leans out over the clean light-warmed pavement, one feels the wind brush chillingly along the house; outside the city, the distance to the edge of a forest, a railroad crossing, a small mound, is a clear grayish blue that forces itself upon the onlooker; and even riding across the Elbe River inside the blond wood of a long streetcar, blinking into the powerful light screen, one feels the chill. (Has everybody been taken care of? Tickets please. Jakob felt so strange, without his uniform and his pass, he had been clutching his twenty pfennigs since the moment he got on, afraid he might forget to pay.) And it doesn't take an open door sucking in the wind: one needn't know that it gets darker sooner, it's enough to look at the water. The water looks cold.

Jöche's hands were drying each other on a torn smudgy towel, the towel flew onto a wheel, dangled, hung still. Jöche mumbled something to himself and backed down the narrow steps. He stood still, pushed one hand against his forehead making his cap slant even more jauntily above his hair; he looked at the weather. The sky was not so blue any more, but still very clear. Angrily, without a word, Jöche shook his hard bony angular head and walked along the tracks past the high signal poles over to the passenger station. Whenever he walked alone, he walked with eyes cast down. He hoisted himself onto the high ridge and paced the platform from end to end. He held himself very straight which became even more evident because of his long dangling arms and bent neck.

He couldn't find Jakob at first. Then he noticed a young man under the clock at the window of the newsstand, he only saw his profile and a dark blue Sunday suit with a high-collared shirt and a black tie, a stranger with a light short coat over one arm; the heavy thought-bowed head under the short hair, seen this way, from the side, a simple silhouette, made one think of reproductions of old coins in encyclopedias. Funny: thought Jöche (this was his word): whether he looks at one or not—and he's visibly looking at me—one feels like a spectator. Funny. Jakob picked up his change, looked up without

surprise, took a step forward toward Jöche. They shook hands.
Jöche made some remark about how elegant Jakob looked.
Jakob answered with a wink. He offered Jöche a cigarette. He
only had his coat and a smallish suitcase that one could have
carried under one arm, he might have three shirts in it and a
towel. The platform was not particularly crowded, isolated
travelers stood here and there in the blinding sun that came
slanting down the roof. The wind swept through in chilly
asthmatic gushes.

"That one can't do a thing about it," Jöche said bitterly.
Jakob asked how long he had had to wait last night. But that
wasn't what Jöche meant. "I don't know if I'd have driven
them," he said doubtfully, ponderingly. His teeth caught a
corner of his mouth. He had very light gray eyes that looked
like his character: a narrow hard unbending bridge of friendship memories reliability. Jakob spun his cigarette between
two fingers before he looked up. He had always squeezed his
eyes together but today he looks as though he did it by
frowning, not even a frown, more like a muscle swelling under
the skin between his eyes, it doesn't move doesn't change
doesn't get smaller. I shouldn't have said that to him. Of
course I'd have driven them. I might have been unfriendly.
"And why, I mean: what do you want to do something
about?" asked Jakob. He had thrown the coat over his
shoulders and was looking at Jöche, direct, attentive, he
wasn't smiling. "Because they're a bunch of liars, they take
a word right out of your mouth and wipe their asses with it."
But the violence in Jöche's voice was mainly surprise. They
dropped the subject. Jakob's eyes hadn't moved. The right
corner of his mouth twisted once, then it was over.

"So you're off, ole boy," Jöche said and smiled and watched
the coming and going on the platform with interested pleasure. The train board had already been hung up. It was
express-red and bore various West German names that filled
one with a sense of loss and distance. The loudspeaker even
took the trouble of informing the few passengers of the car
locations. "Listen to that braying," Jöche said with enthusiasm,

pointing his cigarette to the loudspeaker. "And you've got a dining car," he gave Jakob a worried look. "Come back," he said.

Jakob smiled: "I'm going to see Cresspahl's daughter," he said. They both laughed. That had been no answer. Jöche now knew that, if anything should happen, he was to get in touch with Cresspahl. Otherwise nothing. Because in those days you took a passport photograph and your identity papers to your police station, laid them on the banister in front of the tables and made a short application on an ordinary sheet of paper. Ten minutes later you walked out with your exit permit and straight to the station if the case was pressing. (Those who were in a hurry gradually gathered on the opposite platform where the express from Berlin was due any moment.) And this permit would have been refused Jakob, if instructions had not come from Berlin over teletype after an extremely brief conversation between Herr Rohlfs and the personnel director of the Railroad Head Office. . . and of this Jöche had no idea. And Jakob himself knew the precise details only through Sabine.

"I signed," said Jakob. Declaration! I was told today that I am not allowed to set foot on or drive through West German territory—or West Berlin—unless I have a special authorization from my personnel director. / And when and if authorized, I may not carry any official documents while setting foot in or driving through said areas. / This also applies to private trips outside of business hours. / Place, date, signature. II/15/52 — C 324/55 16: great. They had given him the wrong form. They had no others. Actually this was supposed to be a pledge that he would come back. They merely took his railroaders' pass away and reminded him that, through his work, he knew much that was secret; they even issued him a free ticket although free tickets were no longer supposed to be issued to West German destinations. Herr Rohlfs' memory was extremely accurate. "Well, so long as you signed," said Jöche. "Give my regards to your mother," he said.

For the last three minutes they talked about Dr. Blach and

therefore that same afternoon Jöche was let in by Jakob's landlady and found a longish envelope on the table which he was to hand over to Cresspahl, or to Jonas himself if he could manage to recognize him from the description—if not, ask him to show you his identity card—and don't stick it in the bookshelf. "To think," said Jöche, quietly perplexed, "to think that this train will be at Gesine's tonight, and every day it comes through here. . ." Jakob only nodded. It didn't feel like parting. They both looked toward the end of the train where the conductor was folding his arms above his head. The hoses stiffened under the compartment floor. "I'll go now," said Jöche. He stepped back and ran off across the platform. When the train passed the locomotive office, one engine suddenly let loose a short shriek, Jakob bounced from his seat and pulled at the window, waving with his other hand. But Jöche was nowhere to be seen and long left behind.

Toward noon the wind shoved hard against the train, a wet wind. The sky stayed a leaden white until nightfall.

— You WANTED JAKOB to explain my world to me.

— I didn't mean to imply that you needed tutoring. I relied upon your democratic high school to teach you some of the rudiments of the class struggle. The causes and the history of injustice: about capitalist economy and the essential aims of the revolution. At least for the duration of a class, a lecture (minutes are sufficient), you must have tried to apply these notions to reality, to test them; in one arbitrary second the traffic, a bombed-out house, always symbolizes the First German State of the Workers and Peasants in which traces and chronology point to the annihilation of fascism, exploitation, and inhumanity; in such an instantaneous surprising involuntary realization one's learning becomes reality, even if it does not correspond to absolutely everything one sees. And it has nothing to do with one's teachers.

— You have a peculiar conception of adolescence. That must

have been your own experience, it applies mainly to yourself.
— Already in class the theory of the surplus value seemed
alien, like the compulsory lectures on Marx and Lenin, probably stayed that way voluntarily; but you dropped it without
having gotten over it, without having refuted it; it became
the memory of justice.
— You thought Jakob a person of justice, but that was not
your brand of justice.

GESINE

*my entire being was contentment. I knew one thing only:
what I wanted began to happen (together with the fear of
possible loss). "Hello," I said. In my haste I had crawled over
my legs on the couch to the phone, one knee was squashing an
ankle, my dress was no longer a dress but a straitjacket,
tight across the shoulder blades, pulled and pushed out of
shape. I was nothing but a hand a mouth a head at the telephone. This is how a desk clerk puts through a call, not the
operator. It couldn't be long distance. "The way you welcome
me," said Jakob's voice. When Jakob telephones, the receiver
lies in the hollow of his hand, with two fingers stretching
along his temple; things always have a way of fusing with
him. "How are you?" I asked. I was afraid to hear him say
where he was, I wanted my hope to grow, to diminish in small
bearable portions. "I'm playing deaf and dumb," said his
voice. "I did everything Cresspahl told me, I took the streetcar and carried my suitcase, but they took it from me. I'm being served right and left. Anything else the gentleman might
desire? I said I'd call them to help me take off my shoes. They
saw my permit. They know where I'm from. That they needn't
bother. They wanted to take me on a guided tour through
the house. I think deaf and dumb is the height of distinction."
I cradled the phone in one arm and crawled along the couch
to the window, not letting the receiver from my ear. Under
the blue neon letters over the hotel entrance, the lights of the
waiting cabs shone in the wet haze of thin fog mixed with the*

*precious smell of gasoline; in one of the cosily illuminated
windows opposite, below me, Jakob was lying across his room
phone, reporting to me on the differences. I realized that this
was meant to amuse me. It wasn't as simple as waiting in the
station any more, as the disappointed hurt, the furtive going
home, although we had merely missed each other; on the
table before me lay his last letters, the one about bridge-
building among them, a letter in which I had apparently read
only Jakob, the way Jakob tells something, watches something,
understands something—about two masons and an enthusiastic engineer ("he worked like a dog. Then we didn't give
him the okay, he wanted to save money. We made him tear
it down again, only later they told us the business about his
overtime") and something that can hardly be referred to as
socialism. I had seen nothing but a project in it, imagined
Jakob leaning on his spade, talking to the others on the high
river bank among the bushes; not before now, only now did
his stern disgusted anger about the reception in a West German hotel prepare me for changes in my way of living, he
would examine and not just let pass the things I innocently
overlooked, he is angry about so much service. Who wouldn't
like to let himself be served? I would. And I would cross the
streets and let the revolving door propel me out of the chilly
humidity into the dry commercial radiator air of the hotel
lobby. The doorman would be waiting to lead me from the
vestibule to the armchair with a deaf and dumb Jakob sitting
in it, not comprehending, ultra-distinguished, and I'm forgetting the fear of cleanliness that would make its appearance,*

— but in one respect you are right. All during dinner we
spoke of nothing but those hopelessly decadent British. Nothing else seemed to matter to me any more even.

HERR DR. BLACH was staying at his friends' house.
In the morning he'd lie awake in a bright friendly room with

bookshelves along the walls, furnished for a life of the mind, he could have described each piece from the memory of countless evenings of discussions and friendship that were sufficiently detached not to make demands on him. Cool happy sunlight filtered in through the blinds. Outside, the gardens wore thick fog-mufflers. The day was expecting him like a splendid possibility, without appointments. His tongue recalled the alcohol's bitter taste, former conversations rehearsed themselves in his head, without direction, last evening was the promise of new darkness for tonight: he had long been accustomed to working to deserve the end of his day rather than participating simply in the natural satisfying process of nightfall when lights were no longer just bright but also warm, this time of year.

Soon after the mailbox flap clicked and a thick paper package went plunk on the foyer floor, he heard his friends move into the bathroom. They were walking on tiptoe, they didn't want to wake him, he was the guest. Manfred left for work. Soon after, he got up. Lise looked pretty as a picture from head to toe, all washed and happy, dressing her child, setting the breakfast table, a picture of hospitality: seen through hot tea and fresh rolls and loving housewifely care the world stopped at the door of their apartment; in a certain sense she had been right, known the better way, she had her child on the chair beside her, was feeding it tenderly, one couldn't dispute that. They knew each other from college days, besides: he was fond of her now that she had become happy. (*Jonas*) *But I sat wishing that time had stopped in Cresspahl's bright sun-warmed room next to his workshop, her fingers springing into the keys, wild completely untrained graceful precise, she'd wait for the next sentence her head to one side, a smile digging into the corners of her mouth, the eyes narrow with thinking—before she said it. Before I realized that I had been looking at her, and at me, at us (since when. For how long) from the outside, petrified in the wished-for studious harmony of endless living together. I too let myself be deceived by the way it looked: and to this day I see her, I imagine seeing her, put the newspaper down against the shaking light-speckled back of the seat in front of her, in the bus, in the streetcar, and stare straight ahead of her and say in a low bitter voice, to no one but herself, "those hopelessly decadent British," is it because she doesn't just watch, the way I do, but disapproves as Cresspahl's daughter? shaking her head, stubborn, refusing to understand? True, I understand her. Now I do. I would not have wanted to impose a breakfast table upon her, every morning.* He insisted that he had appointments in town. One can't just be a guest for want of something to do, therefore (although the newspaper had been unfolded invitingly next to his cup and the study had been heated especially for him and the latest scientific books and magazines lay fanned out for him on Manfred's desk) he helped her carry the dishes to the kitchen and rode the cold rattling streetcar for half an hour into the city, carrying nothing except gloves, waiting all day for evening to come. He was not surprised that he got into the habit of watching.

Some days he'd go to the library after lunch. He'd take the sidewalk parallel to the streetcar under the dirty wind-plundered linden trees, the wind spun the leaves like tops about his shoes; however, he'd also watch himself and to his satisfaction he did not slip into the poetry of falling leaves and autumn paths. He didn't feel like ordering a book, it would have meant waiting for it, making arrangements for the following day; he ended up in the magazine section; there was a wait for official publications, West European Communist papers were finally coming through. He understood the language of the city, he did not stand out as a stranger, and in the evening especially, in the bright busy noisy midtown streets, he'd compare the empty stretches and the gawky sinister ruins to the bustling crowds and think of picking up the broken-off social thread, to live in this city: but then he'd think that newness, the attraction of a different place, were not enough after all to make a fresh start. He merely said and remembered: that the suburbs are all around the city, separated by wide parks from the city proper, for each street road path a sign told you whether you were allowed to drive or walk or ride, and at what speed. The willows were still green. The rivers spread endlessly under gigantic bridges, the water stood knee-high about the sturdy pillars; and when people tossed bread into the water gulls came swooping down, obligingly, and glided above the food which they refused to pick up and then they silently disappeared. The evening fog had a taste of chimney smoke: it could have been any city. It was not his fault alone that he saw it that way, but that was the way it was.

Herr Bessiger made a great number of phone calls on his behalf, and apparently conscious of his scientific abilities a certain Herr Dr. Blach would sit and wait outside offices of directors of institutes; moreover, he had come equipped with regards from his boss and made an amiable pleasant visitor also insofar as he readily agreed that things were extremely uncertain for the time being, except, perhaps, the prospect of a third world war.

He accepted an invitation to a lecture in his field. He began to feel good immediately, that afternoon, in the narrow high seminar room with books standing shoulder-high along the walls, with their black spines and neatly pasted white labels, their sheer volume affirmed the tangibility of scientific research and insight. The lamps suggested evening. From the bombed-out part of the building, through the scantily repaired fourth wall came the incessant worried cooing of pigeons. The students arrived in wet coats, wind-fresh out of the twilight, Jonas was glad of Manfred's arm about his shoulder, glad to be led into the warmth in a constant stream of words, glad to be sat down in the back row with more intent cordial confidential talk, because it established him to quite a number of persons as: Herr Dr. Blach from Berlin, a guest. (And later they would drive out and eat supper with Lise and talk on until midnight, the three of them, in the warm night-quiet house as though, all through the day, they had been waiting for this undisturbed afterwork gathering get-together discussion.) Smoking was permitted. From his

protected seat in the dry heat near the radiator against the
wall with the pigeons he could see the students and remember the many-voiced sound of learning, of news passed
on, the progression of knowledge reminded him of the passage
of light (a comparison to physics except for the onrush of
early-morning radiance) and when the professor turned to
him and he answered and all the faces turned toward the back
of the room, he felt completely accepted, completely at ease,
and everybody listened to what he had to say and drew him
into conversations and he had no reason to doubt his official
capacity as a guest-participant; the arrival of the professor—
who sat lost in his armchair, tired with age, but held his head
high, extremely awake, and kept glancing about as he talked;
words were not enough too polished threadbare to express
the giant maze of proved and assumed facts, tirelessly he'd
add to his sentences, break them off ruthlessly as soon as they
led to something new, he had completely renounced clocktime
and the present, he moved exclusively in the past that filled
his mind with its time and space: the arrival of the professor
revived certain moments in Herr Dr. Blach, again he felt his
boss' thin bony old man's arm as he led him down the high
marble halls to the auditorium, again he felt himself sitting
at the foot of the podium watching the yellow-skinned spotted
hands lie casually across the notes, the overstrained distinct
voice wove an artful pattern of a remembered reconstructed
past—only at that period did Anglo-Saxon lyricism find its
subjective expression. Today's changes can be understood
from more than the shifting of social structure, once again
nothing mattered more between four and five P.M. He did
not take notes. His waiting for it all to be over could only be
impatience, he was not wishing for anything else. He analyzed
it further: thought his uneasiness was the result of his personal situation, had no importance. Because, apparently, other
people were able to take clean conscientious notes and to raise
their hands and suggest additional problems that had been
prepared long in advance, like Herr Bessiger (whose mind
was not wandering) who had been equally eager to discuss

the tremendous tension of the comparison—that could be calculated in its details but not conceived in context—at home. For instance: July twenty-six was the fourth anniversary of the Egyptian Revolution. I would not have nationalized the Suez Canal on any old Tuesday either. The Aswan Dam was as vital to them as heavy industry to the German Democratic Republic: at the risk of prosperity and prestige. Of course they needed credit . . . which the West refused them, imperialism in the guise of capitalism, so they seized the Canal, the moral angle is apparent: the total profit, in 1955, had amounted to one hundred million dollars—of which Egypt got three. Anybody who doesn't happen to own half the shares, like the British government, will say: this is the only honest issue. Let's apply for a visa. How come then that we immediately change our attitude when we hear that these honest people have outlawed the Egyptian Communist Party? Which, as long as it is not in power, is supposed to represent the truly progressive element; a single infraction against the theory scares us away, but what if it was necessary? Consequently, the bombers that British and French capital send flying over Egypt are supposed to represent a plausible reaction with the rules of political physics. And the Red Army's advance against the Hungarian revolt is nothing but a successful experiment in the physics lab. Is it tolerable that reality takes place and we censure it according to its adherence to or infraction of theoretical rules? At least for one's personal situations one ought to make decisions. The question Why don't you go to the West should be properly phrased Why are you staying here.

"Because the theory of the surplus value is right, because socialism won't always stay the way it is," said Lise.

The way we learned it. What we grew up with. What we must keep in mind at the start of the spiral which we measure and remeasure in sure-footed leaps, up, always upward, up to that certain point from which a man can fall and break his neck if his life is based on it. What is certain is not certain, what is will not stay that way, and never becomes today right

now. I don't understand. As though I didn't feel the rain.
Which I see.

"Where are you staying?" asked the professor when Jonas bid
him goodbye. He nodded when he heard Herr Dr. Blach was
staying with old college friends. It seemed to reassure him
somehow.

— BUT YOU COULD HAVE asked him why he wanted to go on
that trip.

— And he would have repeated what he said on the application he sent in to the Railroad Head Office through the official
channels, according to regulations: that he wanted to see his
mother. He probably figured his application wouldn't remain
where he put it. But perhaps he preferred not to discuss it
with the State in person, and besides I would not have gained
anything from additional information.

— And every time Jakob saw a wine-red mud-speckled Pobyeda crawl across the street . . . he thought of Herr Rohlfs and
knew that he was watching over him day and night.

— And every time I drove home at night through the tunnels
along the railroad tracks, every time an express thundered
across a road, with the cool clear outlines of its lighted windows in the dark and one guessed the bright warm space
inside the racing oblong, I thought: this is the kind of oblong
he rode off in; or we'd walk down a platform, deeply engrossed
in other things, and it would be one of the lesser-known
details: a squat leather rectangle of a conductor's satchel for
instance, leaning against a pillar together with one of the sooty
red lanterns on the end of a train. . . and every time I go on
living Jakob's—to me unknown—day, up to the moment of
remembering, and because the express coaches were the West
German type as I happen to know, I'd continuously see
Jakob arrive behind one of these low roundish windows in
West German stations, and I'd look at a poster with the

standard of living it portrayed, and I'd think: Take a look at it, Jakob. But take a good look.

— Yes. If he had been you. You would have come and told all of us on the other side of the border that our way of life is wrong.

— I know: whereas Jakob only went to see his mother.

— Why won't you admit the difference? You would call it: he went to see capitalism. Which doesn't exist, I might add, as long as the boom lasts. First, we have the tangible consequences of the proletariat's relative impoverishment—or the inevitable crash—then comes the class struggle, and finally it all boils down to the laws of economics; however, the reality of such a viewpoint decreases with every step.

— The personal experience potential decreases.

— The personal experience potential if you like. The theory of the surplus value is that kind of abstract recognition, it can't be readily applied to concrete persons and circumstances, like the theory that socialism must triumph in the end—which may be even more abstract since socialism has not yet materialized and exists solely in the institutions which try to establish it: in the form of lectures. My thinking isn't abstract enough to see a hopeful future (a hope that nothing warrants, in the present) behind the Hungarian uprising and its suppression, like you perhaps, or Dr. Blach: each advance provokes a reaction, and vice versa; I don't even know the meaning of those two words.

— Let's take Jakob's visit to City Hall. (I don't know if he went there.) It varies from place to place, approximately it goes like this: The visitor from the East is requested to furnish some kind of proof of his actual factual presence in the city. Upon which he receives a welcome, possibly ten West marks, a free ticket to the movies, a booklet of bus or streetcar tickets and free access to the swimming pools.

— We knew all about that. Cresspahl tried it once, so Jakob didn't bother. We spoke of it and I'm sure he shook his head. (With the same—how shall I put it—distinction he used with the hotel employees to protect a visitor from the East: by just not giving in to anything, by simply not "behaving" himself. He wanted nothing, wanted to be considered for nothing but the use and payment of his room, only the business angle seemed worth mentioning.) Actually his headshake showed such a lack of understanding (irony or annoyance would have been preferable) he seemed like a complete stranger: and bewildered.

—And that isn't proof enough for you?

— It isn't. Because he'd come to visit, not to examine. And because all day I was waiting for evening, for the bus that takes the German employees back to the city from a forest some fifty miles of superhighway along the Rhine (I'm giving you a geographical detail. I hope it's of no use to you) and I forgot to imagine what kind of day he'd had. When I saw him again it was evening, he was standing on one of the traffic islands outside the central station; it wasn't as though he'd spent all day waiting, except that he didn't stand there like a young man from around here with plans and appointments who knows how to while away ten minutes, usefully, elegantly with newspapers and a cigarette, he looked lost standing there with his hands behind his back, immobile, it looked as though he were going to stand there forever. I asked him how he'd spent his day; he pursed his lips and looked pensive, finally he laughed and said: doing nothing; then he began telling me about various incidents, it wasn't supposed to be criticism, just amused surprise: like his first telephone call from the hotel that had been supposed to be amusing. The next morning he called and invited me over for breakfast, and although it takes at least three minutes to run across

the doorman rose at the first sound of her shoes on the grating, he walked to the door and held it open for her. To him she seemed to arrive out of the morning grayness with her mist-shimmering kerchief, the way she stood in the lobby with her head down low as though the black grooves between the shiny wet slabs of the pavement had pressed themselves into her brain through her eyes, with her feet stepping over them;

the sight of her careful planned arrival and her breakfast
with Jakob in the morning-cool, tidy, empty dining room
looked more important secret interesting to an hotel employee's anticipation: one day the visitor would no longer be
sitting in the dining room, so she could no longer arrive at
this hour from afar and enter the temporary rationed home of
this hotel, and then nobody would wish her a good morning
the way he (the doorman) was wishing her a good morning:
formal, with fatherly concern—which was surely permissible,
the way she looked. Because in a conversation with the waiter
he expressed the opinion that the lady didn't look like she'd
come from the East, "but when you can't live without visits
from back there, first the parents and now this one, then you
can't be happy here. Either one or the other, but you can't
have both"

— each time I was surprised to see him without his uniform,
without the silver epaulettes and stars and collar mirrors,
without a trace of purpose and reliable occupation. I left
him my keys, but on my way out to work I saw him stay in his
chair as though he would sit there until noon, in smoking
thinking immobility, even to the waiter it can't have looked
like experienced idleness.

HERR ROHLFS
*But that part I'll leave her, I won't take it away from her.*
*Surely he went up to her apartment from time to time, looking*
*the place over to see if there wasn't a job for him somewhere.*
*Perhaps Cresspahl had talked her into buying an antique*
*armchair, such things have a way of getting broken, I can*
*picture Jakob examining the damage between thumb and*
*forefinger, perhaps bits of veneer have peeled off, old wood*
*is fragile, he puts his coat back on and goes downstairs to buy*
*sandpaper and plastic wood and glue and a screwdriver, and*
*in the evening, when she hangs her coat over the back of the*
*chair, it feels different, the chair looks different. He may have*
*kneeled on the floor for an hour and sanded out the damaged*

*spot and filled it with putty and let it dry and pressed the
veneer back into shape and driven the dowel in, carefully,
turning the screwdriver in his hollow hand, and felt the spot
with his fingers to see if it was all right now. . . or he might
have shopped for their supper before he went to meet her at
that stupid NATO bus, standing in grocery stores choosing
each item with the greatest care, thinking how he might surprise her, what's her favorite sausage, and because he was the
thoughtful type he'd feel a certain satisfaction as the shopping
bag grew heavier and heavier, and he'd go home and set the
table. . . or she'd find a book started, open on a shelf, when
she came home, a sign that he had been sitting in her room,
been using her apartment, had looked out of her windows
from time to time. . . : we can't quarrel about where he really
was at home. After all: I did let him go.*

— As I think about it now, I didn't let him go for any special
reason. Just because he wanted to. We'll go into that later.
— Yes. What sort of cigarettes are those? Do try one of mine.
No, they're not Phillip Morris. And because you had no
qualms about his going, and not only because of that special
sense of justice some people deserve from you
— But also because of a kind of thoroughness, you'd have
another word for it, let me explain: You have
— we capitalists have
— certain deceptive comforts, I mean a certain result of un-
hampered private initiative, of free competition. In certain
respects the consumer doubtless fares better. You see, we—
let me say—socialism cannot, at present, for the moment,
afford to have a man stand at a corner in one of the suburbs
and count the people who pass there every day on their way
into the city. He counts them going to work, to the office, to
school, the women who go shopping, the people who come
home for lunch, the moviegoers, couples who go out for the
evening; at the end of the day he has a certain number of
checks on the back of his cigarette box and he adds them up.
When it looks like it might pay off, he buys ten buses on credit

and runs a commuter service and after three weeks he has recovered his investment, with the prospect of a sevenfold return: it's nice to take the bus into the city instead of a twenty-minute walk. But it wasn't for the passenger's benefit. It looks like service to the customer, it is so surprising to a visitor from the East that he gets caught up in it, he may forget that the principle of free competition has other, less pleasant results, like overproduction, mass unemployment, armaments, war. Even without these scientific facts in back of him, Jakob would have been embarrassed by the salesman's nervous anguish: that the customer might walk out without making a purchase. This "thoroughness" probably made you too painfully aware of certain minor aspects, which was enough in itself, one needn't immediately speak of: proofs of the inhuman sides of capitalism. For instance: he liked the technical perfection of the *Bundesbahn* and the so-called traveling comfort, but he made envious comparisons
— "to think that they run their expresses with one man," he said. He was shocked. Again he didn't understand, disapproved. Naturally I didn't understand before he explained to me that putting a train together and getting it ready and all the wasted cars and the maintenance and the service of the conductor and the engineer on a three- to five-hundred-mile run with eight or ten cars seems something of an exaggeration for one single conductor, besides being too cheap for so much work. But it wasn't his intention to disgust me with trains and buses. And besides.

GESINE

*"I want to show you something," I said. I took him by the arm and steered him through the station to the top of the stairs; from there you can see the traincaller's booth. "Look at him," I said; I had wanted to show this to Jakob, but I found myself fascinated with the head of the man behind the glass, he was wearing a cap that said Information in yellow letters, his eyes roved so mechanically officially over the train schedule that*

*hung before him, his brain translated the figures into pre-
cise inhuman lip movements; we couldn't hear him from
where we were standing, his words were spilling out of loudspeakers somewhere down over the arriving passengers; he
didn't pause to breathe, didn't welcome them, had no emo-
tions: Frankfurt am Main express seven - oh - seven* P.M. *platform four Cologne express seven-twelve* P.M. *platform three
Basel seven twenty-one* P.M. *ten nineteen thirty six twenty five
four," I forgot to watch Jakob. When I turned I found him
leaning against the banister beside me, a cigarette in his
mouth, bending over the flame between his hollowed hands;
he didn't know I was eager for him to say something, expected
somebody to say something, finally he looked up to the man's
window without a trace of surprise and said: "How do you
think I sit all day? Let's go." If only he hadn't been so silent
with his answers. If only we had asked him the right questions.*

— The way you describe Jakob's visit I can't see it after the
first day. Because he isn't timid. People always interest him.
He must have made lots of friends right away, been out all
day trying to find out: how do they live here in the West?
what's there to do for a man. . .?
— What you imagine would be the conduct of an East
German agitator who goes back once his mission has been
accomplished; or the restlessness of a refugee from your Republic preparing to settle here. I don't know at what point
Jakob decided to go back. He never intended to stay, he
absolutely didn't want to.
— You know I can't interrogate you.
— And if I tell you how he waited for me once, in one of those
suburban restaurants, a men's glee club just happened to be
holding a meeting there, crowded around the piano with a
cigarette and a glass of beer hesitantly humming the melody
after their leader, every so often they'd come over to the
dining room where Jakob was sitting at the bar discussing with

the proprietor all the rain we'd been having, and after some time they got into the depth of Western defense, the singers overheard some of that and right away they wanted to have communism explained to them first-hand by the refugee fresh from the East, when had he come over,

*a beer for our brother from the East*
*have a cigar*
*I'm no brother from the East*
*because you're staying of course*
*No, I'm going back*
*you are? But can a man live back there? Or must you? Family obligations?*
*don't like it here*
*what!*
*listen, what do you mean you don't*
*I'll tell you. It's not so hard to understand. Take that juke box for instance, plays all by itself, a man goes over with his ten-pfennig piece, picks a record, drops the coin into the radiant red-green-angelblue box, a robot arm gropes forward, stops at the selected record, bends, seizes it, lifts it, deposits it on the turntable that has started to spin, goes back, another robot arm with the needle poses itself in the outermost groove, and now the Badenweiler March bellows through the narrow arm into the warm resounding room*
*and why don't you like that*
*because it's the favorite march of the Führer*
*precisely*
*but he's dead*
*and you people are bringing him back to life*
*nonsense, it's beautiful music*
*not to me*
*ah, you've been sent over*
*he's a Communist, all Communists are traitors*
*And Jakob pushed the table over as he got to his feet, care-fully measuring his blows into the smooth smug forgetful faces, a good punch in the nose*

— you hope then that he tried to talk to them (to persuade them), but there was no talking to them. They didn't understand him. I was a little late, I didn't see him. Until it dawned on me that he was sitting at the big table under the noisy cloud of cordiality from the many refilled glasses. I went over and stood close by and heard Jakob trying to explain to a nice young man (who was neither conceited nor prosperous nor arrogant, a good-natured chimneysweep who genuinely loved singing), I listened to Jakob explain that people weren't keeping him alive because of his blue eyes but because they wanted their chimneys swept: that he was a part of society; they all thought that hilarious, and I had to join them for a drink and Jakob received many invitations for the next few days, to lunch, to a workshop, for a drive.

— But he didn't go.

— Why do you take that for contempt, animosity? Embarrassment.

— I can't imagine. He can't have forgotten that it makes sense to be opposed to war.

— Certainly not. Neither did he forget a single principle he had learned in "the Germany that chose the road to socialism," where everything and everybody always encouraged him in these principles, making them seem absolute, as reasonable as life. That was the baggage he came with on his visit, and he couldn't understand the citizens in the West because they'd never heard of these notions. And besides (you interrupted me), when we rode home at night through the brilliant crowded rainy streets and saw the people in the bus, in the hotel, or waited with them at the curb for the traffic lights to change, and heard them talk, or we watched them riding in their cars, squeezed together proud stubborn shoulder to shoulder, or met them on the stairs and wished them a good evening, he cannot have wanted to call their way of living "bad," actually it all seemed very real to him. You think I'm not a good witness, you think I'm prejudiced. You might have been polite earlier.

— It isn't politeness. But I can't listen to you without prejudice or else I mislay Jakob. I can no longer fit him into my memory. What did he have to say about the convoys of the *Bundesarmee* when he saw them appear suddenly, an armed superhuman power, in the midst of everyday traffic, with all the rights of way? I know, you'll say: it made him think of our army. It's obvious, I can even imagine it, but I don't like it. — Yes: before it was less important and occurred in different situations. And it was within the legal authority of the German Democratic Republic. Whereas this is still a tavern in West Berlin, not far from the border. In seven minutes you can take the elevated back to the East (I believe the subway has already been extra-territorialized), and it's ten minutes walk to the elevated station, seventeen minutes make an immeasurable distance.

— You know what makes you so clever?

— My cynicism: I left the progressive Republic years ago. I've made my home here. Even expeditions to Jerichow are no longer necessary now. What do you do with facts you don't like? How do you think Jakob paid his hotel bill?

GESINE

*"Did you sleep well in this luxury hotel of yours?" I asked when the waiter brought hot coffee and was pouring it into our cups, leaning forward between us, I didn't realize what I was saying, I was forgetting that a waiter is an employee of the hotel, all I wanted him to be was a shield in front of my face, to protect me from being looked at. When I did look up, Jakob had nodded and said "yes," his eyes narrow and pensive as though he were trying to remember his sleep, and if that wasn't it, his thoughts had been wandering elsewhere, to the same country where I was at home, and where I suddenly had trouble finding him sometimes: he was right not to have listened to my flippancy—it was the dreaded dreadful strangeness in which he didn't understand me any more, because here, now, I was supposed to be the "West" to him, what would he have said in Jerichow: had a good night's sleep I*

*hope, is that better? And how did I sleep in my luxurious one-room apartment three houses away.*

— But I know about it. It's a sound business principle. First: the products of our people-owned camera industry are too precious to be flooded out onto the market, and second, our economy cannot afford to do without exports. However, each purchaser must present his identity card and the number is copied down. According to my files, Jakob purchased a camera a day before he left. And since it was nowhere to be found when we searched his room, he must have taken it across the border and sold it in the *Bundesrepublik* for something like five hundred West marks. That was plenty to pay his hotel bill with, he must have had something left over. Perhaps he changed it.

— Two legal offenses in one: smuggling and illegal transfer of money. Isn't that how you would phrase it? Jakob trafficked in foreign currency, he harmed the people's economy?

— I don't see why I should call it by another name. But I'm sure he didn't especially plan for the customs, he didn't remind himself to sit honorably, unsuspiciously; when the loudspeakers appealed Please hold your identity papers money and valuables ready for the Border Control (because everything is noted down, to be checked upon return) I'm sure he didn't lift his suitcase down from the rack—with the camera lying on top of his three shirts. If they had opened his suitcase, they would have found it at once, perhaps he waited, smoking, smiling a furtive smile he didn't even bother to hide. I mean: it didn't look like the comportment of a criminal, unless one thinks one can spot a criminal by his awareness of guilt. Incidentally, the purchase slip with Jakob's name and the camera number made me think of the trip to Jerichow.

— Where he would have tricked you to the end if he could have; when you appeared on the highway half a minute after we made it to the quarry, and you played your searchlights to let us know that you knew, then it was impossible.

— He said that?

— No. I do. And you should take into account that you earned
distrust for yourself with a persistence, as though that was
what you were after.

— I take into account that he wanted to trick me.

— But can't you see that you are belittling reality? Is Jakob's
life nothing but a job with the railroad and smuggling a camera? Then you don't understand him. Who would have given
him the money, in the West, to buy a ticket to the refugee
camp? Can't you understand that he wanted to see his mother,
that was all there was to it, that's the important angle?

— We can't ask him.

— Nobody is made of opinions. Do you still know what he
looked like?

— Yes.

But these are photos you selected for the tenth of November,
there were a few others for Jakob and some for his mother, am
I correct? I don't know what you might have been thinking
(Jakob would have said: never mind. At least there'll be
something left of those days), and if you knew of Jakob's
leaving, these photos make me think that he was already
aware of it then: this follows that. But it's not so at all: seen
from today it looks like a sequence, but to Jakob it was only
that particular Saturday; that's what I mean to say.

— We're making up for our oversight. We can be just as
wrong today. These are a few selected photographs. We went
to see her over the weekend. We took the photographs late on
Sunday when it was already half dark, because I didn't want
her to notice. It was to be a surprise. This is the first one, from
the bus stop. You stand on a little hill and look down into the
camp. It is barren earth, nothing grows on it, it was ravaged
and scorched in the war; and scrap heaps. Close to the out-
skirts of the city, little gardens, bungalows, a few scattered
villas; and there's the shopping street as you can see by those
lights. But they looked much paler that day against the sky.
Even the shops are one-story, with corrugated roofs, they
look as temporary as everything else. And the camp, the usual
barracks.

— For labor brigades, foreign war prisoners, convicts, army hospital, German war prisoners, the homeless, and now refugees. With small flower gardens, according to the occupants. There are lovely flowers in the fall.

GESINE

*"Wait a second," he said. He let go of my arm. He stopped under the naked light bulb of a fruitstand halfway down a sidestreet; it had a wooden roof, but the wind came through the open sides. The woman was pointing to the multicolored apple-pear-lemon-orange-tangerine-grapefruit crates, I saw him shake his head. "Here," he said. I gave him my bag in exchange for the flowers. A thick white paper cone full of flowers. I stood still and opened the paper to see their heads, asters from everywhere, and their colors mingled with the poisonous neon signs. "Thank you," I said. "Since nobody else buys you any," he said.*

— They don't seem to have any now. What you see from the gate. . . does the fence run around the whole camp? What is it: barbed wire?
— No, just plain wire. And you need a pass to get in. The refugees are not allowed to go out very often, they wouldn't let us in at all.
— Whereupon you showed the guard your NATO HQ pass, while Jakob
— Jakob stood behind me, hands in his coat pockets, his chin in the collar, trying to look impressive, someone important *"ouas ist ase"* he asked, he had copied that from me, was pretty good at it actually. He thought the whole thing was a laugh.
— But aren't the refugees often questioned by American military personnel?
— That's why they let us in finally. How can you be so interested in everything he said and did! Here is the next one.
— He didn't bother to take his coat off. . . there were other refugees living in that room, were there? I would have recog-

nized her immediately. That's her suitcase, she never un-
packed it. Just sits there and waits. With her hands in her
lap. Did you take it on purpose that way: Jakob's profile half-
shadowed in the foreground and her face behind it, so clear
and sharp with all its wrinkles, and those strained eyelids, it
looks as though everything had stopped.

— They scarcely said a word. Here we are outside again,
when we took her into town.

— You actually see the wind, the way her coat billows. How
tiny she was, and Jakob so enormous beside her with his
hands behind his back . . . but that effect is your doing: their
walking toward the background that way, into a dimmer and
dimmer distance cut by lower and lower lines of wire. Of
course the fence happened to be there. May I see another
one?

— Here. She refused to go into one of the big restaurants,
that's why this one is so dark. She was talking to him and
each time he managed not to listen. This was the one time
he looked at her and answered. Very hesitantly and baffled, I
find, of course she didn't understand him, but then he didn't
understand either that he could have stayed. I mean her half-
open mouth and the staring narrowed eyes, her head seemed
to be weaving all the time, softly, unconsciously. Maybe it
doesn't quite show up that way, they made the print too
light. She's old.

— Yes.

Incidentally, I didn't pay attention to it at the time, but now
I seem to recall: didn't you have this camera in Jerichow
and didn't you take a photograph on our way back to the
autobahn? It's long and narrow, hardly more than a fountain
pen? and completely soundless?

— That was just for fun.


And the picture was already across one wall in Gesine's room
when Jakob arrived. The photograph had been blown up to
something like sixty by forty-eight, reminding one of the in-

dustrial or advertising photos, or of the visual-appeal posters along the streets of the German Democratic Republic on important political occasions; one could tell by the slightly blurred contours that the film had not been larger than the nail on her little finger. The photograph had been taken without light, a certain brightness filtered in from the invisible background in several flat bars: the neon signs of a gas station that was, itself, not in the picture. The right edge ended in the soft shadow of what had been the driver's back and part of the seat; beside him one could make out a corner of the window. There was a hint of Herr Rohlfs' face projected upwards by the glow of his cigarette; the wrinkles across his forehead looked particularly lively, humid, as though quick-frozen, the pensive expression of the half-open mouth may have come from holding the cigarette. Its glow threw light on Jakob's face, making it shimmer gray out of the shadow, his head was slanting backward, the area around the eyes stood out, strangely sharp (the rear window sits high in a Pobyeda), and since the enlargement exaggerated the natural proportions slightly, the onlooker's eyes halted at the raised lower lid: the pupils had furtively focused on the lens, now they were caught in an indifferent stare. Gesine had hung the picture in such a way that one looked at it from the bottom, not the way the camera had seen it. The right and bottom edges were again crammed full with blurred forms of a car's inside in the dark. When Jakob came for supper the next evening he stopped and looked at it. He didn't ask anything. After a while Gesine thought she saw him shake his head. She went over to him. His eyebrows were raised. "I don't think one ought to . . . use a camera that way," he said. "Everything looks alike, you understand? as though Rohlfs might just as well be working for *your* secret service . . . ?" Gesine walked around him and looked at the picture from the other side. Slowly her eyes wandered over to Jakob, compared him to the photograph. Then she too shook her head, but with a pout. Jakob threw up his hands, laughed soundlessly, sat down at the table. "Never mind. Leave it where it is," he said.

HERR ROHLFS

*Should I have gone about it like the dogcatchers? He would not have approved; still, I might have proved to him that I was right. And finally Jakob would have agreed that crimes must be punished to the extent to which we fail to realize the obligations of our time. To the extent to which we miss out. Everybody had been told what to do. I left no doubts about the importance of socialism: anyone who hurts the enemy, helps us; anyone who hurts us, helps the enemy; anyone who holds back, cheats us of a possibility and gives the enemy leeway for a different possibility; the one who does the wrong thing with good intentions is the stupidest of all. Cui bono. Who will benefit. The way the dogcatchers would have gone after Cresspahl for organized singing. She would not have understood. Nor going after Blach for conspiratorial activity. Makes no sense to her. If anybody had claimed that Jakob held up and impeded the railroad traffic? then she would have understood and come running lootshe galoobkee na krishye. Indisputable insofar as Jakob's mother's Sunday churchgoing had nothing to do with socialism, or Blach's applying for a two-year government-endowed research project (fools), or Miss Cresspahl's lying crouching stretching across her table penning letters to her father, for this excursion she had borrowed a car and showed Jakob how to play autobahn: what a fascinating game: you pass me, I pass you, and Cresspahl never went to church; everybody leading his life as though he hadn't been told what to do. The State doesn't degrade itself if it worries about clean sidewalks among other things, and I can't even say that I dropped the reins, it never occurred to me, I allowed a photograph to be taken of me because it made sense under the circumstances: this is my face, take a look at it, Jakob. My words are what count, I mean what I say, no more. I put the decision up to you. I give you*

*the time to think it over, I won't run Cresspahl in for tax
evasion. And she claims I'm less interested in freedom than in
Jakob's esteem and friendship for the authority of the State.
Which I represented . . . and represent. That is part of it:
compulsory decisions are no decisions. To hell with the intention. The intention also includes the knowledge and taking
into account of given circumstances. But man is fickle, only
those who have made up their minds are reliable. Anyone who
can decide his life is also able to decide about other things,
one day the birdie would have decided to stop flying down
on my hand, I'd have turned into a dogcatcher no matter
how. No, not to hell with the intention; I didn't urge anybody
to go to the West, I didn't tell Jakob: you're risking your
life. I thought there was only one answer. And I expected it
from people who don't have my interests at heart. Conversation is an error. "Perhaps you'd have done better to refrain
from this democratic fraternizing. From the question of
choosing between two absurdities. Between the major and
the minor evil." Reality is not absurd I said to him.*

They returned Sunday afternoon from their visit to the refugee camp. The car had a radio, they heard about the suppression of the Hungarian uprising at usual newstime. They
turned off the autobahn and got stuck in the traffic jam on
the sideroads, cars coming home from weekend trips. They
sat bumper to bumper at the intersection, waiting endlessly.
Gesine showered the cars before and beside her with juicy
expressions, but softly, under her breath; she was half lying
across the wheel, staring out into the gray rain, listening with
bent head to the newscaster's voice who was, at this point,
speculating about British and French troops landing in Egypt.
"I bet they're going to land," she said grimly. Jakob shrugged.
He didn't look up. And Gesine had declared that, if they did,
she'd quit her job with the headquarters. She was no longer
watching the road. Her head was lying sideways on the wheel
on top of her right hand; sad and worried, she saw nothing

but her thoughts. Jakob touched her elbow. The traffic was
moving again. At the crossing people were ready to come
running: she had stepped on the starter so violently, she
hardly managed not to hit a car that was coming from the
other side around the corner; their tires screamed on the
pavement: the usual signal for an accident. But they were
already out of sight, and when they listened to the late news
on Monday night and heard that English and French troops
had, sure enough, landed in Egypt, Gesine laughed and said:
"The way we jammed our foot on the brake he and I . . . and
the way we stood there, two strange animals suddenly face to
face . . . " And Jakob said: "You mustn't be so violent, you
hear?" Her face was near him on the edge of the couch, on
one side, lying on her folded hands, she opened her eyes and
let them wander up to him. She examined him gravely,
sensibly, and pouted. Jakob shook his head. Smiled. She
turned her eyes away and stretched out under the cover. "You
know," she murmured. Her voice sounded muffled, she
seemed half asleep. Jakob looked at her tousled hair over the
raised sleepy shoulder, he laughed softly, tenderly. After a
while he stood up, switched off the light, then he went back
to the armchair and sat for almost two hours in the grayness
of the light from the street. She was breathing evenly, the
reflections of the neon signs flitted across her face like flashes
of lightning; she slept as though she were alone.

Jakob got up and stood at the open window in the damp draft.
He heard her stir. "Jakob!" said her voice, emerging from
sleep. He turned and quickly went over to her. She seemed
awake. "What is it?" he asked. She pulled over to one side
and tucked the covers around her to make room for him to
sit down. "I dreamed I couldn't find the way out," she said.
"In Cresspahl's house, you couldn't find the door?" he asked.
She shook her head. She seemed to have difficulty moving.
"Here," she said. Jakob put an arm around her shoulder and
pulled her toward him and said: "See that gray thing on the
left, know where left is? that's the door, then out into the
hall and down the stairs with the light switches glowing red

in the dark so you know where they are." She sat up, she stopped his hand that was going toward the lamp. She lay back, with eyes open. "Where were you?" she asked. That's how they used to ask each other's thoughts. "My dear," said Jakob: "on the Rehberge, flying a kite, and you were there too." And it was even true. Her open eyes in the dim blurred light made him think of flying kites on the Rehberge. She was fourteen, for a week she worked on the kite in Cresspahl's shop, now it was dancing in the huge shredded sky above them. It was very high up, an oblique blue square with a yellow tail. When the sun came out, the whole sky shone because of the kite and her eyes began to grow restless: the clouds looked like white mountains, with artfully constructed crests, they seemed tangible, one might have walked on them. "Stay," she said.
"Come back," he said. Imitating her intonation, mimicking her. But he hadn't wanted to tease her.

GESINE
*I could have said: I'd like to be up there on those clouds.*

She would not let herself be dissuaded from seeing him off. Tired, lost, she stood beside the train; she didn't look up until it started, a soft gliding jolt that came to her as a shock. Jakob did not see her wave. She stood motionless, looking after him, growing smaller and smaller, he might have held her between his two hands finally, when the train left the lighted station, clattered through the first sidings, she was completely left behind, and out of sight.

REPORTS KEPT PILING UP on Herr Rohlfs' desk. He was sitting at the Elbe, in his temporary office, and spent his nights writing preparatory summaries on the birdie-in-the-bush case. His real reason for being here, however, was not to miss Jakob's return. Every now and then he'd drive to the station to meet the incoming interzone trains and stand outside the gate and look for Jakob in the arriving crowd, although he had enough watchers on their toes who would have informed him immediately had Jakob come in. "This waiting is unbearable," Hänschen said at one point. Which meant they had started waiting three days too soon.

Toward morning, while Jakob was getting close to the Elbe (the train was almost empty toward morning. The only other person in his compartment was a young girl who sat, shivering, across from him, too tired to understand the heavy November light and the steady rain and the harsh hasty rattling of the wheels, such children should not be traveling alone through the night, after Jakob had looked at her for a while he remembered the chocolate he had bought in the dining car to get rid of his last West marks before the Border Control, he took it out of his pocket and broke it inside the wrapper and tore the paper open and wordlessly placed the chocolate on the window table, he took a piece, so did she, he chewed the bitter stuff, pulled his coat over himself and went back to sleep. The conductor came and tapped him on the shoulder: it was time to get off. He was a colleague, they nodded to each other, take it easy they said),

toward morning Herr Rohlfs was informed over teletype that Herr Dr. Blach had disappeared. He must have gotten wind of the police raiding the editorial office because the police found his room in a condition that suggested a precipitous departure. If Herr Rohlfs was quite honest with himself he had to admit that his immediate assumption was not that Jonas was, this very instant, rolling toward him in an express from the opposite direction, hardly toward West Berlin; when he was told, it did fit rather neatly into his speculations about the missing manuscript (although one could merely surmise that he had stored it with Jakob or with Cresspahl. Still, Jerichow was a bit out of the way). And Jonas sat up with impatience when his train slowed down and came to a stop in the middle of nowhere; he climbed over the legs of the other sleeping passengers and stood in the corridor, smoking, figuring how many minutes approximately they were away from the Elbe, and from the tower in which Jakob (or one of them) was sitting and had ordered his train to stop. The nerve of that guy.

But Jakob had not gone back to work yet. We know the exact time from his landlady. She heard him come in, very quiet and considerate, but she's always wide awake at this hour before her alarm goes off, she waits for it to ring (she says) she heard him go into the kitchen and he must have changed his clothes because, when she came into the kitchen later, he was standing at the table in his uniform, she remembered saying how tired he looked, but she didn't remember what he answered. But everything else she remembers perfectly, especially what time it was, since that's when he always gets up. Jakob opened the window. They could hear the rain in the silent deep abyss of the courtyard, in the house across from them one window after another lighted up. Then he left as usual to go to the busstop. She doesn't know if he fixed sandwiches for himself for lunch (he still had some chocolate in his pocket). And the gentleman who rang about an hour later and asked for Herr Abs, she was sure she'd recognize him. A young man with hair cut very short, but she'd recognize him by the eyes, he excused himself for the disturbance.

Because Jonas knew only Jakob's address, besides he had been under the impression that Jöche also lived in town, what's he thinking, with the housing shortage. Jöche lives in Jerichow. In the booth outside Jakob's house Jonas dialed the number Jakob had given him, he managed to get as far as Peter Zahn, but nobody knew where Jakob was, we sure could use him, he's on vacation. How long, we've no idea, we'll switch you back to the operator, ask for Miss So and So. Who didn't answer her telephone, and if Jonas had not been struck by a resemblance between her name and Sabine's, he might have hung up then and there. Instead he asked for Sabine and was told that Sabine had been called to a hospital. He inquired how one got there by streetcar, but changed to the wrong line at one point and arrived long after Sabine, the receptionist sent him to surgery across the gray wet courtyard, but before she asked him if he also worked for the railroad. They kept him standing in the hall. Eventually Sabine came out, still pale but much calmer. They left together, Herr Rohlfs heard from one of the nurses that Sabine had given them quite a bit of trouble. She had been dreadfully upset. They had asked her about his next of kin, but she couldn't think of anybody. Cresspahl did not occur to her. Jonas suggested him and they sent Cresspahl a telegram. He arrived early that same afternoon. Sabine also dictated the press release, someone else might have done that of course, but they probably didn't think of it in their surprise and besides who could have said it better: early this morning an employee of the German Railroad was crossing the tracks on his way to work and had just stepped out of the way of a northbound locomotive

— What's this story about Sabine?
— Yes, that's a story all right. But we had no time to go into it.

when he was scooped up by another locomotive coming from the opposite direction. Emergency surgery was unsuccessful (he died on the operating table). No one can be blamed. The victim had worked in this station for many years and was familiar with every corner of it. Moreover, the clear signal had been given for both directions. The heavy fog, almost impenetrable this time of the year, made it virtually impossible to watch the tracks.

And he was always cutting across the tracks.

# V

Cresspahl arrived in the early afternoon and Jonas was able to catch the express north; they had approximately ten minutes to talk things over in the station, they wanted to meet again the following morning. My father will drink himself to death.

IN THE EVENING train to Jerichow, Jonas sat across from a young soldier of the People's Army. That's all he remembers of the trip. He had a sleepless night behind him; only that morning he had been told (by Sabine) that Jakob had been to West Germany. To see his mother. The soldier was studying Russian, the train was a local, he was probably going home on furlough, every minute counts, make the most of it, learn as much as you can, knowledge is power, assimilate the socialist philosophy, the Warsaw Treaty is nothing but the reaction to the Western Powers' aggressive attitude. The girl beside the soldier seemed to know the lesson, completely uninterested, helpless, obliged, she kept staring into the book, recognized certain words, repeated them to herself, memorized them. From time to time the soldier's stern compressed longing lips would blow his impatience into the sticky hot noisy shivering compartment, and Jakob's voice said, we tried it on an eight-mile run, we welded the joints in the rails, how noisy these locals are, can't hear yourself think, besides, each jolt wears the metal down, you don't realize how much impact there is! Wouldn't hurt to save a little steel. But in that case the ballast has to be level with the head of the rails, for the stones to draw off the heat. Further back in the soldier's grammar at lesson 63 lay a passport photo enlarged to post-card size, four by six, universal standard postcard size. At lesson 63. He'd look at it (never for long) and immediately go on with his reading: and he went on reading during the stops, when the generator gave out, up at the locomotive and the lights dimmed because the battery was that much feebler. A few minutes after they'd started again the lights would jump back to brightness. The soldier read as long as he could see at all, he raced through the verb aspects and didn't slip the book into his pocket before the train stopped in Jerichow; Jonas forgot to watch if anybody came to meet him.

Jöche hadn't come home yet. His wife made the visitor wait in the living room. Jöche's apartment consisted of two sublet rooms separated by a hall. There were three parties using the kitchen, three bells at the door on the landing. The cupboard in the living room looked brand new, richly carved. A broad-based clock sat behind the glass, surrounded by porcelain animals, a pelican, an Easter bunny, a dog, an owl, a mush-room, and a deer in the lower shelf and on the upper shelf four books with glistening impeccable spines and a battered dictionary. Jöche's real books were behind the other door of the cupboard. On top of the cupboard stood a biggish vase between two smaller ones filled with heather. Next to the visible books was one row of cordial glasses and one row of wine glasses on straw coasters. The couch looked unused and the plump multicolored cushions seemed judiciously arranged. Among them a bluish dog face and a yellow teddy bear with a red bow. Over the couch in a dull silver frame hung a picture of cornfields on a hill near a pine forest, with blurred houses in the distance. Briquets were neatly stacked in front of the stove. The carpet was red, with an oriental pattern. An enormous radio with a small empty vase on top and a photograph of Jöche's wife in a streamlined standing frame. Two armchairs, two chairs. She had wheeled the baby out into the kitchen although Jonas would have been glad to have it stay where it was. She had showed him the tiny narrow bedroom and said: "We've been hoping for an apartment of our own for ages, perhaps something will work out at Cresspahl's place, since it's also a railroader's apartment. But so many people are still living in much worse conditions. In the barracks. Naturally they come first." Jonas said that the living room reminded him in many ways of his parents' house. To which he had not returned even now.

When Jöche arrived, he suggested going to the Inn, his wife had to get up so early for work. The Jerichow Inn consisted of a small room next to what used to be Peter Wulff's shop. From the street one came into a vast empty room with brown labeled boxes and shelves still along the walls, they were as dusty as the windows, the glass looked like gray hard frozen earth; the floor was covered with all kinds of junk, except for a path to walk through. Actually the bar was the back room where the peasants used to drink beer and brandy over their deals, in the old days. The counter was still the same, Peter Wulff had merely had new tables built in, and they were already white from thirty years of scrubbing; they were attached to the floor and the benches stood around them very much like a dining car on a train, you could only get through on one side. Peter Wulff put his finger on the radio dial and looked questioningly at Jöche who shook his head. They sat in the corner that was farthest away from the counter, there were few customers that night, the room was lighted only by the lamp at the door and the lamp above their heads. They had walked over in silence from Jöche's place, for a long time they sat facing each other in silence. Finally Jöche raised his head and looked at Jonas and said: "But he always cut straight across the tracks."

THE NEXT MORNING, of his own free will, Jonas got off in the station outside which Herr Rohlfs was sitting in his car having breakfast. A shadow glided past the windows, coat but-

tons scraped the glass, a second later they saw the assistant
(on whom Herr Rohlfs had spent some of his time) weave
his way through the parked cars and step onto the traffic
island in front of the streetcar stop. Not far from him, Jonas
was leaning against the stop sign, waiting. They saw his
profile raised toward the streetcar schedule, he had a cigarette
in his mouth but didn't take his hands out of his coat pockets;
he looked cold. Nevertheless, he climbed in with a straight
back and immediately leaned against the frame of the open
door where the wind would hit his bare neck. Softly humming, the Pobyeda made a half-turn and crept forward
straight across the parking lot and out of the streetcar's sight.
In front of the post office, Herr Rohlfs was just handing the
milk bottle back to Hänschen and the bag with the rolls that
he had held for him during the ride. The car tipped and
swayed softly when the back door was opened and the assistant slipped noiselessly into a seat behind him. "No tape,"
said Herr Rohlfs. Cresspahl speaking: what is this. Hello hello
hello. Have you heard. "The facts. I have no objections. My
appointment with the lady is not to be mentioned." The voice
behind them repeated the instructions. Cold air came blowing
in from the street as the car door opened once more, the car
swayed, stood still, Herr Rohlfs got out with yesterday's paper
and the milk bottle, he crossed the street to a dairy shop.
Came back empty-handed, stopped at a newsstand and began
a conversation with the man inside whom Hänschen could
not see. He switched the radio on.
The morning was bright and gay, with the coming and going
of cars and streetcars and pedestrians, dense and manifold
they crossed the square outside the post office and Herr Rohlfs
delayed his return because his car was standing in the shade
from where one could keep an eye on the post office. He felt
calm and sober, a crystal clear lucidity—without object now—
and he thought of tomorrow, that the sun would rise anew,
that they'd be somewhere else, nothing but files would be
left of today and of the day before; still, he could not imagine
how anybody could be bored with life. The sky was limpid,

the cars were passing so briskly, sharply, the shadows under
the glistening gables looked so black and luscious. He got
back into the car. Hänschen turned up the volume on the
radio, to a half-loud intelligible dialogue; he looked invitingly
around. "And if the conductor happens to come and ask the
passenger whether anyone has . . . die Notbremse gezogen?"
It was a woman's voice with a small flexible intonation. The
voice of the smiling young man answered, bewildered:
"Whether anyone has . . . pulled the . . . emergency brake?"
They both burst out laughing, the man in a good-natured sort
of way, she sounded less surprised. Herr Rohlfs turned the
radio up as loud as it would go. As though he were sitting
right in the car with them, the man's voice rose to a polite
naive question: why need one know the names of things that
were taken care of by the "eisenbahners?" "I am only traveling, see." The woman argued: then he'd know how to answer questions, after all he was in a foreign country, it might
come in handy in case of an accident. "In case of an accident," grunted the still reluctant young man in English.
But he couldn't be unfriendly to his partner, as the conversation progressed the listener had the impression: the American
wasn't listening to his teacher as much as he was looking at
her. He was admiring her so much, at one question he actually
seemed to jump, managed only a completely distracted half-
hearted reply. "The coupling? Yes of course. The coupling.
Uhmmmm . . . Die Kupp-lung, isn't it?" Whereupon Gesine
smiled and said: yes, and repeated the word for the correct
pronunciation. Herr Rohlfs was convinced that all these incidents were in the script, carefully put in to attract the listen-
ers' attention; even Hänschen said something to that effect,
but he laughed more than anybody and was surprised again
each time. Herr Rohlfs pictured how they'd been lying across
the table in Gesine's room those evenings writing it up, with
Jakob leaning back, hands behind his head, saying slyly:
maybe we should explain the difference between an ordinary
local and an express to our foreigner, huh? No kidding: they
call that "through train"? What a beautiful language! See,

said Gesine, Jakob why won't you stay? This program can keep both of us alive, and it's much more fun than head-quarters. "And how does it work?" asked her voice, bantering, provocative. "There is an airhose that links the brakes of every car?" "I see," said the American friendly and distracted with his hesitant, slightly hoarse voice, he was still looking at her out of the corners of his eyes.

When Jonas got into the car and held out his wrists for the handcuffs, the announcer said: "Our program SPRECHEN SIE DEUTSCH with Pfc. Reiners and Miss Gesine." This is the voice of education and information. Our next broadcast will give you interesting details about other fields of transportation: navigation and aviation. "You're not a good loser," Jonas said to the back of Herr Rohlfs. Who did not turn around. Who kept silent when the assistant roughly invited the prisoner to shut up. But in his heart he thought that it wasn't true. That Jakob would have understood. Not with words, in a brief casual silence, just looking at each other. That Jakob would have been fairer.

THE PLACE WAS inexpensive. She had thought of it because she liked their blond scrubbed tables. She arrived a few minutes late, Herr Rohlfs got up when he saw her at the door. I'd be glad to have a sister.

And she didn't look as though she had been crying; that's a point we do want to make.